PRAISE FOR *DON'T MAKE A SOUND*

"A heart-stopping read. Ragan's compelling blend of strained family ties and small-town secrets will keep you racing to the end!"
—Lisa Gardner, *New York Times* bestselling author of *When You See Me*

"An exciting start to a new series with a feisty and unforgettable heroine in Sawyer Brooks. Just when you think you've figured out the dark secrets of River Rock, T.R. Ragan hits you with another sucker punch."
—Lisa Gray, bestselling author of *Thin Air*

"Fans of Lizzy Gardner, Faith McMann, and Jessie Cole are in for a real treat with T.R. Ragan's *Don't Make a Sound*, the start of a brand-new series that features tenacious crime reporter Sawyer Brooks, whose own past could be her biggest story yet. Ragan once more delivers on her trademark action, pacing, and twists."
—Loreth Anne White, bestselling author of *In the Dark*

"T.R. Ragan takes the revenge thriller to the next level in the gritty and chillingly realistic *Don't Make a Sound*. Ragan masterfully crafts one unexpected twist after another until the shocking finale."
—Steven Konkoly, bestselling author of *The Rescue*

"T.R. Ragan delivers in her new thrilling series. *Don't Make a Sound* introduces crime reporter Sawyer Brooks, a complex and compelling heroine determined to stop a killer as murders in her past and present collide."
—Melinda Leigh, #1 *Wall Street Journal* bestselling author

DON'T MAKE A SOUND

OTHER TITLES BY
T.R. RAGAN

JESSIE COLE SERIES

Her Last Day
Deadly Recall
Deranged
Buried Deep

FAITH McMANN TRILOGY

Furious
Outrage
Wrath

LIZZY GARDNER SERIES

Abducted
Dead Weight
A Dark Mind
Obsessed
Almost Dead
Evil Never Dies

WRITING AS THERESA RAGAN

Return of the Rose
A Knight in Central Park
Taming Mad Max
Finding Kate Huntley
Having My Baby
An Offer He Can't Refuse
Here Comes the Bride
I Will Wait for You: A Novella
Dead Man Running

DON'T MAKE A SOUND

A
SAWYER BROOKS
THRILLER

T.R. RAGAN

THOMAS & MERCER

Text copyright © 2020 by Theresa Ragan
All rights reserved.

Published by Thomas & Mercer, Seattle

www.apub.com

Amazon, the Amazon logo, and Thomas & Mercer are trademarks of Amazon.com, Inc., or its affiliates.

ISBN-13: 9781542093873
ISBN-10: 1542093872

Cover design by Damon Freeman

Printed in the United States of America

In memory of Joe Ragan Sr.,
a kind and loving man who always believed in me and
was fond of saying, "They're going to turn that book of
yours into a movie. Just you wait and see."

CHAPTER ONE

After the pinwheel on the computer stopped spinning and the screen brightened, she logged in to her private group. They called themselves The Crew. There were five of them, and they all had nicknames. Hers was Malice. The others were known as Lily, Bug, Cleo, and Psycho.

Their connection ran deep. Rape, torture, and years of anguish had brought them together. They knew one another's stories, and they trusted each other fully. They hadn't joined forces to provide emotional support, although much of what they did *was* therapeutic. The header pinned at the top of their page read Deterrence, Restitution, and Reformation.

It was The Crew's belief that the only way to get justice was to see criminals punished.

Recently, they had decided unanimously to take control of their lives by teaching sexual predators a lesson or two. The people they planned to go after would come from all walks of life—young and old, rich and poor. The Crew had no intention of committing murder. The lowlifes would get exactly what they had coming—no more, no less. Once the target had been properly "awakened," they would be released back into society.

They knew their hobby could easily become a full-time job. But there were only five of them, and so they would do what they could. They all had lives outside their club. Some of them were married and had children of their own. Some had full-time jobs. They would keep what they did from friends and family, because too many outsiders tended to believe the law would see justice served.

But reality wasn't that kind.

Child abusers and sexual predators were becoming the norm. It was a well-known fact that fifteen of sixteen rapists walked free. Criminals knew better than most that there were police shortages in nearly every city and town across the country. It wasn't easy finding good candidates to recruit for police work either. The pay was shit, and the odds of getting killed on the job were high.

So here they were, after years of getting to know one another, plotting their first target. They were a true sisterhood, committed to their newfound cause. Their motto was *One Douchebag at a Time*.

It was all they could do.

For now, it would have to be enough.

CHAPTER TWO

Sitting in her eight-by-eight cubicle on the third floor of the sturdy brick building that housed the *Sacramento Independent*, Sawyer Brooks, a twenty-nine-year-old journalist, gulped down her second cup of coffee and stared at the blank screen. What would her readers want to know about Jason Carlson, the man who thought it would be a good idea to whip out a rattlesnake to impress the kids at his ten-year-old son's birthday party? While posing for pictures, he'd lost his grip, and the reptile bit the face of the child closest to him and another kid's arm before slithering away.

It had happened yesterday. They'd been rushed to the hospital. One little boy was in critical condition. The other kid was going to be okay.

What sort of moron would think pulling out a venomous snake in front of a bunch of kids was appropriate?

A shadow fell over her.

She swiveled around in her chair.

Her boss stood there, hands shoved deep into his pants pockets. His grayish-blue eyes reminded her of the color of the sky before a storm. Derek Coleman was the guy she reported to, one of two people in the building who made the final decision when it came to what stories she worked on.

Coleman was a young widower at thirty-five. Sawyer wasn't one to pry into the personal lives of others, but being observant, paying attention to those around her, and remembering details was one of her genetically predetermined characteristics. It was also her job to know things.

Three years ago, a driver who'd been too busy texting to pay attention to the road had hit Coleman's wife's car head-on. She'd died instantly. He hadn't removed the silver-framed wedding photo from his desk until recently. The picture of him holding his bride close to his chest, her white satin shoes inches off the ground, their faces brimming with happiness, told half the story. Gossipy staff filled in the rest.

Sawyer had worked for the *Sacramento Independent* for five years now. She'd started out as an intern, basically a gopher, then moved on to researching and editing others' stories, finally landing a job as a news and human-interest reporter after another writer moved back East.

She met Coleman's gaze. His expression told her he had bad news. "What's wrong?"

"The kid died."

Her first thought was: *What kid?* Second thought: *No way.* She'd read the stats on snakebites. Both victims had been given an antivenin within an hour of being bitten. The probability of recovery was 99 percent. Venomous snakes bit seven to eight thousand people every year. About five of those died. "How could that be?" she asked, pushing through her surprise.

"Apparently the boy had an allergic reaction."

She swiveled back around, grabbed her purse from the bottom drawer, and jumped out of her chair.

"Where are you going?"

"To the hospital." She knew Coleman wouldn't try to stop her from talking to the grieving family or friends of the boy. Many frowned on journalists talking to family members too soon. But this was a newspaper, after all. Coleman trusted her as a journalist to tell the story, no matter how difficult. She didn't act callously or hound people suffering from grief.

And yet Coleman still stood there. Again, she met his gaze. "Is there something else?"

"Geezer called in sick."

Geezer was a crime scene photographer who worked closely with the *Sacramento Independent*'s top crime reporter, Sean Palmer. "So?"

"He said you can hold your own when it comes to taking pictures." She nodded. Waited.

"There's been a homicide. Forrest Hill Apartments in West Sac. Palmer wants you there ASAP. He said to bring your gear."

"What the hell?" She pushed her fingers through her hair in frustration. "Why didn't you tell me five minutes ago?"

A thick brow shot upward. "Because I need the snake story on my desk by seven tonight."

She'd pissed him off. "I'm sorry. Didn't mean to curse at you."

He said nothing.

She turned away to shut down her computer. Working with Sean Palmer had been a goal of hers since she'd graduated from California State University, Sacramento. Running through a checklist in her mind, she grabbed her backpack, sliding the straps over her shoulder as it dawned on her that she needed to run home to get her camera. Pivoting on her feet, she was surprised to see Coleman still standing there. "Something else?"

"Are you sure you're ready for this? A woman was brutally murdered. From what I've heard, it's a grisly sight." He looked overly concerned.

"Are you kidding me? All I've wanted since I got this job was to work side by side with Sean Palmer and learn from the best."

"But that's not what you'll be doing. Your job today will be to take pictures." He sighed. "And that's only if you can get anywhere near the crime scene."

"I get it," she said.

"You're not to get in anyone's way."

"Got it." It was a tight squeeze, exiting her cubicle with Coleman in the way, but she managed.

"Seven p.m.," he called after her.

A reminder to get the snake story on his desk, pronto. Without turning around, she raised a hand in acknowledgment. Outside, she ran across the parking lot, the dead boy forgotten.

Nine a.m., and already the July heat was proving to be brutal. The kind of extreme heat that made tree branches break and animals pant.

She slid into her car, a second-generation Honda Civic with a rusty baby-blue exterior and tan interior. The engine jumped when she turned the key. A clunker, but it got her where she needed to go. She had no plans to put old Suzy out to pasture.

Despite traffic and hitting a red light, she made a concerted effort not to speed as she drove to East Sacramento. She made a left on San Antonio Way, and as she neared the house of her boyfriend, Connor, she spotted a car she didn't recognize in the driveway.

She pulled to the curb across from the house and shut off the engine.

A visitor? Had Connor been expecting someone, and that was why he'd rushed her out of the house this morning? Her pulse quickened as she walked toward the entrance. Connor was a bit of a slob. Maybe he'd finally hired someone to clean. A few more scenarios played through her head as she slipped the key into the lock and opened the front door.

Music was playing. It wasn't blaring, but it was loud enough to cover the sound of her footfalls as she made her way down the hallway to the bedroom. The door was ajar. She nudged it open, and when she stepped inside, she couldn't take her eyes off Connor's naked ass as it rose and fell. The girl beneath him had big eyes that grew even bigger when she noticed Sawyer standing there.

"Really?" Sawyer asked.

Connor must have been focused on what he was doing, because the girl had to use both hands to push him off her and then gesture at Sawyer.

Connor peeked over his shoulder. His face was red from exertion, which made sense considering this was the hardest she'd ever seen him work.

For some reason, Sawyer wasn't surprised. Not that Connor had ever cheated on her . . . that she knew of. It just somehow fit. Connor had no integrity and only his own interests in mind. And what annoyed her at the moment was that she'd ever moved in with him to begin with.

The girl used the sheet to cover herself. Connor slid off the bed. His dick was still hard, springing forth and wobbling a bit like a diving board.

"What are you doing?" he asked.

"What am *I* doing?" Sawyer laughed, then thought about Geezer being out sick and Sean Palmer at Forrest Hill Apartments, waiting for her. She didn't have time for this. "I need my camera." She walked to the closet and searched through clothes and shoes. Her camera bag had been pushed to the back corner. She opened it, made sure she had an extra battery and plenty of memory cards before zipping it closed, and headed back the way she'd come.

Connor followed close behind. "Where are you going?" he asked.

"Back to work," she said. "It's what people do to pay the bills. You should try it sometime."

He grabbed her arm. She shrugged it off.

"Come on," he said. "We need to talk about this."

"No. We don't. It's over."

"We haven't had sex in months. What was I supposed to do?"

When she reached the door, she turned toward him. "Don't sweat it. You're like every guy I've ever known. I'll grab my things later."

Walking toward her car, she saw a shadow underneath the frame by the front tire. It was a cat. "Come on," she said, trying to coax the animal out. "I'm in a hurry."

She got down on all fours. The poor thing looked half-starved. Its fur was long and matted, and there was no collar. When she opened the car door, the cat darted across the street and disappeared under a thick hedge. She felt bad that she didn't have time to run after the animal to see if it belonged to anyone in the neighborhood.

In her car and back on the road, Sawyer kept her hands steady on the wheel and tried to tamp down the emotions swooshing through her—a pinch of anger, a dab of disappointment, and a bucketful of reality that she just wasn't that into Connor.

Unlike her sisters, she wasn't plagued with OCD, and she wasn't afraid of conflict. But Sawyer definitely had her demons, and some of them came in the form of heightened distrust. Overall, Sawyer felt as if her self-contained anger kept her in control. But she was clearly at war with the world. Like many people, she suffered from anxiety, much of which stemmed from being touched.

Connor had been one of two men she'd had consensual sex with. When it came to having sex, she had rules. No grabbing hold of her hair, face, or buttocks. No fucking the shit out of her. Connor had known better than to dare press her against the wall or pin her to the bed. She needed to be on top—full control at all times. Otherwise, terror set in and made her feel things she didn't want to feel—wild, feral. Her heart would beat erratically, and she would struggle for breath. Her jaw would harden, her teeth grinding together, and there was no telling what might happen. Not that she would ever purposely harm anyone. It was just that moment of feeling trapped that would set her off, filling her with a burst of energy, like a caged animal breaking free.

Her therapist wrote her a prescription every time they talked, but Sawyer always crumpled it up and threw it away. Not because of any clean-body and clean-mind bullshit. But because she knew firsthand what pills could do to her. They made her loopy and calm and vulnerable. Screw being calm and vulnerable. She'd stick with tight fists and body tremors.

She turned her thoughts to where she was headed and Sean Palmer, one of the best crime reporters in the country. He was the reason she'd decided to apply for a job at the *Sacramento Independent*. Years ago, he'd been invited as a special guest to one of her journalism classes at CSUS. When class ended, she'd worked up the courage to tell him how he'd inspired her to seek out a career in journalism, more specifically, crime reporting. Instead of shaking her hand and moving on to the next student in line, he'd looked her in the eyes and fired off point-blank questions, personal questions about her life. He said he'd easily picked her out of nearly fifty students in class, pegged her as troubled and high anxiety—too much foot bouncing, fidgeting, and shifting in her seat. In a matter of minutes, he'd concluded that whatever baggage she was carrying would weigh her down and prevent her from obtaining the sort of sharp-edged focus it would take to become a decent reporter.

She'd returned to her run-down apartment with its rusty appliances and spotty plumbing, disillusioned but not defeated. Taking his words to heart, she'd decided to do something about the baggage he referred to. Starting with finding the cheapest therapist alive and telling her story.

Of all those tragic memories, the night her sisters left was the most troubling, often as eerily vague as it was disturbingly real. Sawyer had been wearing her favorite nightgown, a light-pink cotton shift with a torn hem that fell below her knees. Out of breath and freezing cold, her heart hammering against her chest, she'd stood on the front porch of their old house in River Rock, staring into the night, praying it was all a bad dream and her sisters would return. That's when a weighty hand had clamped down around her shoulder.

It was Uncle Theo, the person left in charge whenever their parents took off in search of antiques and collectibles for their store downtown.

Earlier that night, Uncle Theo had told Sawyer and her sisters he'd be out for an hour or two and to stay put. But he was back. His eyes were glassy, his forehead covered with sweat. He was angry with her sisters for taking off. It was her oldest sister, Harper, who usually calmed him when he got like this, but minutes earlier, Harper had driven away and abandoned her.

Her uncle yanked Sawyer into the house and slammed the door shut. His hands were cold, but his breath was warm, reeking of liquor. Her shoulder felt as if it might pop out of its socket as he dragged her down the hallway. He kicked open the double doors leading into the living area. Four men waited inside, two of them sitting in her mother's newly acquired nineteenth-century French Painted Rococo Boudoir chairs.

Sawyer had no idea what was going on. She didn't recognize anyone in the room. Why were they here?

"She's younger than the others," her uncle announced in a booming voice that ricocheted off the walls. "Double the price if you're still in. I'll give you five minutes to make your decision."

"I'm in," the man farthest away said without hesitation.

"Me too," said another.

A third man nodded. "Same here."

The youngest man, the one wearing a suit and sitting in her father's recliner, stood. He had a thick neck and a wide, square jaw. He walked toward her, his expression hard to read as he reached out and used one of his slender fingers to move a strand of hair away from her eyes.

Her knees wobbled. "I want to go to bed." She looked over her shoulder. Uncle Theo had left the room.

Rooted in place, she didn't move. Her heart beat so fast she thought she might collapse and die right there in front of the four strangers. Why would her uncle have left her alone with them? Nothing made any sense.

The square-jawed man smiled at her as he leaned over and took her hand in his. "Come," he said. "I'll take you to your room." His smile. Those sky-blue eyes and the soft lines around his mouth. She'd never forget him. For the two minutes it took to get to her room, she'd thought he was her savior.

But he'd turned out to be the opposite.

"Don't make a sound," he'd said after he closed the door and turned her way. He'd been Satan in the flesh, blue eyes and all, there to strip her of all goodness and light, spending hours on top of her, inside her, his sweat and sour breath all over her, leaving nothing for his friends but bones and whatever else made up the human body, including a darkened heart and a newfound aversion to being touched.

A car honked. Sawyer slammed on her brakes. Tires squealed.

Shit!

A pedestrian attempting to cross at the red light slapped his hand against the hood of her car and shouted at her.

Her fingers clutched the steering wheel. Her body trembled. She'd been lost in thought and could have killed him. The light turned green. She drove off. The navigation system on her cell phone informed her the apartment complex was a quarter of a mile ahead to the right. It was easy to find. A row of police cars lined the front of the building, lights swirling.

As she turned into the parking lot, she assessed the area. A group of journalists stood to the left of the entrance, most likely waiting for an update from the police chief or a case detective. To the right, a group of people huddled together, consoling one another—neighbors, friends, and maybe family members.

Sawyer parked in the back, away from the chaos. She shut off the engine. Chills washed over her. Someone was watching her. She looked around, took a breath, relaxed. Although nobody was looking her way, a young man—early thirties, she guessed—was sitting behind the wheel of a nearby truck. He'd backed into the space so that he was facing the apartment building. He had a bushy, dark beard, and his hair was mussed. He looked her way, his big brown eyes glistening and overly bright. Had he been crying?

She grabbed her camera, raised it to eye level, and pressed the shutter button.

His expression changed, his eyes suddenly darker, colder.

Sawyer jumped out of the car, hoping to see a license plate. Tires squealed as he sped off. She raised her camera and pressed the shutter button. Another car pulled into the space next to hers. The driver was an elderly woman with silver hair pulled back with a clip. It took the woman a moment to climb out, retrieve her cane, and make her way to the trunk of her car.

Sawyer looked from the line of police vehicles at the front of the building to the woman opening her trunk.

An idea struck her.

She tucked her lanyard inside her shirt, strapped her camera over her shoulder, and went to where the woman struggled with her groceries.

"Let me help you," Sawyer said.

The woman looked relieved. "Are you sure? I live on the third floor."

"Not a problem." Sawyer gathered two heavier bags, leaving the lightest for the woman to take before shutting the trunk and following her toward the entrance.

"Do you live here?" she asked.

"I moved in a few days ago. My name is Sawyer Brooks."

"Nancy Keener."

"Nice to meet you." After a short pause, Sawyer added, "I wonder what happened."

"A young woman named Kylie was killed last night."

"How do you know?"

"Vivian lives in the apartment next to mine, and she called me while I was getting groceries to let me know. I like to go to the store early before too many people clog the aisles."

"Did you know Kylie?"

"Not well. She lived on the third floor too, but she's usually gone during the day and tended to keep to herself. Vivian thinks it was Kylie's boyfriend who killed her."

"Why?"

Nancy shrugged. "He spent more time at her apartment than she did. Who else could it be?"

She had a point. Fifty-four percent of murder victims were killed by someone they knew. Thirty-five percent of female victims were killed by their husband or boyfriend. Sad, but true.

"Did he drive a red truck?"

"I don't know," Nancy said.

As they approached the front of the building, Sawyer caught sight of Sean Palmer at the edge of the crowd. He made eye contact and gave a subtle tilt of his head. Apparently, he'd been shut out and didn't want to risk her being stuck outside the crime scene too.

The woman Sawyer was following showed security her key card. He entered both their names into a logbook and let them through. The lobby was long and narrow, one wall covered with mailboxes, the other with mirrors. "I've never signed in before," Sawyer said. "Have you?"

"No. They probably don't want a bunch of lookie-loos coming around right now."

Sawyer looked around for any signs of a camera. Nothing. A key card would get anyone inside. Crime scene tape blocked the stairway while evidence technicians took photographs of what looked like bloody footprints. Chills swept over her as she followed the old woman to the elevator, where they were quickly herded inside. A uniformed officer stood next to the control panel, her gaze unforgiving as she appeared to consider them as potential killers. "What floor?" she asked.

"Third," Sawyer said confidently.

"When you get off, stay to the left," the officer said. "You'll have to go the long way around. We'd appreciate it if you stayed in your apartment for the next few hours."

The elevator lurched to a stop. The doors opened. As Sawyer walked slowly behind the old woman, she had to stop herself from looking over her shoulder, since she could feel the officer's gaze burning a hole into the back of her skull.

She hardly took a breath until she heard the buzz of the elevator as it returned to the lobby. While Nancy dug around inside her purse for her keys, Sawyer looked at the apartment across the way. Markers dotted the walls. The door was wide open; an officer stood guard.

When Nancy opened the door, Sawyer followed her inside. A minute later, Vivian, the next-door neighbor Nancy had mentioned earlier, joined them in the kitchen. Caught up in the drama of having a homicide right across the hallway, neither woman paid Sawyer much attention as she emptied the grocery items onto the counter, taking her time, hoping they would forget she was there.

According to Vivian, Kylie Hartford worked for *Good Day Sacramento*, a popular morning show. "She was dressed up as a banana the other day, and it made me laugh," Vivian told Nancy.

"I thought it was a bit corny," Nancy said. "But I did chuckle. Funny girl."

"That was Kylie," Vivian said. "She was a bright and shining star. A dose of morning sunshine."

"Nancy said you thought Kylie's boyfriend might have killed her," Sawyer chimed in.

Vivian looked her over as if seeing her for the first time. "Do I know you?"

"She just moved in," Nancy told her friend.

The suspicious look on Vivian's face disappeared. In a low, conspiratorial voice, she said, "I heard that Kylie's boyfriend was some sort of engineer . . . No, not an engineer, an arborist?" She swatted her words away as if they were gnats. "Something to do with trees. Anyway, Kylie and this boy had been dating for five years, but according to Ruth on the second floor, Kylie recently went on a date with a handsome young man who also works on the morning show. Jealousy. Motivation. Makes sense, doesn't it?"

"Do you know the handsome man's name?" Sawyer asked.

"Of course I do. His name is Matthew Westover."

Sawyer made a mental note of it. The two women chatted on about their favorite crime show and how the murderer was usually the most obvious suspect. Once it was clear Vivian was merely playing a guessing game, Sawyer said goodbye and made a quick exit. This might be her only chance to chat up the security officer she'd seen outside the crime scene.

As she approached the elevator, she realized she might have lucked out. The uniformed officer she'd seen earlier was gone.

Sawyer grabbed her camera still strapped around her neck, ready to shoot, and walked toward the apartment. Voices sounded in the back room. She knew how important it was not to disturb anything. Evidence had to be protected. Reaching into a bucket stationed outside the door, she grabbed a pair of shoe protectors and slipped them on.

The place was a mess. From the looks of things, Kylie had put up a good fight. Plants had been knocked over; there was an open book on the floor and a broken picture frame. Fingerprint powder covered the coffee table. Drops of blood made a path across the hardwood floor. Markers followed the same path.

Click. Click. Click.

Down the hallway, she saw more blood. Had Kylie encountered her killer in the main room and then run to her bedroom? Sawyer had never seen so much blood. It was smeared on the walls and floor. She passed a closed door where someone was clearly losing their breakfast. Before reaching the room at the end of the hallway, she heard voices.

"He'll be fine. Give him a few more minutes."

Drawers were being opened and closed.

"Looks like the girl lived alone."

The voices quieted. Sawyer took another step forward. She was about to turn around and head out when she glanced toward the room to her left and saw her.

The dead girl.

Kylie Hartford.

She'd been strangled to death. Wire was still wrapped tightly around her neck, cutting into flesh. Her face was ashen, her eyes open, staring up at the ceiling fan. Other than Kylie's body, a sewing machine, and a toolbox, the room was empty. *Why,* Sawyer wondered, *did she run into this room and not straight ahead into her bedroom?*

She adjusted the lens of her Canon.

Click. Click. Click.

A puddle of blood had gathered to the left side of Kylie's head, where Sawyer could see a gash. Her hair was matted and clumpy. In her grasp was a hammer. That's why Kylie Hartford had come to this room. She zoomed in. Click. Click. Click.

"What are you doing?" a male voice asked.

Shit!

He grabbed hold of her shoulder.

"Get your hand off me," she warned. Her heart pounded as she felt his fingers dig into her skin. Her vision blurred. She bent over, removed the memory card, then came up fast and grabbed hold of the man's arm, twisting hard until he cried out.

A second man appeared. "What the hell is going on?"

"Let me go!" the first man said.

The second man held up his badge. "Detective Perez. Do as he says. Release him."

She grudgingly let go of the man's arm. He stepped away, his face red, his pride damaged. It took a moment for her mind to clear. The panic she'd felt when he'd touched her morphed into worry. Would she be arrested for entering the apartment?

"Who are you?" Perez gestured toward the lanyard that hung around her neck and disappeared inside her shirt.

She pulled the lanyard free and showed him her ID.

"Are you here with Palmer?"

She nodded. "He's downstairs."

"Where's Geezer?"

"Out sick."

"Do you have pictures of the crime scene on your camera?"

"No."

His eyes narrowed. He reached for her camera, and she hesitated before pulling the strap over her neck and handing it to him. After a moment, he gave it back to her. "Get out of here before I have you arrested."

The detective followed her through the apartment and out the main door. He stopped to look up and down at the uniformed officer standing in the hallway. "Where the hell were you?"

"I had to pee."

"Leave this spot again and I'll report you. Got it?"

"Yes, sir."

Sawyer had already pushed the elevator button when she saw the detective marching toward her. She forced her shoulders to relax. *Don't check my pockets.* If he did, she'd be up shit creek. The elevator doors opened. She stepped inside and turned around. His eyes bored into hers. "What's your name?"

"Sawyer Brooks."

"Step out here. I want to—"

"Detective Perez," someone called from inside Kylie's apartment. "Found something you might want to see."

The doors clamped shut.

Sawyer inhaled and tucked her lanyard back into her shirt, then hid her camera as best she could before the elevator lurched to a stop and the doors opened again. She walked toward the exit.

"Hey, you," a security guard called out as she passed.

She could make a run for the parking lot, or she could see what he wanted. She stopped and waited.

"I need you to sign out."

She walked his way, signed her name, jotted down the time of day.

"I couldn't find your name on the tenant list."

"I'm Nancy's granddaughter." He grabbed another list and was looking through it when she added, "Bad day to pay her a visit, but I'll be back." She left before he could question her further.

Outside, Sawyer took in the sea of faces as she walked back to her car. The crowd had doubled. Sean Palmer was nowhere to be seen.

CHAPTER THREE

Sawyer was back in her cubicle, clacking away on her keyboard. It was ten minutes after six when she finished writing about the birthday party gone amiss. She ended the sad tale with key points about safety precautions around reptiles, then connected to her email service, composed a message to her boss, attached the file, and hit "Send."

Immediately after leaving the apartment building in West Sacramento where Kylie Hartford had been murdered, Sawyer had called Sean Palmer to tell him what she'd seen and heard. When he didn't answer, she drove to the hospital where the boy had died from the venomous snakebite. Sawyer had been surprised to walk into the hospital's main lobby and find Jason Carlson, the man who'd thought it was a good idea to pull out a poisonous reptile at his son's party, sitting alone.

When she found him, he'd been crying—noisy sobs between short, convulsive gasps. He must have needed to talk to someone, because all it had taken was for her to offer a bit of sympathy for him to open the floodgates. He hadn't seemed to care that she was a reporter from a local paper. The man had talked freely, grief-stricken by what had happened.

Sawyer had found herself feeling sorry for him. Not a reaction she'd expected after first hearing the story. Her sisters had accused her, on more than one occasion, of lacking empathy. But Sawyer disagreed. Rather than feeling overwhelmed by the suffering of others, she believed her compassion allowed her to keep emotion out of moments like this.

Jason Carlson and his children had grown up around snakes. He swore his snakes were not aggressive and believed all the commotion that day had prompted the attack. But he also admitted to being naive to think something like this couldn't happen. He wasn't sure whether the boy's parents intended to press charges, but he said he wouldn't blame them for doing so.

If only the snake had bitten him instead, he said, over and over again.

If only.

Negligence. Accident. It wasn't her job to judge or tell her audience how to feel. Her job was to tell the story. Be fair. Let readers make up their own minds.

Her phone buzzed. The screen showed DAD. She picked up the call and said hello.

"Are you at home?" he asked.

"No. I'm at work."

"Gramma Sally passed away last night. She died in her sleep."

Her heart sank. Gramma Sally was her mom's mother. "Is Mom okay?"

"She's fine."

It helped to know Gramma hadn't suffered, and yet guilt for not being there for her weighed heavily. When Gramma Sally had moved from Florida to River Rock to live with Sawyer and her parents, she'd been diagnosed with Alzheimer's. Despite her failing health, she'd lived another seventeen years, and made it to eighty-three. The thought of never seeing her again left an ache in Sawyer's chest. Gramma had taught Sawyer that life wasn't always fair and people needed to learn to suck it up. *Be brave. Be strong. When life gets tough, you need to get tougher,* she used to say.

"I'll let you go," her father said into the silence. "The funeral will be held at the River Rock Chapel on Friday at one p.m."

"Why so soon?"

"You know how your mother is."

She did know. Mom couldn't sit still or relax. Everything needed to be done yesterday. Mom and Gramma Sally had never gotten along. No doubt Mom was of the belief that the sooner Gramma was buried six feet under, the better.

Sawyer's mom had always been stubborn and strong, passionate about the Rotary Club she'd formed. Admired by many but liked by few. Sawyer had always wondered if Mom's behavior was the reason Dad locked himself in his office.

"Are you still there?" Dad asked.

"Yes. I'll come down for the funeral," Sawyer said. "I'll leave tomorrow."

"Have a safe drive. We'll see you soon."

Sawyer's chest ached. Gramma Sally was gone.

She had mixed feelings about returning to River Rock, but it was only a few hours' drive, and she wanted to pay her respects to Gramma and say goodbye.

Her cell buzzed, letting her know she had an incoming text.

Sean Palmer wanted to see her in his office.

Although they worked in the same building, Sawyer never got the opportunity to see or speak to Sean Palmer. His office was on the floor above with a view of the American River. In his late sixties, he possessed flyaway white hair and a neatly trimmed beard to match. He was fond of black turtlenecks, wool jackets, and eyeglasses with square, black frames. He always smelled like his last cigar: earthy, woody, sometimes fruity and nutty.

His office door was open, but she knocked anyway.

His back was to her. He waved her inside, and after he finished what he was doing, he pivoted around in his chair and reached a hand toward her, palm up.

It took her half a second to realize he wanted the photos she'd taken inside Kylie Hartford's apartment. Something bubbled at the pit of her stomach as she reached around inside her pants pocket before she realized the USB was in her left hand. It irked her to know he had that effect on her.

"Relax. Have a seat."

While he worked on uploading the digital files to his computer, she settled down and took note of his work space. On the shelf behind him were rows of fiction and nonfiction novels, starting with *Killings* by Calvin Trillin and ending with *The Journalist and the Murderer* by Janet Malcolm. Also in the work space were an ancient police scanner, a printer, and stacks of files. Framed pictures of Palmer posing with various local celebrities covered the walls. At the beginning of his career, he'd won the Livingston Award for Young Journalists when he covered criminal justice and the death penalty. He'd won the Investigative Reporters and Editors Award in 2007, and myriad other medals and certificates for his outstanding work.

Pulling her back to the moment, Palmer said, "Interesting choice of photos you took." He leaned back in his chair and clasped his hands over a slight paunch.

She wasn't sure what to think about that comment. "In a good way or bad way?" she asked.

He smirked. "Both." A painstakingly long pause followed before he added, "I remember you."

She lifted a brow.

"Journalism. CSUS. Correct?"

She nodded.

"I believe I told you to get out of your head."

She was surprised he remembered. "You pegged me as high anxiety and said all the baggage I was carrying would prevent me from attaining the focus needed to become a good reporter."

"Sounds about right. I guess you didn't listen. Good on you."

He was being a smart-ass, letting her know he didn't have to be psychic to see that she hadn't let it all go. "Not true . . . about the listening part," she told him, chin held high. "I took care of the baggage—most of it—and committed myself to learning how to observe and pay attention to my surroundings."

He swiveled his computer screen so he could share one of her photos with her. A bloodied young woman on the floor, her leg twisted awkwardly. "A little grim, don't you think? Focusing on blood and gore."

"Scroll back to the first picture," she said.

He did.

"That man was in the parking lot when I pulled up. He was sitting in his truck, watching, crying. Under the circumstances, he stood out, so I snapped his picture."

"Boyfriend?" he asked.

"Not sure. But if he is, according to a neighbor, he and Kylie have been dating for a few years. The neighbor believes jealousy played a part in the murder after Kylie went on a date with a man she works with."

"Interesting."

Interesting? His demeanor and tone set her on edge. Not only had she gotten inside the apartment where the murder took place, she'd managed to talk to people who lived next door to the victim. What the hell did he want?

"Did you leave your business card with the neighbor?"

"No. I rushed out of there so fast, I didn't have—"

"Did you get their names?"

She nodded.

"How did you get inside the victim's apartment—a crime scene?" He turned the computer screen back around and scrolled through the rest of the pictures.

"My plan was to talk to the officer standing by and see if he would allow me to take a few pictures. That's when I noticed the door to Kylie's apartment was wide open and unguarded. I saw an opportunity and I took it."

"Do you think that was ethical?"

Was he serious? "Yes. I didn't lie to get inside the apartment. I walked in, and nobody stopped me."

"But you knew you shouldn't be there?"

"I didn't think about it."

His jaw hardened. "I got a call from Detective Perez."

Ah. His attitude was beginning to make sense.

"He told me you attacked one of his men."

"Only after he grabbed hold of me."

"Perez asked you if you took any photographs—"

"He asked me if I had any pictures on my camera. I said no because that was the truth. The pictures were on the memory card in my pocket."

Palmer did not appear to be impressed by her cleverness.

"You told the security guard at the front of the building that you were the elderly woman's granddaughter."

Shit. She said nothing.

"What do you think would happen if I used your photos in my write-up?"

"Probably not a good idea," she said. "I hoped to use them to help solve the case."

"It's our job to report on crime, not solve it."

"I realize that, but—"

"If you're serious about becoming a crime reporter, I suggest you do your homework."

Heat rose in waves from her toes all the way to her face, but she willed herself to stay seated. "I know what I'm doing."

He leaned back in his chair, his frustration with her obvious. "What is this all about?"

She felt cornered, trapped. "I don't know what you're asking."

"These pictures of yours. The crime? What's it about?"

"Kylie Hartford," she answered confidently.

"No," he said, sitting up again and planting a firm hand on the top of his desk. "This isn't about Kylie Hartford. It's about crime as a whole and how it affects the community. The true purpose of investigative reporting is to let the general public know what's going on. Keep them informed so they can be active participants in society. That's our job."

"Interesting," she said, mirroring the same tone he'd used earlier.

"Being a smart-ass isn't going to help your cause."

"Interesting," she repeated with less sarcasm. "Because I clearly remember reading about the story you did on Heather and Dean McKenzie when you were first starting out."

His silence spurred her on. "The newly married couple were bludgeoned to death in their front yard in the middle of the day. No witnesses. No suspects. *You* happened to be the reporter who covered the story. *You* caught a scent, and like any good tracking dog, you followed the trail. In the end, if I remember correctly, you received an award or two for helping to find the killer and solve the case."

"I'm beginning to think you've made it this far because of pure stubbornness," he said. "Maybe you want to prove something to some-one—maybe me, maybe yourself—but you should be careful not to overestimate your cleverness."

She came to her feet, arms stiff at her side. "In class that day you said a good reporter is direct at all times. No beating around the bush. Go to the scene, you told the class. Talk to anybody who moves. Find out the who, what, where, when, and why, and if you're lucky . . . how."

He scratched his jaw. "I guess you do listen."

Her heart raced, her temper flaring, getting the best of her. Why had she stood? *Because you always react first and think second, dimwit.* Afraid if she said anything more it would only make things worse, she remained still and inwardly counted to three.

Sean Palmer set about stacking files and sorting mail. "Anger issues aside," he told her, "I wouldn't say you're the super reporter Derek Coleman touts you to be, but I am intrigued. I called you in here today to see if you might be interested in being on my team."

What the hell? If someone had asked her what this man was getting to, an offer to work with him would have been the last thing on her list. She pointed at her chest. "Me?"

His smile was stiff, but there was a gleam in his eye too. "You."

"Working—on a team—with you—together?" *If only she could untwist her tongue.*

"Yes," he said. "You. Me. And my team. All working together. What do you say?"

He was playing games with her. She felt as if she'd just gotten off the craziest roller-coaster ride ever made. The kind with steep drops and winding turns that flipped you upside down and made you beg for it to stop. "I'm being promoted?"

"If you take the job, yes."

She tilted her head. "Did you say that Coleman touts me as a super reporter?"

"He does."

Hmm. Her boss was a man of few words. She couldn't remember him ever praising the work she did. *Whatever.* "I can't start until Monday," she said. "My gramma passed away last night. I'll be leaving for River Rock tomorrow to attend her funeral and won't be back for a few days."

He frowned and absently tapped a finger against the edge of his desk. "I'm giving you a promotion, and you're already asking for time off?"

Shit. She didn't know what to say. *Think, Sawyer. Think.*

"I'm sorry about your loss," he went on as he glanced at what looked like a short list of names, hers being at the top. "But we're short staffed, and I need content."

She spouted the first thing that came to mind. "I'll get you content," she said with more desperation than intended. "My hometown of River Rock is practically around the corner from here. It's a small town that reeks of death, abandonment, and abduction—chock-full of the sort of stories told around the campfire, the sort of stories that make people feel uncomfortable." She kept her gaze fixated on Palmer's. "I'm not talking about made-up tales of zombies and vengeance-seeking ghouls. These stories are real."

"A little dramatic?"

"Possibly," she said. "Is it working?"

"River Rock," he said under his breath, ignoring her question. "The name rings a bell."

"That's probably because in 1996 the murder of Peggy Myers got national attention. School was out, and Peggy, a fourteen-year-old girl, was found dead by the edge of the river. She'd been mutilated, her skull smashed in with a hammer, a chunk of hair chopped off. Authorities were baffled." She shrugged. "But many people in River Rock are poor, and investigations are expensive. The killer was never found."

He opened his mouth to say something, but Sawyer wasn't finished, and she was quick to the punch. "That's not all," she said. "Four years later, it happened again. Avery James, fifteen years old. Hammer to the back of the head. A clump of hair chopped off. No signs of sexual assault."

He nodded. "Another unsolved murder in River Rock."

"That's right. And if all that wasn't enough to frighten a young girl, that girl being me," she said, pointing to her chest, "five years later, my best friend, Rebecca, disappeared on her way home from swim practice."

"Was she ever found?"

"No."

"I don't remember that story," he said.

"I'm not surprised. By that time, River Rock had gotten so much airtime, even the media yawned." Sawyer was done. That's all she had.

Long pause, and then: "I have limited resources. And the *Independent* doesn't circulate in your hometown."

"Anything I look into over the weekend will be on my own time and dime," Sawyer said. "I only need a few days after that to talk to people and gather information."

Palmer was a tough one to read. Judging by the serious look on his face, it could go either way. "I believe this story is important," she added calmly. "People travel to River Rock from Sacramento every weekend, just like they travel to Reno. We've done stories in Reno, Auburn, Roseville. Why not River Rock?"

He smoothed a hand over his beard. "What could our audience learn from it?"

"That victims of murder need justice," she said passionately. "Peggy Myers and Avery James should not be forgotten."

Silence.

"Give me a week to talk to people, interview them, and dig deep for new information. I know how to scramble. I can make this work."

"I'll expect impartiality."

"Of course."

"And gobs of content. Good stories that will make our readers take notice and send me emails congratulating our good work."

She nodded.

"I want you back here on Wednesday."

She exhaled. "I should talk to Coleman, let him know what's going on."

"He knows. I'll tell him you agreed and that you'll be starting when you return from River Rock."

Maybe that was why Coleman had been acting so strange this morning. "Okay," she said. She stood there for a second longer than necessary before starting for the door. Then she turned back to face him. "Will I be getting a raise?"

"Three percent now. Three percent in six months if all goes well."

"Sounds reasonable. I should go."

He nodded.

And that was that. One of the worst and best days of her life, packed into one. Life could be funny that way.

CHAPTER FOUR

Malice opened her laptop to see what The Crew was up to. They didn't want to glorify vengeance by calling themselves The Enforcers or The Avengers. They were merely five women who'd had the misfortune of being wronged.

They had met on Reddit, a massive collection of online forums where people shared news or commented on posts. After Reddit banned the darker markets, which were basically a swamp of disgusting internet activity—child abuse images, drug markets, gore, stolen shit, terrorist chats—The Crew moved to a Dark web forum dedicated to harm reduction. Media coverage on some of the high-profile cases in their group had died down long ago. Life went on . . . for some. For others, it wasn't so easy.

Psycho had had the misfortune of being kidnapped on her twenty-first birthday, then held captive for three years in an underground room built beneath a small cabin in the woods. She was raped often and sliced open with a hunting knife, her wounds sewn with fishing line. It wasn't until her captor was stopped during a routine traffic check that he was caught. He'd made the mistake of carrying around Polaroid pictures of Psycho, naked and bound. A couple of photos lay scattered about on the passenger seat, along with an empty soda cup and a crumpled bag from McDonald's. The monster was ultimately convicted and imprisoned. That was twenty years ago. He would be released soon. His projected release date was sometime next week. The Crew planned to be the first to greet him when the time came.

Cleo had been gang-raped during a three-day-weekend party at a fraternity house. When it was over, Cleo did everything right. She went to the hospital, told her parents, and talked to the school board. Her case went to court. The frat boys—young, rich, and privileged—stuck together like flies on sticky paper. The boys, their parents, and the media painted the victim out to be sexually promiscuous. She'd been looking for it, they said. She'd wanted it. A dozen boys came forward, all friends of the accused, to swear before the judge that she was no virgin. As if that mattered. They knew because they claimed to have been with her. The only *proof* the lawyer provided were pictures of Cleo's short skirts and semi-see-through blouses, and skimpy-bathing-suit shots while on vacation with her family. It was enough for the jury to wipe their hands of the mess and let the boys off without so much as a scolding. Cleo had a list of six names.

Lily had been thirty-five when she made a connection with a man through an online dating app. She met him at the restaurant and was surprised to see that he looked like his profile picture. She was even more surprised that the conversation was good, bordering on great. He made a lot of effort to get to know her, asked all the right questions, and regaled her with childhood stories that involved the ups and downs of growing up in a big family. They talked for hours, ate, shared a bottle of wine. It wasn't until they walked out of the restaurant that she began to feel dizzy and slightly nauseated. She knew immediately that something was terribly wrong.

Her date showed no sign of disappointment when she turned down his offer to go back to his apartment. He simply walked her to her car. While she fumbled around for her keys, he pulled out his key fob and clicked the button. The black car parked next to hers whistled. His car had not been there when she'd pulled into the parking lot earlier, which meant he must have moved it when he excused himself to go to the men's room.

Before she could question him, her legs buckled, and he caught her in his arms, almost as if he'd been waiting for her to pass out. That was the last thing she remembered until she woke up in his bed the next morning, naked, her wrists and ankles tied to the bedposts. It was the weekend. She lived alone. Nobody would worry about her until Monday. For the next forty-eight hours, her blind date did unspeakable things to her. She fought him until 11:58 on Sunday. She knew the time because there was a clock on the wall, and she'd been staring at it throughout her ordeal. At 11:58, he untied her, dragged her into the bathroom, where he had the shower running. He washed her hair, scrubbed every inch of her body, then tossed her a towel and told her to get dressed and get out.

She went to the hospital. The police were called. She filled out a report and told them he'd forced her to shower. They used a rape kit anyway. The whole procedure was invasive and time-consuming. She went home, showered again, and went to bed. The next day, she had her locks changed and the windows in her apartment inspected. She took a week off from work and had way too much time to think, analyze, and wonder when he'd spiked her wine. She had never once left the table. Follow-up with the doctor showed genital injuries. Semen was found. The authorities talked to her "date," and he convinced them that their time together was consensual.

The system for date-rape-drug testing didn't help her either. The equipment used wasn't sensitive enough to detect substances at low concentrations. Days had passed between the time Lily had been given the drug and when she arrived at the hospital.

It was over. Only it wasn't. Not even close.

Bug. Twenty-seven. Five foot two inches. Smart. Dreadlocks, dark eyes, perfect teeth, wide smile. Cheerleader for the varsity football team. Held down by a defensive linebacker and raped by the quarterback and a wide receiver. She hoped to see them at her ten-year reunion. All The Crew did. She'd reported the football players to school authorities and had gone to the police station with her parents. The rapists were from affluent households, though. Bug was not. They were white. She was not.

Malice. Verbally and physically fucked by those she trusted most.

CHAPTER FIVE

Sawyer climbed into her car. She needed to stop by Connor's apartment and grab some things for her trip to River Rock. But first she pulled out her cell and sent Harper a text, asking if it was okay if she slept on the couch tonight, telling her she'd explain everything when she got there. There were a half dozen missed calls from Connor and double that number of texts. She deleted all of them without bothering to read them first.

By the time Sawyer buckled her seat belt and turned on the car's engine, her phone buzzed with a reply from Harper, letting Sawyer know she could stay the night.

On the drive, Sawyer's mind swirled with thoughts of her sisters. Their relationship was complicated. Sawyer couldn't find it in her heart to forgive her older sister, Harper, for abandoning her. *Let it go . . . Live in the now . . . Take responsibility.* All good advice she'd received over time but not at all helpful. The thing that stung her most was that Harper was too messed up to talk about those dark days, holding them deep inside as if she thought that might make them disappear.

To be honest, it was a wonder the three of them had come from the same two people. Harper had been a wild child who had since morphed into a cleaning fanatic and control freak. Aria was a worrier who shied away from conflict, intent on keeping everyone around her satisfied. Although many people pierced their bodies as a form of expression,

Aria once admitted to Sawyer that she did it as a form of self-therapy and stress release.

And then there was Sawyer—paranoid, unable to trust, and angry. Angry with her uncle for abusing her and Aria. Angry with her parents for being blind to it all. Angry with Harper for abandoning her. And especially angry with herself for being unable to move on.

At the advice of a counselor, Sawyer had hired a private detective she couldn't afford and had gone in search of her long-lost sisters. Five minutes after she'd handed the PI her money, she had an address for a Nate and Harper Pohler.

She was twenty when she found them living in the same house they lived in now. Harper insisted Sawyer live with them while she worked on getting her degree. Sawyer hadn't liked the idea of moving in with her sister, but neither did she enjoy living in a run-down apartment.

Once she moved in, every day was like *Groundhog Day*. Sawyer woke up, went to school, came home, studied, and went to bed. Nobody talked about the elephant in the room. Everyone simply went about their business as if everything were hunky-dory.

Her sisters' ability to wash their hands of the past had only made things worse for Sawyer. For eight years she hadn't heard from them, and yet they wanted to pretend everything was fine. It was bizarre, and it pissed her off. She struck out in the only way she knew how, by ignoring them, including all their small talk: *How was your day? How are you doing? Do you need anything? Are you hungry?*

Fuck you. Fuck you. Fuck you, and fuck you.

Except she also made sure they knew she was around by being loud. She walked loud, talked on the phone loud, made coffee loud. She wanted to punish them for leaving her behind, and she had been doing a pretty good job of making all their lives miserable until Aria had taken Sawyer aside and told her what had happened, starting with her own nightmarish childhood—every disgusting detail.

Until that day, Sawyer had thought she was the only sister who'd been abused by Uncle Theo and his friends.

But she'd been wrong.

Aria told her that every time Mom and Dad had left Uncle Theo to watch over them, Harper would put Sawyer to bed and then run off to party with her friends. At first, Aria had enjoyed her time with Uncle Theo. He would make her hot cocoa, and they would watch movies together. She would often wake up the next morning feeling nauseated. It turned out Uncle Theo had drugged her and taken her to rape fantasy parties where she was passed around.

It all sounded much too familiar. Until their little talk, Sawyer had no idea there was a name for that sort of perversion.

Rape fantasy parties. Big business. Big money. Who knew?

Aria said Uncle Theo had threatened to kill family and friends if she ever told a soul. So she'd kept quiet. He'd done the same with Sawyer. Threats were a common tactic used by many sexual abusers.

Aria also went on to explain—something she'd often heard from Mom too—that Harper had been a rebellious child who drank and did drugs, nothing like the uptight woman who now used a lint roller on the floor of her bedroom to get every hair.

It wasn't until Harper was dropped off at one of her uncle's parties, where she stumbled into a back room and saw what was happening to Aria, that a plan to escape River Rock was set into motion.

The only thing Aria remembered about the night she and Harper left River Rock for good was being jostled awake, then staggering barefoot down the gravelly drive before being shoved inside the back seat of a truck, where she blacked out. It dawned on Aria only later that Uncle Theo had drugged her before he'd left the house after warning them to stay put until he returned.

That same night had been seared into Sawyer's brain to relive over and over again—crying and out of breath, cold and shivering, she'd stood on the front porch, watching the twinkling back lights of a truck disappear down the road, her sisters inside, leaving her alone, and then Uncle Theo's hand clamping down around her shoulder before he dragged her into the house and handed her off to four strangers.

Nothing was ever the same again.

The days had melded into eternity until her parents returned home. Sawyer had cried with relief, but Mom and Dad hardly batted an eye when they learned that two of their daughters had run off. Her parents had always been neglectful. They'd allowed their daughters to wander miles from home when they were much too young to do so. Sawyer and her sisters used to walk home from school, never worried about the time. They made their own meals, did their homework unassisted, figured things out on their own without much supervision.

Most parents would have called the police and spent day and night searching for their missing daughters. But Mom and Dad were certain Harper and Aria would return. When a week passed and that didn't happen, Mom blamed Harper, committed to her long-held belief that her eldest daughter was hyperactive and out of control, determined to disrupt their family since the day she was born.

Sawyer had tried to work up the courage to tell her parents about Uncle Theo, but his threat of doing them harm stopped her every time. Without her parents, no matter how negligent, she would have no one. If not for Gramma being diagnosed with Alzheimer's and moving into their home months after her sisters ran off, Sawyer wasn't sure she'd still be around. She imagined she might have taken her uncle's life, or worse, her own.

Sawyer parked at the curb in front of Connor's house. She climbed out of the car, and as she walked toward the house, she realized she hadn't thought of Connor all day.

The door opened before she reached the welcome mat. "I knew you would come back," he said.

"I'm here to collect my things." She stepped inside and walked to the bedroom they had shared for eight months. She grabbed her duffel bag from the closet, opened it wide, and began stuffing it with her clothes and shoes.

"Please stay. That girl meant nothing."

Sawyer turned toward Connor and looked him in the eye. "I should have moved out a long time ago."

He stepped forward, reaching for her.

She raised her hands high to avoid his touch. Connor, she realized, had been nothing more than an experiment. Every rape victim reacted differently, but Sawyer had been left with an extreme aversion to being touched. Her therapists said she suffered from haphephobia. She had many of the symptoms, and things hadn't been any different with Connor. The first time he'd kissed her, she'd felt as if she were on fire. Every touch burned her skin. The first time they'd had sex, she'd spent the rest of the night in the bathroom throwing up. She knew in her heart that she'd used him in an attempt to desensitize herself, also known as self-exposure, something she and her therapist often discussed.

Connor had backed off. He stood a few feet away, hands shoved into the front pockets of his pants. "I love you," he said.

He'd never said the words before, and she was glad for that. She grabbed a tote bag that hung from a chair in the corner and took it with her into the bathroom. Connor stayed close, watching as she plucked toiletries from the shower, bathroom cabinets, and drawers.

"I only slept with her because—you know—you've been distant. I can't remember the last time we made love."

They had never made love. They had fucked. There was a big difference. She put the strap of the tote over her shoulder, walked back into the bedroom, picked up her duffel bag from the floor, then exited the bedroom and headed for the front door. It wasn't until she stepped outside that she turned to face him.

His eyes pleaded.

She sighed, trying to think of what a normal person might say under the circumstances. "I'm not the girl for you, Connor. Not even close."

"Stay," he tried again. "We'll talk it out."

She couldn't do this—deal with Connor, talk to him, set him straight. It would serve no purpose she could conceive of to tell him the truth—that being with him had been a mistake, and she didn't love him. Hell, she hardly liked him. "My gramma passed away," she said flatly. "I'm going to River Rock for her funeral. Please don't call me again."

She shut the door and walked away. The night air was warm and sticky as she put her things inside the trunk of her car. When she opened the car door, she noticed the same cat she'd seen earlier hiding behind her front tire. It was gray and white with black fur around its eyes.

She leaned over and grabbed the cat by the scruff before it could run off. Holding the animal close to her chest, she slid in behind the wheel and used her free hand to shut the door. The cat freaked out, clawed its way out of her hold, and jumped over her to the back seat.

Ouch! It had scratched her neck.

She released a long breath. What was she doing? She didn't have time for a cat, and yet she couldn't leave the animal to fend for itself. Aria would help her out. She turned on the ignition and drove off.

CHAPTER SIX

Sawyer sat in her car, parked outside a green, single-story, cookie-cutter house. She'd already shut off the engine and pulled the key from the ignition. Her neck stung where the cat had clawed her. She leaned over the seat to look for the cat, but it was hiding. She adjusted the rearview mirror to see a crisscross of bloody scratches on her chin and neck. *Great.*

For a long moment, she simply sat still and observed the house where both of her sisters lived. It was growing dark, but the lights were on, and she could see movement inside.

The house belonged to Harper and her husband, Nate. They had a boy, Lennon, fifteen, and a girl, Ella, ten. Aria lived in the garage, which sounded worse than it was since Nate was a contractor, and he'd fixed it up nice. There was a small kitchenette, lots of storage space, and plenty of light.

She could count the number of times on one hand she'd seen Harper since moving in with Connor. Her sister tended to treat her like one of her kids, hovering and smothering, which was one of the reasons Sawyer had been eager to move in with Connor.

Sawyer's fingers turned white from holding on so tightly to the steering wheel. Her heart beat wildly within her chest. She'd caught Connor in bed with another woman. She'd found herself alone in a room with Kylie Hartford, murdered and lying in a pool of blood, eyes wide open. And Gramma Sally was dead.

And yet she'd managed to keep it together.

Until now.

All it had taken was sitting outside her sister's house to feel the full breadth of her anxiety. All sorts of images floated around in her mind. She squeezed her eyes shut to stop the panic from taking hold.

She needed to calm down before knocking on the door. Heeding the advice she'd gotten from her therapist, she closed her eyes and imagined a long stretch of beach. She sank her toes under the warm sand, and when she opened her eyes again, she saw Connor's slowly sinking dick.

Shit.

She blinked the vision away. No, she didn't love Connor. But that didn't stop his betrayal from making her gut ache, a mixture of anger and disappointment twisting and turning like clothes in a washing machine.

She got out, opened the trunk, and grabbed an old towel that had been there forever. She then opened the back door, and when the cat made a run for it, she grabbed hold, rolled it in the towel like a burrito, and rushed across the stone walkway with its perfectly manicured lawn and rows of tulips, which defined her older sister perfectly. She'd never been diagnosed, but it was clear to anyone who knew Harper that she suffered from OCD.

Her middle sister, Aria, wasn't anything like Harper. Aria liked to pretend everything was okay. It seemed to Sawyer that all the horrible things that had happened to Aria had been tamped down, shoved beneath layers of false forgiveness and pent-up rage. Sawyer hated the thought of what might happen once the plug was pulled and Aria's anger was let loose.

Bottom line was, terrible things had happened in River Rock.

Aria was convinced that something bad had happened to Harper too. Something worse than Uncle Theo and his friends, which was why Aria and Sawyer agreed to leave her alone and never talk about the past.

But that hadn't stopped Sawyer from being angry at Harper for leaving her behind.

Sawyer knocked on the door, doing her best to hang on to the cat.

Lennon opened the door. He'd been so small when Sawyer had found her sisters. Now he was taller than his dad.

She stepped inside, told him to hurry and shut the door before she set the towel on the ground. The cat took off in a blur.

"Was that a raccoon?" Lennon asked.

She rolled her eyes. "It's a cat."

"A feral cat?"

"I have no idea."

"Did it do that to your neck?"

She'd already forgotten about the scratches. "Yes."

"Mom is going to be pissed."

"It's our little secret, okay?" She folded the towel and set it down by the door.

He rolled his eyes. "I'm staying out of it."

"Thanks for the support." She headed inside and found Harper in the kitchen making lunches for the next day.

Without missing a beat, Harper pointed at the refrigerator. "Grab three yogurts and a bag drink from the bottom drawer, would you?"

"Sure." Sawyer handed the items to her sister.

"Your dinner is over there," Harper told her. "We couldn't wait any longer."

"Thanks."

Nate entered the kitchen. The man took up a lot of space. He reminded her of the Brawny guy in the paper-towel commercial. Nate ran a construction business. He always looked the same: jeans, T-shirt, plaid shirt, and work boots. His hair was shaved around the ears, longer on top. He'd grown a beard since she'd seen him last. "Hey, Sawyer."

"Hey, Nate."

"Lennon!" Harper shouted. "Tell your sister she has five minutes to get in the car!"

Sawyer gestured toward the sleeping bag and other items near the door. "Is someone going somewhere?" she asked.

"Ella is off to summer camp first thing in the morning," Harper said. "She waited until the last minute to pack and realized she didn't have everything on the supply list she was given."

"What are you doing this summer?" Sawyer asked Lennon.

"I guess I'm working with Dad."

"At least you'll make some money," Sawyer said as she searched the kitchen cupboards for two small bowls. She filled one with water and the other with a scoop of tuna from the Tupperware she'd found in the refrigerator and set the bowls on the ground, out of the way.

"Are those for the raccoon?"

"What raccoon?" Harper asked.

"Sawyer brought a raccoon inside," Lennon told his mom.

Harper scowled. "No, she didn't."

Lennon smirked.

Harper looked at Sawyer. "Where is it?" Her eyes widened. "And what happened to your neck? You're bleeding."

"It's not a raccoon. It's a cat. It has no collar, and its ribs are jutting out," Sawyer said. "I thought maybe Aria could take it to work with her."

"Don't let her take it to the SPCA," Lennon protested. "They'll kill it after three days."

"Maybe someone will take him home," Sawyer told him.

"Look at you!" he said. "The cat ripped your neck to shreds. Nobody wants a cat like that."

Ella raced into the kitchen. "Hi, Sawyer."

"Hi, Ella." Nobody bothered to hug Sawyer. They knew the drill. *Say hello. Be cordial. Don't touch.*

"There's a cat under my bed," Ella said. "Can we keep it?"

"No," everyone said at once.

Ella's head dipped.

"Off you go," Harper said, waving everyone toward the front door. "The store is only open for another forty-five minutes."

Lennon moaned. "I don't know why I have to tag along."

Harper waved him off. "Just go."

"I don't know how you do it," Sawyer said when they were gone.

"Don't try to change the subject." Harper ushered Sawyer toward the dinner table and put a plate in front of her as if she were one of her children.

Sawyer sat down. Beans, rice, and chicken. "I'll find the cat a home. I promise."

Harper sighed. "Do you want hot tea?"

"No, thanks."

Harper plopped down on a stool, took a sip from her mug, and said, "I heard about Gramma Sally."

Sawyer lifted a brow. "Who told you?"

"Dennis left Aria a message," Harper said without emotion.

It used to bother Sawyer that Harper referred to their parents by their first names, Dennis and Joyce. But Harper could be like their mother at times—cold and set in her ways. If Sawyer wanted any sort of relationship with her niece and nephew, it was best if she chose her battles with her older sister carefully. "I thought you and Aria no longer talked to Mom or Dad."

Harper shrugged. "You know Aria."

Yeah, she did. Sweet, forgiving Aria. "The funeral is Friday."

"You can't possibly go."

"I'm going," Sawyer said. "Gramma Sally was the only good thing left in River Rock. I want to say goodbye."

"And yet you haven't been to see her lately, have you?"

"I don't want to argue with you. You know I've been busy." Sawyer used to drive back home once a month. Once a month became every other month, and finally once or twice a year. First it was studying that had kept Sawyer away, and then the internship with the *Sacramento Independent*. The last time she'd seen Gramma was a year and a half ago. By then, Gramma Sally could hardly move and had lost her ability to communicate through words.

"There's no way you can make a three-and-a-half-hour drive alone with your anxiety. You told me yourself that the mind does funny things when you have too much time to think."

Had she told her sister that?

"The panic and fear will set in," Harper went on, "then the dry mouth, nausea, tingling hands. Terrified, you'll pull to the side of the road to call me. You'll need me to come get you, and this time I will say no."

"That only happened once," Sawyer reminded her.

"Twice."

"I've been working on my anxiety. I'll be fine. I haven't had an episode in months."

Harper's gaze roamed freely over her. She was scrutinizing, judging as she often did. "So what happened to you today?"

Before she had a chance to tell her about Connor, they heard the front door open and close. Aria stepped into the main room where she could see them in the kitchen.

The last time Sawyer had seen Aria, her hair had been purple. Today it was turquoise. At five foot three, Aria was the shortest of the sisters. She was also the prettiest, and all the tattoos and piercings merely added to her cool, edgy look.

Aria looked from Harper to Sawyer. "What's going on?"

Sawyer lifted a brow as she chewed. *Where to start?*

"What did Connor do?" Harper asked as she moved to the sink and began scrubbing perfectly clean porcelain.

"Oh," Aria said, as if she'd figured it all out in a matter of seconds. She joined them in the kitchen and took a seat close to Sawyer. "Did Connor mess around with someone else?"

Sawyer turned to her. "Why would you say that?"

Aria clamped her mouth shut.

Sawyer nudged her arm. "Tell me what you know."

"Nothing that you don't know already," Aria said. "He's a narcissist. All he wants to do is talk about himself, and he's the most uninteresting person I've ever met."

"You told me you liked him."

"Did I?"

"Spit it out," Harper demanded. "What happened between you and Connor?"

Sawyer chewed, swallowed, then said, "I went home to get my camera for work and found Connor in bed with another woman."

"Awesome," Aria said. "Now you can move on and forget he was ever in your life. He did you a favor."

"You can move in with us," Harper said, looking at Sawyer as if she could be her newest project.

Sawyer groaned. They had no idea what she and Connor had been through. It had taken forever for her to trust him enough to let him kiss her and touch her. It disheartened Sawyer to think he'd so casually tossed her trust in him aside. Sawyer set her fork down. "I'm not hungry." She stood, and Harper took her plate before she could take care of it herself. "I should get my things from my car and make the couch up. I want to be sure I get plenty of sleep before the drive to River Rock."

"River Rock?" Aria asked.

"Yes," Sawyer said. "I'm going to Gramma's funeral."

Aria blinked. "Why? She's dead."

Sawyer's head was already throbbing when the cat shot through the house.

"Was that a raccoon?" Aria asked.

"It's a cat I found. He was starving."

"You brought a cat with you?"

"He's not staying," Harper chimed in. "I think Nate might be allergic."

"Can you take care of him until I get back?" Sawyer asked Aria.

"Of course."

Harper moaned.

Aria pointed to Sawyer's neck. "Did the cat do that?"

Sawyer nodded, then gestured toward the door. "I need to get my things."

"So you won't go to Gramma's, right?"

"I have to go. In fact, I *need* to go. Gramma was my rock. I need to say goodbye." Sawyer ran a hand through her hair. "What are you two so afraid of anyway? We're not little kids any longer. Both of you should come with me so we can sit Mom and Dad down and have a real conversation about everything that happened when we were growing up." Sawyer didn't mention that she'd be staying to interview people about the Peggy Myers and Avery James murders. She'd save that for another time when she wasn't exhausted.

"Did you know that Uncle Theo was released from prison?" Aria asked.

Sawyer fixed her gaze on Aria. Uncle Theo had gotten fifteen years for aggravated assault after raping and robbing a coworker at the cable company where he worked. Her stomach heaved. "How do you know?"

"I keep track of these things."

"After all Dennis and Joyce put you through, why would you bother trying to talk to them?" Harper asked. "You still don't get it, do you? They don't care about any of us. They never did."

"Please don't go," Aria pleaded, her voice soft.

Poor, sweet Aria needed to grow a pair.

Sawyer looked at Harper. "Mom and Dad kept a roof over my head and food in the cabinet. At least they never ran off in the middle of the night, leaving me to fend for myself, never to be seen again."

Harper stabbed a finger her way. "That is exactly what Joyce and Dennis did. They were your parents, *our* parents, and yet they abandoned us all."

"Nothing good ever happens in River Rock," Aria reminded Sawyer.

Sawyer was at the door, her hand grasped onto the knob. Her phone wouldn't stop buzzing. She pulled it out and glanced at the screen—a missed call and three texts from Connor. She shut her phone off and shoved it back into her pocket.

As soon as she stepped outside, she inhaled.

Once she returned from River Rock, she would need to find an apartment, anyplace but here. She loved her sisters, but sometimes, like now, they made it difficult for her to breathe.

CHAPTER SEVEN

Six o'clock the next morning, Sawyer woke up. At the end of the couch where her toes peeked out, the cat had made himself comfortable. Last night, she'd dreamed the cat had ruined Harper's couch, and in retaliation Harper had made a coonskin cap out of him. When the cat lifted his head and saw her looking at him, she said, "Hi, Raccoon."

Raccoon darted away.

She got up and trudged to the bathroom down the hallway, brushed her teeth, changed out of the gray sweatpants and back into jeans and a T-shirt, then slipped on a pair of sneakers. In the living room, she quietly tore blankets and sheets from the couch, folded them neatly, and put the cushions back the way she'd found them. Hands on hips, she glanced around to make sure she wasn't leaving anything behind. She heard soft footfalls closing in on her.

"Leaving already?" Harper asked. "I was hoping you would stay for breakfast. You know, say goodbye to Nate and the kids."

"I want to get on the road early, before there's too much traffic. Besides, Mom and Dad might need help with last-minute funeral arrangements."

Harper made her way into the kitchen and returned with a brown paper bag like the ones she'd made for the kids.

"You made me a lunch?"

"A few snacks and a water bottle to tide you over." Harper gestured toward the kitchen. "I'm going to make a fresh pot of coffee. If you wait a few minutes, I can send you off with a coffee to go."

"Sure," Sawyer said, unable to turn her down. She followed her sister into the kitchen and took a seat on one of three stools framing one side of the granite island. As Harper readied the coffeepot and started the brewing process, she rambled on about the excessive heat Sacramento had been experiencing and the list of chores she needed to get done.

"Gramma died," Sawyer cut in before her sister could read off another to-do list.

Harper turned her way, clearly perplexed.

"We," Sawyer said, "all three of us, used to spend whole weekends at Gramma's when we were small." Recalling those times made Sawyer feel a lightness in her chest. "We painted rocks, played tag, and made bouquets of wildflowers. Do you remember?"

Harper tightened the sash on her robe. "I remember."

"Gramma Sally used to talk about you a lot," Sawyer said.

Harper snorted. "All good things, I'm sure."

"Yes. All good. She always thought you were the most like her."

Harper wasn't having it, and she set about finding a to-go coffee cup for Sawyer. Sawyer noticed the deep frown lines and jerky movements and wondered if the two of them would ever find a way to connect.

Lennon appeared before any more could be said. "Hey, Aunt Sawyer."

Sawyer inwardly scolded herself for bringing up the past. She could tell by the paleness of Harper's face, and by the way her hands trembled, that she'd upset her. Her sister was fragile.

"Hey, Lennon," Sawyer said, giving him her full attention.

Lennon leaned over to give her a hug and then quickly backed off, trying to be funny.

It wasn't.

"Are you guys fighting again?" Lennon asked.

"What do you mean, again?" Harper asked him. "This is the first time I've seen Sawyer in months."

Lennon swept his fingers through his curly mop of dirty-blond hair. "My bad," he said. "Sorry I said anything."

Sawyer ignored them both. Harper filled a to-go cup and slid it across the counter to Sawyer along with some creamer.

"Do I have to work with Dad today?" Lennon asked his mom.

"Yes."

"All my friends are going to the water park while I'm handing tools and shit to a bunch of old guys."

"Watch your language."

"Aria swears all the time, and you don't give her sh—crap."

"She's Aria."

After screwing on the lid, Sawyer crooked her neck and looked up at Lennon. "How tall are you now?"

"Six one." His eyebrows shot up. "Hey! If you're going to be living with us for a while—"

"A few nights at most," Sawyer cut in.

Harper crossed her arms. "You don't like living with us?"

"It's not that at all. I just prefer to have a place of my own."

"Anyway," Lennon tried again, "I was thinking maybe you could let me practice driving that beat-up heap of yours?"

"That's not a nice thing to say about someone's car," Harper scolded.

"He's right," Sawyer said. "Old Suzy is falling apart. She's a piece of shit—I mean, crap."

Harper exhaled heavily as she set about making a cup of coffee for herself.

"It would be a good car for him to learn to drive in," Sawyer said. "When I get back, I could take him to the school parking lot."

"Lennon and Nate are going to be gone next week, helping Nate's father with his fence."

"Once we're both back and settled," Sawyer told Lennon, "I'll take you driving."

"Cool," Lennon said.

"I'll think about it," Harper said.

Sawyer stood, grabbed the brown paper bag and coffee. "I should go. Thanks for taking care of Raccoon while I'm gone."

"Raccoon?" Harper asked.

"That's the cat's name."

Harper sighed.

Sawyer set her gaze on Lennon. "I'll see you when you get back from Tahoe. Have fun putting in that fence."

Once she was outside, Sawyer breathed in the fresh air. It made her sad to see her sister so rigid and uptight. If Harper could be honest with herself and others and let all her feelings out, the good and the bad, maybe all three of them—Harper, Aria, and Sawyer—could help one another heal properly.

Aria was of the mind that Harper was riddled with guilt for scaring Uncle Theo off when he'd come to her room, and yet failing to save her sisters. Apparently, Harper had grabbed a pencil from her bedside table and gouged Uncle Theo's face, making a jagged line from eye to ear, warning him that if he ever touched her or her sisters, she'd go straight to the police.

Before Aria had related the story, Sawyer had always wondered where Uncle Theo had gotten the scar.

Now she knew.

Chapter Eight

On the drive to River Rock, Sawyer nearly turned around twice. Returning to her hometown always left her feeling weighed down by sadness and grief. Sometimes she wondered if she were the only person in River Rock who thought about Peggy Myers and Avery James. And what about Sawyer's best friend, Rebecca? Was her family still looking for her? Or had life simply moved on without her?

Sawyer thought of Rebecca all the time. How they used to walk to the park where Sawyer would lie on the grass and watch the clouds make shapes while Rebecca pumped her legs on the swing, her head back and her eyes closed as she floated through air.

The drive felt longer than Sawyer remembered. The last time she'd visited was eighteen months ago. Although she hadn't experienced any of the anxiety Harper had prophesized, as soon as she reached Frontage Road, her chest tightened. It was as if something were lodged in her throat, making it difficult to breathe.

She pulled into the gas station up ahead, next to an available pump, figuring she could fill up her tank and take a breather at the same time. She climbed out and slipped her credit card into the slot, then removed the cap from her gas tank.

"Sawyer Brooks," she heard someone say.

She looked up, surprised to see Aspen Burke. She smiled at him, squinting into the sunlight. After Rebecca disappeared, she and Aspen had spent a lot of time together. He looked different. He'd filled out in the chest and shoulders, and his acne was gone. He used to have long, stringy brown hair that fell to his shoulders, but now he had a taper-and-fade cut around the ears, leaving his dark hair longer on top. He wore a short-sleeve tan uniform and a dark-blue flat-bill cap. A badge pinned to his left breast pocket read "Reserve Deputy."

His smile reached his eyes, and before she knew what he was up to, he wrapped his arms around her and gave her a long squeeze. "It's good to see you, Sawyer."

Her heart raced, and she tried not to panic. Relief washed over her when he finally released his hold. "Wow," she said as she took a step back. "You're a deputy now?"

"I am." He pointed to the back of her car. "Broken taillight," he said. "Might want to get that fixed. If it were anyone else, I would have to ticket you."

Thankful that he didn't pull out the little book sticking out of his pocket, she said, "I had no idea. Thanks."

"I guess you're back for Sally's funeral?"

She nodded.

"I'm sorry for your loss. I know the old gal meant a lot to you."

"She did." Sawyer's gaze fell back to the badge he wore. "How is River Rock? Still toxic?"

"In what way?"

"You know what I mean—two girls murdered and the killer never found. It all sort of left a bad taste in my mouth."

"The homicide rate is much higher in large cities like Sacramento. We did have some Halloween decorations stolen last year, and we have the occasional bike taken off a front porch." He smiled. "You have no idea how damn good it is to see you."

"It's good to see you too, Aspen." It was true. Although Aspen was older, he'd had a difficult childhood and had dropped out of school at a young age. She and Aspen used to go out into the woods and find a shade tree by the river where they would fish or play checkers. And yet after leaving River Rock, she'd never once reached out to him. She could taste the guilt as it trickled down her throat. "How long have you been working for the sheriff?" she asked.

"A few years now. I can hand out tickets for traffic violations and such, but I can't arrest anyone. What about you? Last I heard, you were writing for some paper?"

"I was promoted," she said. "I'm a crime reporter now. In fact, while I'm here I figured I might as well look into the unsolved murders."

"Ahh. So that's why you were asking about River Rock?"

"Since you're a reserve deputy, any chance you can find out if the Peggy Myers and Avery James murders are still on the chief's radar?"

"I'll ask, but before you go around knocking on doors, you should know that people are sensitive about that stuff. Most of them want to put all that behind them."

"I understand."

A few seconds of awkward silence followed before Sawyer asked, "Will I see you at the funeral?"

"Of course." He tipped his hat. "I better go now. I'll keep you in the loop if I find out anything from the chief about the murders."

"That would be great. See you tomorrow," Sawyer said. She watched him climb in behind the wheel of his truck and drive off.

After getting gas and talking to Aspen, she breathed easier as she drove along Frontage Road through town, past Dominick's Doughnuts, the old Fish and Hook store, and the Roasted Bean.

The only thing that *had* changed was her.

It was weird. Being back in River Rock made her feel as if she had tumbled down Alice's rabbit hole. Only it wasn't a colorful, fantastical world she'd landed in. It was dark and immoral, secrets hidden in every corner.

She made a left onto Cold Creek Road. When Gramma still had her wits about her, she had warned Sawyer to leave River Rock at the first opportunity. "Get out of here and never look back. Do you hear me?"

But Sawyer hadn't listened.

Moments later, Sawyer sat quietly inside her car, engine rattling, idling at the bottom of the driveway leading to the house where she'd grown up. Since her job offered health benefits, she'd been able to seek therapy, hoping to find a way to put the past behind her. Every therapist she'd talked to told her she had some form of anxiety. One therapist said she suffered from *high* anxiety, the same diagnosis Sean Palmer had given her. Sawyer's research on the subject convinced her that no matter what they labeled her abuse and trauma, it wasn't going away. It had become a part of her, and now it was all about managing her emotions.

People with anxiety often worried about things they couldn't control. That might be true for Sawyer too. She didn't fear heights or flying. She wasn't self-conscious. She didn't worry about her job or her future. She worried that the resentment and anger buried inside her might eventually harden to the point of no return. She didn't like touching or being touched. She never cried. She trusted no one. There were times she felt like an emotionless shell. Only yesterday, she had observed a young woman lying in pools of blood, and yet Sawyer had hardly given the woman a second thought. How could she be a good crime reporter, let alone a decent human being, if she didn't feel or care?

Don't count on anything, and you won't be disappointed.

No one is really happy, so don't worry about it.

Those were just a few of the things people had told her over the years to make her feel better, but their words only made her feel as if she should keep silent—as if they were letting her know that everyone has problems, so stop complaining.

If she continued down this path of feeling anger and bitterness, wouldn't she eventually become coldhearted like her mother?

Her parents had always been gone a lot. When they hadn't been off searching for treasures for their antique shop, they were ghosts in their own house. Dad had spent most of his time at home locked in his office, while Mom had either been on the phone with one of her Rotary Club members or at a meeting.

Not everyone could be the perfect parent. Mom and Dad never argued like a lot of parents do. But Sawyer knew that unless her parents confronted their own issues, the likelihood that they would ever accept responsibility for their role in any of their children's lives was doubtful.

With that thought in mind, she stepped on the gas and headed up the driveway.

CHAPTER NINE

Cleo found Brad Vicente at the far table of the restaurant in a darkened alcove.

He stood as she approached. "Brad," he said. "You must be Cleo."

"I am. Nice to finally meet you."

He held her chair while she took a seat. Their wine had already been poured, just as Lily had suspected it would be.

"I hope you don't mind," he said. "I went ahead and took the liberty of ordering for you."

"Under the circumstances, I appreciate it. Work was crazy. Traffic was just as bad."

"Cheers," he said, holding up his glass.

"Cheers." They clinked glasses, and she took a sip. A little sweet, but not bad. No weird aftertaste. She set her glass down and looked around. "This is a nice place you chose."

He smiled.

The restaurant had lots of windows with views of a courtyard made up of a weeping willow and mossy rocks. A candle flickered on every table. She looked him over. She'd been talking to him online for weeks now. She and the rest of The Crew had dissected every post and then decided as a group how to respond. "You look exactly like your profile picture," she said.

He chuckled.

"I'm serious. It's refreshing. You have no idea how many men I've met face-to-face only to learn they look nothing like their photos."

He lifted a brow. "So you do this often?"

"You're my fourth." She frowned and reached a hand over the table. "You have something on your tie." As planned, she knocked over his water, drew her hand back, and gasped as if it had been an accident.

He scooted back in his chair and jumped to his feet. Ice cubes fell to the floor, and water dripped from his shirt and pants.

"I'm so sorry."

"It's okay," he said. "Enjoy your wine. I'll be right back."

As soon as he disappeared, she went in search of their server and told him the wine was sour and she wanted a fresh bottle of the same wine brought with new glasses. She slipped him enough money to cover the wine plus a tip and asked him not to mention it to her date. By the time Brad returned, she'd filled both glasses and drunk hers.

"Good as new," he said as he took his seat.

He didn't waste any time refilling her glass. She took a sip and smiled. "Your profile mentioned you had a large family and that you're the outdoorsy type, but what I want to know is why you're still single."

He chuckled again.

"No, really," she went on. "You're handsome, successful, good-humored—"

"I have flaws, like everyone."

"Such as?"

"I'm an exercise addict. I go to the gym twice a day, sometimes three. I can't get enough."

She sipped her wine, observed him over the rim of the glass. "What else?"

He leaned toward her. "I'm also addicted to sex."

It was her turn to laugh. "Seriously?"

He shook his head. "No. I'm kidding. I wanted to see your reaction."

"Well, that's too bad."

Before he could respond, the server brought their dinner. Miso-marinated sea bass for her and porterhouse steak for him.

"So," he said after the server left, "you were saying?"

"I forget," she said before sliding a bite of fish into her mouth and chewing. She sipped her wine. "Maybe I'll remember before dessert is served."

"You intrigue me."

"You've only known me for twenty minutes." She ate while he stared at her, his eyes probing.

"Should I be worried?" he asked.

She smiled. "Most definitely."

Before they finished the bottle of wine, Brad appeared antsy, less patient. They skipped dessert, he asked for the bill, and quickly ushered her from the restaurant.

She stumbled slightly as she walked across the parking lot toward her car. What the hell was going on? She'd watched every move he'd made, and she'd only drunk one glass of wine.

He linked her elbow with his. "Why don't you come to my place for dessert?"

She wobbled, then stopped and held on to him for support. "I don't think so. Isn't there a three-date rule before I go home with you?"

His jaw hardened. "I didn't take you for a tease," he said under his breath.

The man had gone from happy-go-lucky to suppressed fury in a matter of minutes. The look on his face scared her. "What did you say?"

"Maybe I should drive you home."

"I'll be fine." She hoped that much was true. She didn't feel well. She inhaled deeply. "I just need to get some fresh air."

"The least I can do is walk you to your car."

"No need," she told him, but he kept his arm hooked around hers and continued onward as if he knew exactly where she was parked. She'd taken only a tiny sip or two from the first bottle of wine. Whatever he'd spiked it with couldn't possibly have been enough to throw her off her game. Her gaze darted from one side of the parking lot to the other. *Someone from The Crew is supposed to be here. Where are they?*

Her car came into view. If she could get inside and lock the doors, she might be safe.

He pulled out his key fob. The headlights of the car next to hers winked.

The same thing happened to Lily.

Her insides turned. She was going to be sick. *What the hell is going on?* In that moment she recalled the look Brad had given their server as they walked out the door, their hands in a viselike grip. Had Brad slipped their server another tip? The server must have found him in the bathroom and told Brad what she'd done, then spiked the new bottle, knowing Brad would pay him for his troubles.

"I'm not feeling well," she said. Her vision blurred suddenly, her car now resembling a gray mass. Dizziness overcame her.

"Don't worry," he said as she melted against his chest and into his arms. "I've got you."

CHAPTER TEN

Jolted awake by the sound of the front door opening, Sawyer jumped to her feet. She'd fallen asleep on the living room couch. The lights came on. Her eyes strained against the brightness.

Mom and Dad were home. It took a moment for her vision to clear. They stood side by side. In the time since she'd seen them last, Dad appeared to have aged twofold. His dark hair, his best feature, had thinned considerably and was mostly gray. He held a cane in his right hand. Mom had never been what Sawyer would consider a beauty, but she always managed to hold herself regally, spine stiff and chin jutting, as she was doing now. Her silver hair had been blown dry into a classic bob, her bangs swept to one side. Her face appeared pinched, her lips so tightly drawn they made a white slash beneath her nose.

"Where have you been?" Sawyer asked, not intending to sound accusatory, merely curious.

"Your dad had no idea what time you were coming. When dinnertime rolled around and you still hadn't shown up, we decided to head into town for something to eat."

"It's ten p.m.," Sawyer pointed out.

"Don't get sassy with me," Mom said. Before she could go on one of her tirades, Dad put a hand on her mother's arm.

She scowled at her husband. "What? We've hardly seen her since she left home, and yet we're supposed to pull out the banners and whistles when she decides to make an appearance?"

Mom had always been an angry person. Sawyer's therapist told her that many people's anger stemmed from their inability to deal with fear, disappointment, or frustration. It annoyed people like Mom that they couldn't control every little thing that happened in life. Her mom's anger could be rooted in past trauma, but until she recognized her behavior, she wouldn't be able to see that her anger was only hurting herself.

Sawyer was used to her mom's outbursts, and most of it went in one ear and out the other. But it was the reason she rarely visited. If Sawyer could afford it, she would have stayed at a hotel. But money was tight, and her mom was harmless.

"Joyce," Dad pleaded, "this isn't the time to—"

Mom looked down her nose at Sawyer. "I'm assuming you brought your outfit for the festival next week."

Sawyer glanced at Dad to see any telltale sign that her mom might be joking. Dad took a breath. Mom wasn't kidding.

"I didn't bring an outfit for the festival since I won't be staying very long. I have to get back for work."

"I'm going to bed," Mom said with a huff.

They listened to the sharply accented footfalls as Mom disappeared down the hallway. The bedroom door slammed shut.

"Your mother has had a long day," Dad said to Sawyer.

"I should have texted before I left." Neither of them made a move to step closer and wrap their arms around each other. Dad and Mom had never been the affectionate type, so it worked out well all around.

Dad's posture relaxed some once Mom left the room. "I'm glad you came. It's good to see you."

"You too, Dad."

"I guess I'll head off to bed. Unless you want to stay up and chat, or—"

"No," she said, surprised by his offer. "We should both get some sleep. It'll be a long day tomorrow."

He nodded. "Your room is ready for you. There are clean sheets on your bed."

"I was thinking I'd sleep in Gramma's cottage."

He shook his head. "The mattress is stained. The place is a mess." He turned to leave, didn't get far before he glanced back at her and said, "Gramma Sally would be glad to know you came to say goodbye."

She nodded but said nothing as he walked away. He didn't know his mother-in-law, the woman he'd lived with for the past seventeen years. Gramma would not be happy to know Sawyer had returned to River Rock. Gramma never wanted to live with the daughter who despised her for leaving her father, a man Sawyer's mom never talked about. Their family was built on secrets rooted in shame, secrets that only served to lead to trust issues and anxiety.

Lack of funds had made it impossible for Gramma to turn down her parents' offer to live with them. The same reason Sawyer wasn't staying at a hotel. Sawyer had paid rent while living with Connor, but since she had no plans to sleep on her sister's couch for too long, she needed to save every penny for a deposit and first month's rent on a new apartment.

She grabbed her duffel bag and purse from the floor, turned off the lights, and made her way down the hallway to her bedroom. Shadows crossed her path, and the wood floors creaked beneath her shoes. In the blink of an eye, she was twelve years old again.

She held on to the wall for support. She could see him. Smell him.

Sawyer fell back a step, nearly lost her footing. *Breathe. Breathe, damn it!*

Whole minutes passed before she was able to shake the memories away and stop her hands from trembling. She continued on, pausing when her hand grasped the doorknob. Her plan had been to stay the weekend. But already she saw no reason to be in River Rock. After the funeral, she would return to Harper's home, tell her sister she'd been right, and ask her if she could stay there until she found an affordable apartment.

Sawyer opened the bedroom door, brushed her hand against the wall, and flipped the switch before stepping inside. The beat of her heart drummed faster. The bed, the dresser—everything looked the same. This was the first time she'd been in her old bedroom since Gramma came to live with them. Gramma had moved in to the cottage in the backyard, and her parents had never tried to stop Sawyer when she moved her things into the cottage and slept on a cot next to Gramma. The cottage had always smelled of roses growing right outside the window. But her bedroom had a dank, musty, unused smell to it.

The single bed with a patchwork quilt and flattened pillow had been pushed against the wall. There was also a dresser. Curtains with a washed-out, flowery print covered the small window above the dresser. A slumped-over Raggedy Ann doll sat on a straight-back chair in the corner of the room. She considered taking the quilt and pillow to the main room and sleeping on the couch.

You're no longer a little girl. You're in control now. You're strong. You can do this.

She searched through her duffel bag, pulled out her camera, and scrolled through the digital pictures she'd taken at the murder scene. Sitting on the edge of the bed, she stared at the picture she'd taken of the living room. A woman's coat had been tossed over the arm of the couch.

Had Kylie gotten home right before someone knocked on the door?

If the person didn't have a key card, Kylie would have had to buzz them through, which meant Kylie would have been alerted. That told Sawyer that her killer had to have been someone Kylie knew. Maybe the killer had come home with her.

Another picture revealed a book on the floor. It had fallen on its spine, the pages open so that she was able to read the title page.

Hunted: A Jacqueline Carter Novel, signed by the author: "Kylie, the next drink is on me. Waylan Gage."

Sawyer had heard of Gage. After writing for years, all the while struggling with depression and alcoholism, he'd managed to hit all the bestseller lists with *Hunted*.

She pulled out her phone and searched the internet for his name, then clicked on his website. The first thing that popped up was a list of dates and the cities he would be visiting during his latest book tour.

He'd already been to the Convention Center in Sacramento. She looked at the date and saw that he'd been at the convention, signing books on the same day that Kylie was murdered.

It was too late to call Palmer, but she would definitely tell him what she knew the next time she talked to him.

Her gaze shifted to the broken frame and the black-and-white photo on the floor next to the book. She zoomed in on the man in the picture, then clicked through the pictures until she found the one she'd taken of the man sitting in his truck in the parking lot. The young man in the black-and-white photo was definitely the same guy she'd seen crying.

Tired, she put her phone, along with the camera, back inside her bag, grabbed her sweatpants and T-shirt, and changed her clothes. She took her toiletries to the bathroom down the hall and brushed her teeth and washed her face.

Back in the bedroom, she shut off the light, climbed under the clean sheets, and rested her head on the pillow. Who had killed Kylie Hartford?

The boyfriend seemed the obvious culprit—too obvious. According to the neighbor, he'd spent more time in Kylie's apartment than she had. If that were true, wouldn't he have had time to plan? Judging by the photos, Sawyer would say this was a disorganized killing. From the looks of it, Kylie had been caught completely off guard. Would a distraught boyfriend have chased after her in a thin-walled apartment where people had seen him come and go?

As she lay there, thinking about Kylie's last moments, unfamiliar noises drifted through the dark: a thump, a creak, footsteps? Her gaze sifted through moonlit shadows and landed on the doorknob. There was no lock on the door.

Was the knob moving, or was that her imagination?

To hell with it.

She pushed the covers off and got up, walked quietly across the room, and yanked open the door. She looked both ways.

Nobody was there. She inhaled.

After she closed the door, she picked up the chair with the Raggedy Ann doll and slid its wooden back under the knob. Satisfied that it would hold if someone tried to enter, she climbed back into bed, closed her eyes, and began counting backward from one hundred.

CHAPTER ELEVEN

"Fuck!" Malice said loud enough for everyone connected to the call to hear her.

"What happened?" Psycho asked.

"I was sitting in my car, waiting for Cleo to tase the son of a bitch so I could help her get him into the trunk. But she passed out, literally collapsed into his arms."

"What now?" Psycho wanted to know.

Malice watched Brad Vicente's BMW pull out of the parking lot. They had to act quickly. "Lily, are you there?"

"I'm here."

Malice could only pray that the man was heading home. And if anyone knew the answer to her question, it would be Lily. "We need an address. Where does Brad Vicente live?"

"Fifteen hundred Nineteenth Street, Sacramento. Midtown. There are three entrances. One upstairs, two downstairs."

Malice plugged the address into the navigation app.

"That area is usually crowded around this time," Lily said. "When you arrive at the house, keep your head down, face covered. Parking might be difficult to—"

"I'm a block from the house," Bug told the group.

"How did you manage that?" Psycho asked.

"My night off, remember? Lucky for Cleo, I was waiting for a friend at Shady Lady, which happens to be right around the corner, when Malice called. I can see Brad's house from here. I'm going around back."

"Be careful."

"Always."

Malice found a parking spot on Twentieth. She checked her phone. There was a text from Bug: I'M HIDING IN A CLOSET DOWNSTAIRS. SOUNDS LIKE HE ENTERED THE HOUSE THROUGH THE GARAGE. STAY PUT UNTIL FURTHER NOTICE.

Malice wondered how Bug had gotten into the house so fast. Had she broken a window? Had anyone seen her? Their original plan had been to get Brad to Cleo's car, tase him, and then take him to an abandoned warehouse ten miles away. It had seemed so clear and easy on paper.

But *this* was the real deal.

Her nerves were shot. Nothing was going right. They had no plan B. The pounding in her ears made it difficult to think. Every worst-case scenario imaginable was fucking with her mind. Her instincts screamed at her to call the police. Her friend could be in danger. But The Crew's number one rule was "No police." Because that would mean they would have to file a report. The police would ask for names and IDs.

No police.

She would stay put, as Bug suggested.

It was after 9:00 p.m. Hot as hell. Sweat trickled down her spine. A group of rowdy kids walked by, laughing, streams of smoke trailing behind—teenagers, their hormones working overtime. She didn't want to think about what she'd been doing at that age. Definitely not hanging out with friends. And definitely not laughing.

A car drove past, music blaring. A couple walking their dog on the other side of the street stopped to stare at the teenagers across the way. Thirsty leaves hung from myriad branches of sycamore trees lining the street. Farther down the block, she spotted Psycho, tall and willowy, hard to miss. She made a sharp left into an alleyway.

Unable to sit still, Malice put a baseball cap over the black wig she'd been wearing for most of the night. The mask would draw attention, so she left it in her purse for now. Her wig felt tight and didn't help her throbbing headache. She climbed out of the car and walked at a measured pace toward Brad's house. Twelve and a half minutes had passed since receiving Bug's last text. Then her phone buzzed: COME ON IN. BACK DOOR IS UNLOCKED.

Malice took another sweep of the area. Psycho was nowhere in sight. The couple and the teenagers were a good distance away as she stepped through a side gate. Trees and a tall wood fence covered in ivy made for lots of privacy. There was a patch of grass, and a stone path that led to a firepit surrounded by inviting outdoor furniture. The back door was ajar. After her mask was on, she pushed the door open and stepped inside.

The curtains on the windows straight ahead had been pulled shut. The lighting was dim. The room was a long rectangle. A pool table and a small built-in bar took up the space on one side of the room, and a couch, coffee table, and flat-screen TV took up the other side. Malice stood next to the couch. Somewhere close to the middle of the room, sprawled out on the floor, was Brad, wearing a button-down shirt and navy-blue boxer briefs, his wrists and ankles bound with duct tape to various pieces of furniture, including the legs of the pool table.

Psycho and Bug sat on two of three stools lining the bar. Behind them were glass shelves filled with neat rows of whiskey, bourbon, vodka, you name it.

Psycho had taken off her wig and eye mask. She greeted Malice with a nod.

Bug, twenty-seven, the youngest in the group, raised a cue stick. "Want to join us for a game of pool? I was about to rack the balls."

Brad thrashed about. He'd been gagged and blindfolded, forced into a vulnerable situation, and he didn't like it. He rocked his head maniacally back and forth, his face strawberry red from the effort.

Malice shut the door, locked it, then pulled her mask off. "Where's Cleo?"

"Upstairs, sleeping off the drugs." Bug used the cue stick to point to the laptop sitting on the bar. "I need a password." Bug was the computer geek in the group, the hacker. During the day she worked for an antivirus company, stopping hackers like herself.

"How did you get him tied up so quickly?" Malice asked.

"I heard him going up and down the stairs. After he quieted, I made a noise. He came back downstairs. I tased him and he went down. Luckily for me, he had more than one roll of duct tape in the cupboards in the laundry room. That stuff comes in handy." She smirked. "I think I did a good job under the circumstances."

Malice checked the bindings holding Brad in place. She knelt low and leaned close to his ear. "No use struggling, Brad. If you want to make things easier on yourself, you'll need to give us the password to your computer."

Beneath the tape over his mouth, his roar was followed by a stream of words she couldn't make sense of.

"We're here to teach you a lesson," Malice told him. "The quicker you cooperate, the sooner you'll be released."

"Look what I found hanging on the wall outside," Psycho said.

Malice lifted an eyebrow. They had no plans to dismember Brad or do him any lasting bodily harm, but scaring him was definitely on the table. "Those pruning shears look sharp. What do you plan to cut off first?"

Brad was at it again, wriggling around, screaming beneath all the tape. He clenched and unclenched his fists, attempting to loosen the bindings around his wrists.

Malice stood and headed for the spiraling iron staircase leading upstairs. "I'm going to check on Cleo and take a look around, see what I can find. Could one of you let the others know we'll be staying on schedule?"

"We're going to stay here?" Bug asked.

"Yes. We need to stick to the plan."

"What about neighbors, family, coworkers?"

Malice frowned. "What about them?"

"Somebody could stop by, ring the doorbell, call the police if they think something funny is going on."

"Stop worrying," Psycho told Bug. She pulled her phone from her pocket. "I'll contact the others."

Malice didn't see The Crew members in person often. Psycho wore a tank top that revealed dozens of scars. Some were thicker than others, a mass of raised tissue. Others were shiny and red.

Psycho noticed her staring and said, "He did a good job of stitching me up, don't you think?"

Malice said nothing. Upstairs, she found Cleo passed out on the king-size bed in the master bedroom. She found a strong pulse. "Cleo," she said. "Wake up."

Cleo stirred, moaned, but didn't open her eyes.

Malice left the lights off as she made her way around the bedroom, opening drawers and searching through Brad's things. He was neat and tidy, his socks in perfect rows. T-shirts and boxers all folded in perfect squares. *Impressive.*

"Where am I?"

Malice turned toward the bed. Cleo was sitting up and rubbing her eyes. "What happened?" Cleo asked. An expression of terror crossed her face suddenly, and she scrambled from the bed. "Where is he?"

"It's okay. Bug was able to get to him before he could touch you."

Every part of Cleo was shaking. "Fuck."

Malice nodded.

"Is this his house?"

"Yes."

"If he had taken me somewhere else—anywhere—I would have been literally and royally fucked."

"But you weren't. It's okay."

"It's not okay." She clamped her head between her palms. Seconds passed before she looked at Malice. "Months of planning, texting that asshole, exchanging pictures, and flirting." She shivered. "For what? He was in control the entire time."

She's right, Malice thought. Things could have turned out much worse than they had. Cleo had been lucky. Lily had told them exactly what Brad was capable of, and yet he'd still managed to get the upper hand.

Next time, things would be different.

CHAPTER TWELVE

Sawyer climbed out of bed after tossing and turning for most of the night. The cold crept under her clothes and caused goose bumps to gather on her arms. She grabbed her sweatshirt from inside her bag and pulled it over her head. On her way to the kitchen, she smelled coffee brewing. Mom was putting away dishes.

"Good morning," Sawyer said.

Mom gestured toward the cupboard. "Coffee cups are over there."

Sawyer grabbed a mug on her way to the coffee machine, filled it up, and took a seat at the kitchen table. Since she wouldn't be staying long, she knew the best way to move on from last night was to simply apologize. "Sorry I didn't tell you what time I was coming yesterday."

"Today's a new day," Mom said in a chirpy voice. "It's behind us."

She'd forgotten about Mom's favorite saying: "It's a new day. Let bygones be bygones."

A part of Sawyer felt bad for not trying harder to stay in touch with Mom and Dad. But it worked both ways, didn't it? Was it solely her job to make the effort to connect? She thought of Harper and how she made sure to call Sawyer at least once a week. Their conversations were short, but it was nice being checked on. Harper was a good mom to her kids—a great mom. Since the day Sawyer found her sisters, it was Harper who'd gone out of her way to include her and make her feel welcome.

Mom finished with the dishes and was now collecting eggs and milk from the fridge. "How are your sisters?"

The question blindsided Sawyer. Mom rarely asked about Aria or Harper. They only talked about her sisters if Sawyer brought one or the other up in a conversation. "Aria is doing great. She works more than one job, which keeps her busy." Sawyer sipped her coffee. "Three days a week at the SPCA and part-time at a coffeehouse for the health insurance. Every once in a while, she drives for one of those on-demand transportation companies."

"That's too bad," Mom said without looking up from what she was doing. "I always thought Aria would be a doctor—you know, a veterinarian. She was the smart one out of you three."

"And Harper," Sawyer said, ignoring the impulse to tell her mom that she was also smart and had graduated with honors, "is a wonderful mom to your grandchildren."

"But her children are probably old enough to do things on their own," Mom pointed out. "What does Harper do in her free time?"

"Taking care of two kids and a husband is a full-time job when you do it right."

Mom's gaze tore into hers. "Is there some hidden meaning in that statement?"

"No," Sawyer said, although there was. Being a good mother was a full-time job. Being a shitty one didn't take much time at all.

Mom went back to whisking the eggs and milk. "And what about you?" Mom asked.

Sawyer perked up at the thought of her talk with Sean Palmer. With so much going on, she'd nearly forgotten. "I recently got a promotion. I'm working my first homicide." She sighed. "Well, I will be when I return home."

Mom's face fell, her jaw slack. "Homicide?"

Sawyer nodded.

"I thought you wrote for a little local paper over there in that cow town?"

Here we go, Sawyer thought. Did Mom hate her life so much . . . or was there more to it than that? Either way, Sawyer decided to let it go. "It's the biggest newspaper in the city, and I'll be working in the investigative field under one of the most respected crime reporters in the country."

Mom poured the egg mixture into a sizzling frying pan on the stove. "So you write about dead people?"

"Sure," Sawyer said, already feeling a bit deflated. "I tell a story, let people in the community know what has happened so they can make informed decisions."

Mom stirred the eggs. "As in?"

"As in there is a killer running loose, so you might not want to let your young children roam freely without adult supervision."

Silence strangled the air between them.

Sawyer wondered if Mom remembered doing just that? Letting her three daughters run around town alone, knowing that Peggy Myers and Avery James had been murdered? Did Mom ever feel any remorse whatsoever for not being there for her daughters when they needed her? Two young girls brutally murdered, and Sawyer had no recollection of her parents ever warning her to be careful. And what about Uncle Theo, Dad's brother? Was Harper right when she said Mom and Dad knew exactly what went on under their own roof? Or would Mom go to her grave denying that anything horrid had ever happened in River Rock? A new day and all that bullshit.

"Hello, Theodore!" Mom said.

Sawyer's body tensed as she glanced over her shoulder toward the kitchen entrance. Knowing her uncle had been released from prison was one thing, but seeing him inside the house where she'd grown up, where he'd abused her, was quite another. "What the hell is he doing here?"

"I didn't know you were here," her uncle said, his eyes on Sawyer.

He'd lost a lot of weight. His tattered clothes and scraggly goatee made him look as if he'd been living under a bridge. Sawyer's hands shook, her insides jittery, as she met her uncle's gaze. It wasn't fear she felt, but rage. "I can't believe you have the gall to step inside this house after everything you did. You're a sick fucker."

"I should go," he said.

Sawyer stood. "Yes, you should."

Mom clicked her tongue. "Don't mind her," she told Uncle Theo. "Stay and have some eggs and coffee with us."

Sawyer looked at her Mom. "What is it with you? He was sent to prison for rape. Harper told me you know what this man did to me and to this family, and yet you allow him into your house and offer to feed him?" Heat flushed through her body. "Harper was right. You don't care about your daughters. Today's a new fucking day. Is that how the saying goes, Mom? Yesterday is behind us. Let it go?"

Mom's jaw hardened.

The side door behind Mom, the one leading to the backyard, came open. Dad stepped into the kitchen. He looked from face to face, his gaze stopping at his brother. "I told you not to come around while Sawyer's here."

"I just wanted to stop by and see if you and Joyce needed help this morning. You know, before the service."

Sawyer tried to read the silent exchange between her parents, but it was impossible to tell if the dynamics of their relationship had changed. Mom had always worn the pants in the family. She almost always had the upper hand. When they disagreed, she usually won. But Dad surprised her by pointing his finger toward the exit. "Get out," he told his brother. "Now."

"I helped take care of Sally," Uncle Theo argued. "I'm family too."

"I'm not going to try to stop you from going to funeral," Dad said. "But you're not welcome in this house."

Uncle Theo pouted. "At least tell her how I've changed. How I found God and made amends. I'm not who I used to be. Tell her."

The blood in Sawyer's veins was boiling. If he didn't leave soon, she might just strangle him with her bare hands. "I don't care," she said. "You ruined my life and my sisters' lives. Nothing you could say would ever make up for what you did."

"Go!" Dad said to his brother.

Mom said nothing.

Uncle Theo headed back the way he'd come.

Sawyer heard the door open and close.

She couldn't breathe. The thought that she might see him during her visit had crossed her mind, but nothing could have prepared her for the outpouring of emotions that threatened to bring her to her knees. Her insides quivered. "I'm going to get dressed and then drive to town," Sawyer said, afraid she might break down if she didn't get away. "I'll see you both at the chapel."

"What about breakfast?" Mom asked.

"I'm not hungry."

CHAPTER THIRTEEN

At 8:00 a.m., Malice parked on Nineteenth Street, closer to Brad's house. To the left of his home was an alleyway followed by a Queen Anne Victorian with a large porch and a **FOR RENT** sign in the front window. The house to the right of Brad's was occupied. Last night, through a bathroom window, she'd watched a woman leave the house with a dog on a leash. Thirty minutes later, Malice happened to peek through the blinds from the main room when she returned. The neighbor wore dark leggings and a T-shirt. Her dirty-blonde hair had been tied back in a ponytail. Malice guessed the woman to be in her late thirties.

That same neighbor was now leaving her house again. This time without the dog. She used a key to lock the front door, slipped it into her bag, and walked down the front steps. When she got to the street, she stopped to stare at Brad's house.

A chill washed over Malice. *What was the woman doing? Had she heard something? A strange noise?*

Malice didn't take another breath until the woman started off down the street. Today she was dressed in slacks, heels, and a pink shirt with a froth of petals on the sleeves. The woman suddenly pivoted and looked directly at her.

Malice froze, didn't take a breath until the woman climbed into her Subaru and drove away.

Had she seen her?

Cleo and Psycho had spent the night with Brad. Malice pulled her baseball cap on and tugged it low over her eyes. She grabbed the bag of food she'd brought, climbed out of her car, and crossed the street, making sure the heel of her boots didn't land too hard on the pavement as she went along.

A dog barked in the far distance. Leaves fluttered from trees like rain, sticking to her hair and shirt.

Something niggled. *Am I being watched?*

Paranoia could be a sneaky beast, pressing against her chest, hanging on to her like a needy child. She continued on at a steady pace. *Nothing to see here,* she thought as she made her way through the side gate and slipped into the cover of Brad's backyard. Only then, safe beneath the covered patio leading into the bottom half of his house, did she take a breath.

Her hands were clammy, her heart beating wildly. As she collected herself, she set the food on the bench outside the door and replaced the cap on her head with a wig. Next came the mask that Cleo had made from neoprene.

The paranoia wasn't going away. She found herself second-guessing everything they were doing. *Why am I here? Risking everything? Will teaching one asshole out of thousands make things better for me?*

Her thoughts were replaced by her abuser's face, clear as day. His hands felt rough, calloused, his fingers touching, groping, his tongue wet against her skin, his body heavy, his breath on her ear, his words— threats of violence—holding her captive.

And just like that, she was being violated all over again.

She felt the disgrace, shame, guilt, and embarrassment until shock set in, leaving fear in its wake. Her body had shut down—eyes closed, muscles lax, mind drifting—as he took everything and left nothing.

A car backfired.

Her eyes shot open, surprising her since she wasn't aware that she'd closed them. She filled her lungs with air as anger replaced all else, swirling around her like a mini tornado. It irked her to think, even for one second, she'd questioned what she and the rest of The Crew were doing.

Brad had done his best to break Lily down, take control of her body and mind. What would he have done to Cleo had they not intervened? How many others had he damaged? It stunned her that she felt this sudden need to think of these things at all. Brad was scum, a pervert who needed to drug women and tie them up to give him a momentary sense of self-worth to make him feel secure and manly.

Malice reached out and held firmly to the doorknob, turned it, stepped inside, and shut the door behind her. Facing the bar, she waited for her eyes to adjust to the dark through the tiny slits of synthetic rubber.

The curtains had been tightly drawn. Without any light coming from the downstairs bathroom, the room was much darker than it had been last night. She focused on the spot where she'd last seen Brad. A distorted shadow caught her eye. "Cleo, is that you?"

There was movement to her right. Chills washed over her. A rustling sound, and then a strong hand grasped on to her ankle and held tight.

She struggled to free her leg but was yanked to the floor instead. The contents of the bag she'd been carrying scattered about, and her head struck a hard object, sending a sharp ache through her skull.

Despite the pain, she managed to stay alert. She couldn't see him, but she knew it was Brad who was tugging on her leg. The anger she'd felt minutes ago morphed into rage as he dragged her toward him. All uncertainty left her. She knew what to do. Feigning unconsciousness, she let him pull her closer. How many times had she lain awake at night, imagining what she would do if she were ever attacked?

Too many.

She could hear him breathing. Smell his stench. She was deadweight. He was weak and tired. His other hand reached for her leg, his knuckles brushed against her calf. She drew back her free leg and slammed her booted foot straight ahead, making contact with his chest or face, she had no idea which and didn't care.

He let out a deep guttural sound but refused to let go.

They both knew this might be his best and last chance at escaping.

Drawing back her leg, she kicked him again, this time with more force. The bastard wouldn't give up, wouldn't let go!

Adrenaline filled her. She felt invincible as she pulled her leg back and struck again and again. She didn't stop until she heard the drumbeat of footsteps hitting the stairs.

Lights came on.

Only then did she realize he'd let go of her. Lifting her head, Malice saw the damage she'd done. His face was a bloody pulp. From behind her she felt Psycho latch on to both of her arms and pull her away from the bloody mess. Psycho was strong. She lifted Malice into her arms and onto the couch without much effort. "Are you okay?" Psycho asked. "You're bleeding."

"I hit my head when he yanked me to the floor."

"Lie here for a minute." Psycho left her side.

"You did some damage," Cleo said, "but he's still breathing. How did he get loose?"

"All I know," Malice said, "is that the son of a bitch messed with the wrong person this morning."

Nobody argued with that.

"He's out cold." Psycho knelt down close to Brad, assessing the situation. "Looks to me as if he twisted and turned his wrists all night long and was able to loosen the tape enough to pull one of his hands free. If you hadn't come when you did," she told Malice, "he would have escaped, probably would have run to the neighbors to call the police."

Malice didn't want to think about what could have happened. She reached for a napkin that had flown from the bag of food when she dropped it and used it to dab at the gash on her head.

Psycho dragged Brad back to the bar area, rolled him onto his stomach so she could bind his wrists behind his back before fastening him to an old but sturdy built-in radiator. "Good thing Brad keeps a nice big supply of duct tape in his house," she said as she worked.

While Psycho took care of Brad, Cleo cleaned up the mess by the door. She held something up between her fingers. "Looks like you kicked out one of his teeth."

"Nice," Psycho said.

Malice pushed herself to a sitting position. When the dizziness passed, she stood and picked up the napkins and the breakfast sandwiches she'd bought and put it all on the coffee table. She grabbed a sandwich. "I'm hungry. Did anyone make coffee?"

"It's brewing now," Cleo said.

Once everything was cleaned up, Psycho and Malice ate their sandwiches and drank coffee at the bar as they talked about what to do next.

Cleo sat on the couch with Brad's laptop and a pile of papers she'd found stuffed away in his bedroom closet.

They had no idea Brad had come to until he spit out a mouthful of blood and said, "You bitches will pay for this." He let out a growl as he tried to free himself. "My good friend is a cop. When he finds out I haven't been to work, he'll be knocking on my door."

"The second I find proof of what you've done, your ass will be dragged to jail by that same friend," Psycho told him.

"There are no videos," Brad told her. "You're wasting your time."

Psycho snorted. "Bullshit. All serial rapists keep videos so they can relive that moment when they had power. Because with guys like you, that's what it's all about."

"I'll find you," he said. "Every one of you. You're all dead."

"You try so hard to be a big scary dude, don't you, Bradley? But you need to tie women up to get a hard-on?"

"Fuck you," he said. One of his eyes was swollen shut. His nose had been flattened, definitely broken.

Psycho stood, grabbed a cue stick, and used it to poke at his crotch. "What's under there, I wonder? A tiny little worm, I bet."

"Wouldn't you like to know," he said. "Go ahead and take a look. I don't mind."

"The only reason I would go near your dick would be to cut it clean off and toss it in the garbage disposal." Psycho scrunched up her face. "Make a little mincemeat out of your little willy."

Cleo let out a low whistle and jabbed an arm in the air. "Do it!"

"I'm not sure being here is safe," Malice said. "I saw the neighbor staring at Brad's house on her way out. I mean, she didn't just glance at it, she stopped and stared for a long while."

"That woman is hot for me," Brad said.

Psycho ignored him. They all did. "I thought we were sticking with the plan?" Psycho asked.

The doorbell rang.

Malice cursed under her breath. She pointed at Brad. "Gag him!"

Psycho grabbed one of the washcloths Cleo had used to clean up and shoved it in his mouth before winding duct tape around the lower half of his face.

Cleo set the laptop aside, caught up to Malice, and followed her up the stairs to the front room. The curtains were drawn. Nobody could see them as they made their way to the entry door. Cleo peered through the peephole. "I can't believe it. It's him."

"Who?"

"The waiter who served me and Brad at the Blue Fox."

Before Malice had a chance to let that sink in, Cleo opened the door, took a fistful of the man's shirt, and yanked him into the house.

Malice shut the door and locked it. Her heart was racing. Things were spiraling out of control. By the time she turned around, Cleo had him pinned to the floor, a knife at his throat.

Psycho rushed up the stairs. Her gaze fell to the man on the floor. "What's going on?"

"We need the rope and duct tape!" Malice dropped to the floor to hold the man's legs to stop him from flailing around.

Psycho disappeared back down the stairs and returned seconds later with the tape and used it to bind his wrists, knees, and ankles. It helped that the waiter was young and bony, likely had never set foot in a gym in his life. His eyes were wide open. He'd already pissed in his pants.

Cleo stopped Psycho from taping his mouth shut. "In a minute," she said. "Why are you here?" Cleo asked the waiter.

"He invited me."

"Brad?"

"Yes."

"Invited you here to have sex with me?"

"Yes."

"Have you done this before?"

He looked confused.

"I'm not asking if you've had sex before. I'm asking if you've come here to this house to have sex with one of Brad's dinner dates?"

He shook his head.

"You're a liar. I know you've done this before."

"Okay. Y-yes. Last time I only watched."

"What kind of sick fuck are you?"

"I don't know." His lips and chin trembled. "I'm sorry."

"You're only sorry because we caught your ass."

He was crying now, snot oozing out of his nose.

Cleo looked at Malice. "This is bullshit. He came here to rape me!"

His sobbing was getting out of control.

"Shut up," Cleo told him, "or I'll end it for you right now."

"I think you should take a breath and calm down," Malice told Cleo.

Cleo peered into her eyes, and that's when Malice realized she was pissed but not out of control. She wanted to scare the waiter.

"The asshole," Cleo said through gritted teeth, her spittle hitting his cheek, "was going to do whatever he wanted with me while Brad watched, and then vice versa. I'm livid. You would be too if it had been you," she said. "If he doesn't tell me everything I want to know, I'm going to kill him."

"Please," he begged.

"Psycho," Cleo said, "I want to get his confession on video."

Psycho stood over them. She pulled out her cell, pushed some buttons, and kept it aimed on the man. "Ready."

Cleo glared at the waiter. "Answer my questions truthfully and we'll let you go."

He nodded.

"How long have you worked at the Blue Fox?" Cleo asked him.

"Two years."

"What did you put in the wine?"

"Rohypnol."

"Did Brad give you the drug?"

He nodded.

"Is that a yes or a no?"

"Yes."

"The last time you were at Brad Vicente's house, did Brad video the event?" Malice asked, hoping he would fall for the ploy since they still hadn't found any evidence that he kept images or videos.

He said nothing, prompting Cleo to press the blade closer to his throat. A drop of blood appeared.

Malice hoped she knew what she was doing.

Psycho zoomed in on the waiter's face. "Answer her, asshole!"

"Yes!" he said, sobbing anew. "He took a video. He always took videos."

Malice gestured for Psycho to turn off the video. Once that was done, she said, "Let's cover his face and drag him downstairs. We need to focus on finding those videos."

CHAPTER FOURTEEN

Sawyer parked in an empty lot, climbed out, and walked down Frontage Road toward the doughnut shop. The place was surprisingly crowded.

"Sawyer Brooks, is that you?"

Sawyer smiled when she saw Old Lady McGrady. That's what she and her sisters used to call her when they were small. She and her husband, Harold, used to run a popular tourist attraction called River Rock Gold where they taught visitors to pan for gold in the creeks and streams. Harold used to love talking about the years from 1880 to 1959 when thousands of gold miners were all crowded together, searching for gold, and how ninety ounces was often recovered in a single pan. Harold had been one of the lucky prospectors, able to live nicely off his finds. He knew how to find hidden pockets in the bedrock. Sadly, he passed away months before Sawyer left for Sacramento. Had a stroke while panning and was found facedown in what his friends called a hot spot, leaving his wife with enough gold to pay for his funeral and then some. Old Lady McGrady had to be in her mid to late eighties by now.

Sawyer waved. "I'll be right there." She ordered a coffee and a maple bar and brought them to the table where Old Lady McGrady was sitting alone. "Mind if I join you?"

"I'd be offended if you didn't."

Sawyer took a seat. Old Lady McGrady's long silver hair had been loosely braided in one long strand that hung over her shoulder. Her skin was wrinkled and weathered with age, but her eyes were as clear and blue as Lake Shasta.

"Go ahead," she said to Sawyer. "Eat!"

Sawyer took a bite. The doughnut melted in her mouth. It was delicious. So was the coffee. Her stomach grumbled. She realized she'd hardly eaten in two days.

"I'm going to miss your gramma," Old Lady McGrady said. "I used to visit her once a week and take her for a walk in her wheelchair. She never said much, but her eyes lit up every time a bird chirped or a frog croaked."

Guilt seeped through Sawyer. Despite Gramma telling her to leave River Rock, she should have been there for her. "Thank you for watching over her."

"I did it more for me than for her. She frightened easily, and it always made me feel better knowing she was okay."

"What was Gramma afraid of?"

"She said she heard your mom and dad talking, and she thought they might do her harm."

"What?"

"Your gramma worried about a lot of things, and most days she mumbled incoherently. To be honest, everything scared her."

"When did this happen?"

"Oh, gosh. It was over a year ago. I shouldn't have said anything." Old Lady McGrady reached over and rested a blue-veined hand on Sawyer's forearm. Sawyer didn't pull away.

"Don't beat yourself up," Old Lady McGrady said. "You did the right thing, leaving this town. I would have left myself if I'd had any place to go."

Sawyer knew Old Lady McGrady had a loose tongue and a fondness for gossip, but imagining Gramma spending days and nights alone and afraid sent chills up her spine. "Do you mind if I ask you a question?"

She pulled her hand back to her side. "Not at all."

"It's about the unsolved murders. Did you know either of the victims?"

"Harold and I knew everyone in River Rock. I still do. Peggy used to spend a lot of time with her siblings, panning for gold. She was so smart. Such a tragedy."

"Do you recall if there were any suspects at the time?"

"None that I know of. But Danny Hart was the first person to come forward and tell the police that he saw a young woman with long brown hair running from the woods that day."

"Mind if I take notes?"

"Not at all. It's about time someone around here started asking questions."

Sawyer finished writing and then looked at her. "I'm glad you feel that way."

"Killing someone and then taking a piece of hair as some sort of gruesome trophy. That kept me up at night. I still think of it."

"Why Peggy?" Sawyer asked.

"The only thing I could think of was jealousy. She was a sweet, young, pretty girl."

"Do you think Danny Hart was telling the truth?"

"I don't know," Old Lady McGrady said. "He passed away years ago, so you won't be able to talk to him, but for a week or two, it seemed like everyone had a theory about who and what they had seen. I think Chief Schneider got frustrated and sort of gave up."

"It was probably easier for him to blame it on an outsider," Sawyer said.

"Definitely." Old Lady McGrady looked at her and frowned suddenly. "You and your sisters had a rough go of it, didn't you?"

"I'm not sure what you mean."

"After hearing about your uncle's release, I have to admit I was surprised to see you back in town."

Sawyer had always wondered who, if anyone, in town was aware of what Uncle Theo had done to her and Aria. "You knew?"

"After your sisters ran off, I suspected. But it wasn't until your uncle was thrown in jail for sexually assaulting a coworker that it all came together for me." She narrowed her eyes. "If I'd known what he was up to, I would have brought in the cavalry. Hell, I would have grabbed Harold's rifle and taken care of him myself."

Sawyer would have liked to have seen that. She finished her maple bar and chased it down with coffee.

Old Lady McGrady began collecting her things. "I better get going. I've got errands to run before I go home to get ready for the funeral." She patted Sawyer's arm for the second time. "I'll see you in a few hours."

"Thanks for talking with me," Sawyer said. After waving through the window at the old woman, Sawyer got up to refill her coffee. No sooner had she returned to her seat than a feeling of being watched swept over her. She gazed out at the line of cars parked on the street. They all appeared to be empty. Beyond the cars was the edge of a wooded area, a vast expanse of woods she knew well. A place where she used to read as eagles soared overhead, a serene place where birds sang and young coyotes played. Even within the darkest parts of the woods, she'd always felt safe, hidden from the most dangerous predators of them all . . . humans.

Her gaze traveled to the fishing store across the street. Nobody was coming or going.

Stop being paranoid.

She pulled out her phone and saw she had two missed calls. One from Derek Coleman, her ex-boss, and the other from Aria.

She decided to start with Coleman. She hit "Call back," and when he answered, she said, "Hi. It's Sawyer. You called?"

"I did. Do you mind holding on for two seconds?"

Before she could answer, the other end of the line was muffled. She could hear voices on his end and what sounded like a door closing.

"There. We're good," he said. "I can talk now."

She said nothing. Simply waited.

"Are you there?"

"I'm here."

"First off, I wanted to tell you how sorry I am for your loss."

"Thank you."

"I also wanted to thank you for putting one hundred percent into the story about the birthday party gone horribly wrong and let you know I appreciate your hard work."

Her chest puffed just a little bit. "You're welcome."

"It's a tragic story that you told in a respectful and meaningful way. Your words will bring awareness to what should have been just another party."

She didn't know what to say. She couldn't recall Derek Coleman ever calling her in the past to hand out praise, or for any reason at all. It felt somehow unnerving, and yet she wasn't sure why. It took her a moment to think of what to say next, and by the time she started speaking, he spoke too. They laughed. "Go ahead," she said.

"No. You."

"Sean Palmer told me he talked to you about the job offer," she said.

"That's right. He did."

"He told me there was no need for me to give you notice."

"Correct."

Okay, she thought, *so he isn't calling about that.* She felt a tickle, a fluttering in her belly at the thought of not working with him any longer. "You've been a good boss," she said, then rolled her eyes.

"I could have been better. You and I were sort of thrown together at one of the worst times of my life. I definitely could have done better."

"Oh, no," she offered lamely. "That's not true."

He laughed.

She felt like an idiot, but that didn't stop her from stumbling onward, tripping over her words, probably making a fool of herself. She was good at that. In that moment she realized this was the first time in the three years since his wife's death that he'd so much as hinted at the tragedy. "I'm sorry about the loss of your wife. I should have told you that years ago, but there are simply no words when someone so young is taken too soon. Or maybe there are words, but I certainly was and still am at a loss as to how to express my sorrow for what you've been through."

"It's okay, Sawyer. There was and is no need."

Her nerves had quickly gotten the best of her, and when that happened she tended to talk too much. "Sean Palmer told me about the nice things you said about my work . . . about me. From the sounds of it, your generous praise made me look so good he had no choice but to give me a shot at it."

He laughed again.

She couldn't recall if she'd ever heard him laugh before. Hell, he hardly smiled. This conversation was getting weird. *Stop, Sawyer. Say nothing else.*

Coleman said, "Sean told me you plan to return on Wednesday."

"Correct."

"I realize this might sound as if it's coming from left field, but now that you're not working directly under me, I was hoping you would have dinner with me sometime."

She'd taken another swallow of coffee and nearly spit it out.

"Are you there?" he asked for the second time.

"I'm here. You caught me off guard. Sorry."

"No. Don't be. You've traveled back home for a funeral, and here I am, out of the blue, asking you out on a date. I only called to let you know I appreciated you getting the story to me with all you had going on."

A date. Connor had never taken her on a date. They'd met at the coffee shop where Aria worked part-time. She and Connor had kept running into each other, and the next thing she knew, she was moving in with him.

But this was Derek Coleman—the man who'd been calling the shots for the past three years, the sad, grieving widower who kept to himself.

This was definitely the *Twilight Zone*. She'd traveled to another dimension. Which is where her brain was at the moment—in another world. "I don't know what to say. I'm . . ."

"No need to give me an answer. We'll talk when you return to the office next week."

Before she could think of what to say next, he said, "Again. My condolences. We'll talk soon. Goodbye, Sawyer."

"Bye," she said absently, still in a daze. Derek Coleman had asked her on a date? She rarely discussed her life outside work, so it made sense that he wouldn't know about Connor . . . And now that Connor was out of the picture, that was a nonissue. But the thing that niggled at her was that she hadn't seen it coming.

Not even close.

She finished her coffee, shouldered her bag, and exited the coffee shop, still feeling blindsided by her conversation with Coleman as she walked along the sidewalk. Over the years, she and Coleman had talked about story projects and her work performance. But it never went beyond that. Even so, did she want to go on a date with him? He was six years older than she was. He was serious about his work. He was over six feet tall. He had nice eyes. God, it felt weird, thinking about him this way. She'd always thought of him as the sad, grieving widower. The man of few words.

She wove around a couple. Somebody had once told her about Coleman's large, supportive family. She couldn't remember why they had told her or why she remembered that tidbit at all, except that maybe such a loving image didn't compute—a big family gathered around the table at Thanksgiving, everyone happy to see one another. *Weird.*

Dinner with Coleman? Alone? Just the two of them?

No. She couldn't do it. She didn't want someone like Derek Coleman to get too close and see all the broken bits and pieces. She liked and respected him too much. Besides, he'd been married once, which told her he was the settling-down sort who probably wanted to have kids someday. Settling down with one person for too long wasn't her thing. And the thought of ever having children didn't appeal to her. She loved her niece and nephew. Would do anything for them. But she could hardly take care of herself, let alone a child. No way.

Sawyer noticed the bookstore next door to the coffee shop. Since she was here, she thought she might as well say hello to the owners, Mr. and Mrs. Russell, and ask them what they remembered about the murders, if anything.

Peering through the window, she saw a woman standing behind the counter. *Is that Oliver Quinn?*

A bell jingled as Sawyer pushed through the door.

Oliver looked different. A lot different.

He'd always worn his long brown hair pulled back in a ponytail, but today he wore it loose in highlighted waves that swept over his shoulders. The beard was gone. His skin flawless. He looked thinner, almost fragile looking.

Oliver and Sawyer had been in the same class growing up. They were the same age, born on the same day. Like a lot of kids in River Rock, Oliver had been through some shit in his life. Teachers and parents thought of him as a troublemaker—the rebellious kid who smoked cigarettes between class and did as he pleased. Other kids were afraid of him, and they called him a warlock because he threatened to put a curse on them if they didn't leave him alone.

Like Sawyer, Oliver loved to read. Back then he'd gravitated toward dark fantasy with elements of horror and dread, while Sawyer tended toward mystery, anything involving a murder that needed to be solved. They both spent whole weekends in the bookstore, sitting on the floor or on the beat-up couch in the back room, never talking much, simply reading for hours on end. Mr. and Mrs. Russell never kicked them out. The kindly couple simply worked around the misfits in their store as if they belonged there.

Oliver didn't look up until Sawyer stood right across the counter from him, their faces a foot apart. Oliver finally lifted his head. "Sawyer Brooks?"

Sawyer nodded. "It's been forever. I can't remember the last time I saw you."

"Exactly one week before you left this miserable town for good. You were here at the bookstore, looking for a good read," Oliver said. "And call me Melanie, or Mel if you're in a hurry." Oliver gestured with his hands across the upper part of his body, sort of like the woman on *Wheel of Fortune* might do before revealing a letter on the board. "Hormone replacement therapy alone didn't cut it, so I had breast augmentation surgery to help alleviate gender dysphoria and improve my confidence and self-esteem."

Oliver had always kept to himself. He used to come across as edgy and uptight, so his announcement made sense. Holding secrets and not being able to be yourself would take its toll on most people. Good for him for having the courage to be himself. "Some secrets are too great to keep trapped within yourself," Sawyer said. "I'm happy for you."

"Thanks. TMI, I know," Melanie said. "But life's too short. For the first time I'm content with who I am. It's freeing. What about you? What are you up to these days?"

"I'm a crime reporter."

Melanie chuckled. "That's why you really came back to River Rock, isn't it?"

Sawyer was taken aback but quickly composed herself. "It's definitely part of the reason. I don't have much time, but if you don't mind, I would love to ask you about the unsolved murders."

Melanie crossed her arms over her new chest. The boobs, the voice, the hair and skin—it was hard to believe that this young woman was her old friend Oliver. "You came to the right place," she said.

Sawyer pulled out her notebook.

"Just last week I heard rumors that Robert Stanley beats his wife on a regular basis."

"Bob? The mechanic?" Sawyer asked. "That's horrible, but what does that have to do with the murders?".

"He didn't just beat her. He pinned her to the ground, chopped off a chunk of her hair, and threatened to kill her if she didn't behave."

"Just like the killer did to Peggy and Avery," Sawyer said.

Melanie nodded. "Exactly."

An old cuckoo clock on the wall began to chirp, reminding Sawyer it was time to go. "I want to hear more, but I have to go. Will you be around over the next few days to talk about this?"

"Come by anytime. I'll be here."

Sawyer stuffed her notebook away and then met her gaze. "It's good to see you."

"You too."

When Sawyer got as far as the door, Melanie said, "Be careful."

Sawyer looked over her shoulder at her. "What do you mean?"

"Just what I said."

CHAPTER FIFTEEN

It was nearing 11:00 a.m. by the time Malice, Cleo, and Psycho dragged the waiter downstairs and bound him to the leg of the pool table. Psycho fastened pillowcases over both men's heads, taping the dark fabric around their necks. She'd left plenty of air holes at the sides and back of their heads, so they could breathe but couldn't see.

Once the men's faces were covered, all three women removed their wigs and masks. Then they waited for Bug, who worked for Antiva, an antivirus company, and Lily, who worked as a manager at an outdoor adventure shop, to take time off for lunch so the entire crew could discuss what to do next via video on their cells.

Psycho's and Cleo's phones were used to pull Lily and Bug up on FaceTime.

"I have thirty minutes," Bug said when she called. "What do you propose we do now?"

"I got in. Found the file of videos hidden under 'Attributes!'" Cleo said excitedly.

They all cheered.

"Call the police and hand over the videos," Bug said.

"Not so fast," Cleo said. "It will take me a while to see what we've got. I'm skimming through them quickly, but I can already tell that some are blurry. It looks like Brad used low resolution when he first started out."

"How many are there?" someone asked.

"Dozens. It's going to take me some time to sort through these."

"Keep going," Malice said. "In the meantime, I vote that we stick with the plan and do everything we can to discredit Brad."

"The plan was to disrupt his life by sharing his truth," Lily said. "He's a predator. He should be locked up, but how do we move forward without proof of what he's done?"

"We can tell your story using an anonymous name," Bug said. "Maybe others will come forward."

Malice nodded her agreement. "Great idea. It's up to us to reveal the true Brad to his friends and coworkers. Then it's up to them to decide—"

Beneath the pillowcase, the tape over Brad's mouth must have fallen off because he interrupted. "Your ridiculous masks and wigs won't stop me from finding you," he said. "Every single one of you. You have no idea what I'm capable of. I'll do things to you that will make you wish you were dead."

Malice looked at the screen, where she could see Lily's face redden. She was the reason they were here, the one person in the group who had suffered Brad's forty-eight-hour assault. She had been here, in this house, with that man. Now, listening to him make threats after all he'd done ended up being too much.

"We have dozens of videos, showing you torturing and raping women," Lily shouted from the phone. "You will pay for what you've done!"

Brad cocked his head. "That voice. Who is that? Do I know you?"

Lily opened her mouth to speak, but Cleo cut in before Lily could say anything more. "If you don't shut your mouth, Brad, I'm going to have to shove that pool stick up your ass."

"I'd like to see that," Bug said. "The dirty thug needs a taste of his own medicine."

"My friends and coworkers will see the videos for what they are . . . a bit of kinky sex. Nobody can see my face. I made sure of that. And sorry, ladies, but I don't have any distinguishing marks other than my big cock." He snorted. "My boss won't give a shit about any of you bitches."

Psycho jumped off the stool she'd been sitting on, went to where Brad had managed to prop his upper back against the radiator. His hands were still bound behind his back, his legs in a wide V, his ankles taped to one of the couch legs.

Psycho grabbed the pruning shears and used them to cut off his boxers. Once that was done, she opened and closed the blades, making sure he could hear the snip, snip, snip. "The tree or the apples?" she asked Brad.

Brad struggled to get loose. "Get her away from me!"

Lily laughed.

"Hurry," Psycho told Brad. "Time is running out. Make a decision."

"Fuck you!" Brad said, wriggling frantically, trying to escape.

"Fine," Psycho said. "I'm going with the tree." She slid his penis between the sharp blades.

"Get her the hell away from me!"

At first Malice thought Psycho was just playing games. Now she wasn't so sure. Afraid his screams might be heard outside, Malice jumped up and used a throw blanket to muffle his cries. "Psycho. Stop."

"Are you kidding me?" Psycho asked. "Why are we even here? You heard the man. He's going to come after us. Nobody will give a shit about what he's done to those women. The police have already let him off at least once that we know of. Who's to say they won't let him go again? It's up to us to teach guys like Brad Vicente a lesson."

Malice exhaled.

"Majority rules, right?" Psycho asked her.

"Right," Lily cried.

Psycho looked toward the others. "Who votes to cut off his dick?"

Lily, Cleo, and Psycho raised their hands. "Three to two."

Snip.

Brad let loose an ear-piercing scream, primal and gut wrenching, like something Malice had only heard in the movies. She had to use all her strength to hold him down and muffle his cries. Blood seeped between his legs. That's all it had taken. One sharp snip of the shears, and the deed was done. No room for discussion.

Malice let go of the blanket covering Brad's face, pushed herself to her feet, and went straight for her purse. She pulled out a syringe. Her hands shook as she removed the plastic tip. Brad continued to scream and writhe in pain as she fell to her knees and plunged the needle into his arm, hoping she got a vein.

Back on her feet, she dropped the syringe back into her bag along with her mask. She found her wig inside her bag and pulled it tightly over the top of her head before stuffing loose hairs into the cap. Her head was pounding. Everything going wrong was one thing—it was out of their hands—but purposely deviating from the plan was another. She needed to get away from this craziness.

"What are you doing?" Cleo asked.

"I'm done. I'm getting out of here. Hopefully the drug I gave him will quiet him down." Malice pointed at the cut-off appendage and the puddle of blood. "This wasn't part of the deal."

Brad's legs were trembling, his voice hoarse and barely audible.

"I hope you're not serious," Psycho said, hands on hips. Blood dripped down her pant leg. "You beat the man until he was bloody, and we helped you clean it up. And now you're leaving?"

"The *only* reason he was able to grab me when I came through that door," Malice said, "was because you two weren't keeping an eye on him. Rule number one: 'No police.' Rule number two: 'Never take your eyes off the prisoner.' If I hadn't shown up, your asses would be in jail right now. Rule number three: 'No blood.'" She swung her hand back toward the man with no penis. "You've gone too far. This is bullshit."

Cleo set down her laptop, came to Malice's side, ushered her into the bathroom, and shut the door. "Take a breath," Cleo said. "He's not going to die. We'll clean this mess up and get out of here, okay?"

"If you leave that man tied up, he could die."

"I'll hack into someone else's account to alert authorities."

"What about the waiter?"

"I found him on a recent video, and his face is clearly visible."

Malice frowned. "What's he doing in the video?"

"He appeared to be watching, learning, jacking off. He got in a few feels, enough to keep him quiet. I found him on social media. His name is Doug Glacier."

A sicko in the making, Malice thought. "So we let Doug go?"

"Yes. We'll threaten him, tell him he needs to quit his job and never make contact with Brad again, or we'll take the videos to the police. He may not have seen what happened to Brad, but he heard. I wouldn't be surprised if he moves out of state after today."

"God," Malice said, shaking her head. "I can't believe she did that."

"He deserved it."

Malice rubbed her temple. "That's not the point. I can't work with Psycho if she's not going to stick to the plan."

"The plan went to shit the moment I passed out in Brad's arms. It's going to be okay. We're all new at this. We'll do better next time."

Malice couldn't think that far ahead. But Cleo was right . . . their plans had gone to shit from the beginning. If there was a "next time" and everything went to shit from the get-go, they would call the whole thing off and regroup.

"Come on," Cleo said. "Let's clean up, make sure we wipe down anything we touched."

"We should have worn latex gloves," Malice said.

"Next time."

Chapter Sixteen

The service was held outdoors. It was a beautiful day, blue skies and hardly any clouds. Sawyer stared down into the open casket, surprised to see Gramma's skin looking soft and her cheeks flushed as if she'd returned from a stroll. The funeral director had done a good job. Gramma wasn't overly done up or plastic looking. She appeared peaceful.

Tears didn't come, but Sawyer's heart felt heavy. "I love you, Gramma," she whispered. "Thank you for saving me and for giving me a fighting chance." Turning away, Sawyer headed for the empty seat in the front row next to her father. There were more than fifty people in attendance. Many were here today, she was certain, because of Mom and Dad. By the time Gramma had come to live with them, she was already experiencing forgetfulness and needed assistance carrying out everyday activities. Sawyer's parents, on the other hand, had spent more than half their lives here. River Rock was an old mining town, but panning for gold wasn't the only reason people came to visit. Mom and Dad's antique shop was a big draw and brought a lot of tourists into town. People drove long distances to see their store because of the bizarre collectibles to be found, and because of its size—two stories, each floor long and narrow. Every bit of space taken up by old tavern tables, Empire sofas, and Mission-style settees used to display vintage toys, jewelry, antique photographs, perfume bottles, and whatever oddities struck their fancy.

Sawyer used to enjoy searching for new items whenever she was left to roam the store. The memories prompted Sawyer to look at her parents, reminding her of a time when she was young and so hungry for their attention.

She never got it.

Both parents had been emotionally unavailable. Always too busy. Her therapist had told her it was likely Mom and Dad had their own problems growing up and simply did the best they could. Mom never talked to Sawyer about her childhood, but from what little she gathered from Gramma, Sawyer's mom was angry with Gramma for leaving her father. She believed it was a woman's place to stand by her husband through thick and thin.

The funeral director came forward then, stood behind the pulpit, and asked everyone to take a seat. He talked about everyone gathering today to celebrate Sally's life. As he invited people to speak, the sound of a police siren pierced the air.

Sawyer looked around for Aspen. She spotted him in the last row of chairs, his gaze directed toward the main road where the siren's whirring was now fading. Sawyer turned back to face the casket. She would see Aspen at the house later.

It took a few moments before the murmurs died down and the director was able to finish speaking.

A woman Sawyer didn't know took a few minutes to say kind words about Gramma. Next came an elderly gentleman dressed in an orange-and-brown plaid suit. He admitted he'd never met Sally but wanted to talk about the hazards of old age and how they all needed to keep moving. Apparently, he'd been walking every day for most of his life and was in tip-top shape. That garnered some laughter. He then invited anyone interested to join him each morning at 9:30 a.m. in front of the wood bear carving at Gold Dust Park.

Old Lady McGrady was the third and last person to speak. When she finished, Sawyer thought about getting up and saying something, but her legs wouldn't budge. She couldn't do it. Her feelings for Gramma were too personal to share. Nobody needed to know what Gramma meant to her. Her memories were hers alone.

The director had a few final words, and no sooner had the funeral begun, it was over.

Sawyer stood.

A group of people quickly formed a line, waiting to talk to Mom and Dad.

Sawyer walked toward the back in search of Aspen, closer to the edge of the freshly mowed grass where the tall pines towered over her and she could smell the damp earth.

Someone called out her name. A young woman. A cheerful voice. Sawyer stopped and turned toward her. It was Erika Leonard from high school. She'd been one of the mean girls back then. Every school had their share of them. They liked to mock others and spend most of their time gossiping.

"I'm sorry about your gramma," Erika said. "I know she meant a lot to you."

"Thank you."

"If there's any chance you'll be staying in River Rock for a while, Robert and I would love to have you over for dinner. Robert talks about the Brooks sisters all the time, especially Harper. He had a thing for Harper and used to offer to fix her car for free whenever it broke down."

"Bob Stanley? The mechanic?"

"The one and only," a male voice said behind Sawyer, startling her. She whipped around, surprised to see Bob hovering over her. His broad shoulders strained against his light-blue button-down shirt. The sleeves were rolled up to his forearms. He had big hands, a brawny chest, and a wide smile.

Erika beamed while Sawyer thought about what Melanie had said about Bob beating his wife. She wanted to reach out and pull off Erika's sunglasses to see if she was hiding any bruises.

Sawyer couldn't imagine the two of them together. The prom queen and the bad-boy mechanic. Like mixing oil with water.

Erika held up her left hand. "We're married. Three kids with a fourth in the oven." She patted her stomach.

"Wow."

"That's what I said when she broke the news to me," Bob said.

Sawyer fixated her gaze on him. His smile was long gone, as if his wife had betrayed him by getting pregnant. "I'm happy for you," she said. Before she could say anything more, Uncle Theo approached, stepped between her and Erika, and put a hand on Sawyer's arm. "Don't touch me," she said.

He pulled his hand away.

"I'm sorry," Uncle Theo said, tears in his eyes. "For everything."

He touched her arm. She slapped it away.

"Excuse us," Sawyer said to Erika and Bob.

"Sure you don't need some help?" Bob asked.

"I'll be fine." Sawyer walked away. She felt a stiffness in her neck.

Uncle Theo followed, talking all the way. "The pastor at Holiness Church says that I have paid my debt to society. I'm a new man, and I'm getting help. Please. I'm only asking for your forgiveness."

Sawyer waited until she was far enough away from Erika and Bob before she turned on her uncle. "You're a fucking pedophile. Bottom of the barrel as far as people go." Her hands rolled into fists. "I'll never forgive you for what you did. I don't want to talk to you. I thought I made that clear this morning. I don't understand why you're here. Gramma knew everything. She despised you."

"She was nice to me. I helped take care of her."

"Gramma was afraid of you."

"That's not true. It was your mother who made Sally whimper whenever she came near her. Not me."

Sawyer's jaw hurt from clenching her teeth. "Whimper? What the hell did Mom do to Gramma?"

He didn't answer, which was fine since she didn't believe a word he said. "Nobody wants you hanging around," she said, wanting to hurt him. "You meant nothing to Gramma, and you mean nothing to me. It's like you're not even standing here talking to me. You're invisible."

Sawyer walked away, every muscle tense. Why couldn't he leave her alone? He'd taken advantage of her and Aria when they were much too young to fend for themselves. He should be locked behind bars. He didn't deserve to walk free, and he certainly didn't deserve her forgiveness.

Sawyer bent over, hands propped on her knees, and counted backward from ten. Before she had a chance to gather her emotions, she heard a group of people talking about a young woman who was killed last night.

Up ahead, she spotted Aspen heading toward the parking lot. She had to run to catch up to him. "What's going on?" she asked him when she caught up.

Aspen turned toward her, his expression serious.

"Is it true?" Sawyer asked. "Was someone murdered last night?"

"I have to go, Sawyer." He turned to leave.

She stayed close to his side. "Who was it?"

He looked at his phone. "Isabella Estrada," he said as he walked.

Sawyer's stomach turned. "Her brother, Caden, was in my graduating class. Did you know Isabella?"

"I don't think so. The name doesn't sound familiar."

Hoping to ask him about what Melanie had said about Bob Stanley, she opened the passenger door of Aspen's truck just as the engine roared to life. She hopped in and buckled up.

"What are you doing?" he asked.

"I'm coming with you."

"That's not a good idea. Chief Schneider wouldn't like me bringing gawkers."

"I'm a reporter."

"That's even worse."

"Then tell him the truth," she said. "That I wouldn't get out of the truck, and you didn't have any choice in the matter."

He didn't look happy with her as he pulled out of the parking space. The ride was bumpy as he drove on the narrow, unpaved road leading through the woods to the main thoroughfare running through River Rock.

"You should have stayed with your parents," he said, his eyes on the road ahead.

"They won't even know I'm gone."

"You haven't changed much, have you?" he asked.

"What do you mean?"

"You never did take no for an answer. You were always stubborn."

"Maybe," she answered. "But I also know when to back down."

He seemed to think about that as they drove, then said, "I was surprised to see your uncle there."

"Uncle Theo showed up at the house this morning too. The asshole wants my forgiveness." She shook her head, glad that her hands were no longer trembling. "That will never happen."

Her gaze drifted to the scenery outside. She found herself thinking of the girls who were murdered. "How old is—was Isabella?"

"Sixteen."

"I wonder if there's any connection between this murder and the others," she said.

"First of all," he said, "it's up to the chief to decide whether or not we're dealing with a homicide."

"Got it."

"And as to others, you're referring to Peggy Myers and Avery James."

"That's right."

"I talked to the chief, and he said people don't talk about those girls any longer."

"Why not?"

"The citizens of River Rock want to move on. They no longer want to be associated with murder and death." He made a right onto Cold Creek Trail.

He seemed different from the way she remembered him. He was older now. Mature. "It's nice that everyone wants to sweep all the craziness under the rug and pretend all that horrible stuff never happened," Sawyer said. "But it is what it is, plain and simple."

"What do you mean?"

She kept her gaze on his profile while he drove. "River Rock is death," she said. "It's also misery and rape and neglect. In my opinion, River Rock stands for everything bad in the world."

Aspen visibly stiffened. "You don't live here anymore. The people who stayed, the ones who have nowhere else to go, would like to move on."

Again, she thought about the long summer days they'd spent together, especially after Rebecca went missing. Once Gramma moved in, she'd seen less and less of Aspen.

"You never said goodbye."

His statement surprised her. He was angry with her, annoyed at the very least. She tried to think, tried to slip back in time and remember. Had she left him like that—without so much as a goodbye? She rubbed the back of her neck. "I didn't realize. I'm sorry."

"Don't be."

"No, I am. I was so wrapped up in getting out of here, leaving River Rock for good, that I didn't stop to think about anyone but myself." She wondered suddenly if Harper had felt the same way when she'd left.

Aspen said nothing, his gaze on the path ahead, another dirt road lined by oaks, pines, and thick brush. Before anything more could be said, they had arrived. There was a fire truck and two police vehicles to the left. He parked his truck between two trees and jumped out.

Chief Schneider looked surprised to see Aspen.

"I heard about the homicide on the scanner," Aspen told him.

Sawyer watched Aspen step over the yellow crime tape still being rolled out so he could talk to the chief.

Her insides turned, her gaze fixated straight ahead on the young girl tied to the wide, mossy trunk of an oak tree. Thick rope circled the dead girl's naked body multiple times from neck to ankles. Her skin was milky white, her eyes wide and fearful, mouth gaping open—stuffed to the brim with brittle leaves and stems seemingly scooped up from the forest floor.

CHAPTER SEVENTEEN

An hour after leaving Brad's house, Malice was sitting inside a coffee shop with her laptop and a decaf black tea. The last thing she needed was more caffeine, since she was experiencing a rapid heartbeat after everything that had happened. The knot on her head was now the size of a walnut instead of an egg, but it ached just the same.

She logged in to the group to see how everyone was holding up. They had all agreed to check in at 2:00 p.m. On the left of the screen she noticed Cleo was the only one signed in to the group.

MALICE: Any news?

A few minutes passed before Cleo responded.

CLEO: I saw Brad wheeled out of the house on a gurney and placed in an ambulance. The police are still at his house.

Malice's insides roiled at the thought of Cleo being anywhere near Brad's house.

MALICE: What if they recognize you?

CLEO: I'm walking a friend's dog. I look nothing like the woman who went to dinner with the asshole. Nor do I resemble the woman in the mask. I am the queen of disguises.

She ended her comment with a happy-face emoji, which didn't make Malice feel any better.

Lily's name popped up to the left of the screen, then Bug's.

BUG: I wonder if they'll be able to reattach his dick?

LILY: Not that I care about his well-being, but it worked with that Bobbitt guy. And that was after sending out a task force to find his penis in a field in the middle of the night.

BUG: I hope this doesn't screw up our plans for my reunion with a couple of douchebag football players.

It was too early to worry about Bug's reunion.

MALICE: Anyone know where Psycho is?

CLEO: She's keeping an eye on the waiter.

Malice closed her eyes and prayed Psycho didn't do anything stupid.

BUG: I'm going to have to get back to work, so I'll go ahead and give you all an update. Psycho can read it later. I won't delete the conversation until tomorrow. Out of the dozens of videos I found on Brad's computer, I was only able to find three that showed a decent profile of Brad. The sicko was careful not to get clear shots of his face. He was also able to warble his voice. I'm not sure how he did that without messing up the rest of the audio, but he did.

CLEO: Why would he warble his voice, but not the victims'?

BUG: I can only assume that hearing and seeing the fear in the victims was part of his deal—the thing that turned him on.

LILY: Fucker.

BUG: I also blurred out the victims' faces because the last thing they need is to be victimized twice.

LILY: What about me? Was there a video?

BUG: Yes. I wasn't sure if you wanted to use it to take him to court someday, so I was waiting to—

LILY: I need to think about it.

BUG: Take your time. Let's take a vote on whether or not the best videos of Brad should be sent to the police on a flash drive?

All four of them voted yes.

BUG: Should I post one of the videos on his social media: Facebook, Twitter, Instagram? And what about sending a video to his company CEO?

MALICE: Any chance the police would be able to trace the flash drive or the IP address to you?

BUG: No.

Malice sighed. Bug's confidence in all things was as comforting at times as it was worrying. If authorities were able to trace the video to Bug, then what? They would all be in a lot of trouble.

LILY: When do you plan to post the video on social media?

BUG: As soon as we hear from Psycho.

PSYCHO: I'm here. Sorry I'm late. The waiter hasn't left his apartment. I called the restaurant and asked for him and was told he quit. Give me a minute to catch up with previous posts.

Five minutes passed.

PSYCHO: Okay. I vote YES to all of Bug's questions. I'd like to say that I know this didn't go as well as everyone had hoped, but nobody can argue that Brad didn't get what he had coming to him. I do think our first assignment has been eye opening. At least for me. I have no doubt in my mind that Brad will try to cause trouble. We all knew he was smart, ruthless, and controlling. But I'm ready to move on to assignment #2. I'm looking forward to attending Bug's reunion.

Malice couldn't stop thinking about how badly their first assignment had gone. More than anything, she wanted the predators to pay for what they did. But talking about revenge and doing it were two different things. Fear was setting in and bringing doubt with it. Sure, she'd known from the start that they were taking big risks, but the thought of being caught was weighing heavily.

Assignments had been decided on long ago. Otto Radley, assignment number two, was the man who had kidnapped Psycho and held her captive for three years. She had the scars to remind her every day of the horrors she'd endured. He was the only predator in the group who had been convicted. That was twenty years ago. Psycho was getting antsy. Malice could feel it. Hell, she'd seen it with her own eyes every time Psycho had rolled her shoulders and gritted her teeth when they were at Brad's. Their mission to get justice had gotten real.

BUG: I gotta go. Talk soon.

Psycho logged off, then Lily.

CLEO: You okay?

MALICE: I'll be fine. You?

CLEO: Danger is my middle name. If you need to talk, you know where to find me.

After Cleo signed off, Malice sat there for a moment longer, staring at the blinking cursor. Laughter caught her attention, and she found herself smiling at a toddler who had stopped to stare at her, his pudgy arm outstretched as he offered her a gooey treat before his mother ushered him away.

Somewhere along the way, she realized, she'd become a little less angry.

She had her moments. Only hours ago, in fact, she'd felt the fury after she'd stepped inside Brad's house and he'd pulled her to the ground. The rage was still there, inside her, swirling around like a bubbling witch's brew, but it felt different. The world had become less dark. The people close to her, the flowers and trees, and the kid with the sticky fingers, were all illuminating and real, giving off light, making it easier to breathe.

CHAPTER EIGHTEEN

Sawyer had sat in the car for ten minutes, staring at the dead girl, oblivious to the photographers and forensics team as they worked the scene, before she finally climbed out of the truck. As she approached, she noticed red, swollen bumps on the girl's skin where mosquitoes had fed on her blood.

She pulled out her cell phone and took two pictures before an officer told her to go back to the truck and stay there until Aspen was finished. Sawyer took a few steps in the other direction, and when the officer got busy with something else, she turned back around. The girl's face was haunting, her eyes open and overly bright, as if frozen in that horrible moment of terror. The anguish and torment visible even in death.

Sawyer's stomach cramped. She felt edgy, twitchy, a desire to scream out for Isabella. She wasn't sure why this crime scene affected her differently than the one she'd seen at Forrest Hill Apartments.

She didn't know either of the victims.

And then it hit her. The problem was River Rock. She could feel its tentacles crawling up her neck. This town was like a living, breathing entity, pulsing with an immoral darkness all its own. She turned away from the crime scene, but instead of returning to the truck, she walked toward the woods where the dappled shade covered her in semidarkness.

Decaying leaves, branches, and bark crunched beneath her feet. Despite the team of experts close by, it was quiet. The air had an earthy dampness she hadn't felt when she'd stepped out of the truck. Ferns and brush and purple wildflowers covered much of the land. A spiky branch grabbed hold of her slacks, and she had to bend over to break free. Nearby, a piece of cloth, black and leathery, clung to another branch. She pulled the fabric from the prickly branch and examined it closely— cowhide or goatskin. The edges all around were uneven and torn. She tucked the scrap into her back pocket as she continued on. Up ahead she saw an area of the forest floor that had been flattened, as if a family of wild animals had slept there, huddled together.

"Sawyer! What are you doing?"

She looked up. Aspen was jogging toward her. "Just taking a walk," she said as he approached. "I've been reading and researching crime scenes for years." She shook her head. "But seeing that girl tied up like that . . . it was too much."

"It's a gruesome sight," he agreed. "I've got to head back to the office. Chief Schneider wants me to stay there and man the phones."

"Oh, okay," she said. "Do you mind dropping me off on Frontage Road on your way?"

"Isn't your car at the cemetery?"

"It is, but I didn't want to take more of your time."

"I'm good. I'll take you there."

"Thank you," she said as they walked back to his truck. She climbed in and fastened her seat belt.

He revved the engine, then made a three-point turn to get back on the road, heading away from the crime scene. "So when are you leaving?" he asked as the wheels rumbled over uneven ground.

"Wednesday."

He glanced her way. "You look white as a ghost. You really are shaken up, aren't you?"

"I didn't sleep well last night. There was Gramma's funeral to deal with, and now this." She scratched the side of her head, pulled a leaf out of her hair. "I don't know what I was thinking, coming back here at all. I always feel the weight of River Rock on my shoulders when I visit."

"What about your parents?" he asked. "Don't you want to spend some time with them while you're here?"

"Nothing's changed, Aspen. My parents and I don't see things the same way." She blew out a breath. "What about your mom? What's she up to these days?"

"I thought you knew. She passed away last year."

"I had no idea. I'm sorry."

He said nothing.

Sawyer couldn't stop thinking about Isabella. Would she end up like Peggy and Avery? Forgotten?

The thought made her feel sick to her stomach.

Her cell phone buzzed. It was Sean Palmer. She declined the call. She would call him back after Aspen dropped her off.

"Was that your boyfriend?" Aspen asked.

"*My* boyfriend?" She snorted. "No. Sean Palmer is my new boss."

"What happened to the old one?"

"Remember? I was promoted."

"That's right. Shouldn't you take his call?"

"I'll call him back later." She turned toward Aspen and said, "I know you said that the people of River Rock want to move on—you know—leave those other murders in the past, but what about you? You're a deputy. Doesn't it bother you that two young girls were murdered and yet nobody cares?"

Aspen sighed. "I didn't say no one cares. It's just that at some point people have to move on with their lives."

"I get that. I really do. But forget about all those people for a minute. What about you and Chief Schneider?"

"I'm sure it gnaws at the chief. He loves this town like nothing else. But he can only do so much. He has a lot of stress. He was pressured by the public and the media to solve those cases. He still is. For years people demanded answers he didn't have, and everyone seemed to have their own theory as to what happened. But what's the chief supposed to do when he has to do it all on his own? He has to process the crime scene, sort out the evidence, conduct interviews, and follow up on any leads. I've watched him work. I try to help as best I can, but again, there's only so much we can do. Most of the time, I feel sorry for the man. Even when he does solve a case and get a conviction, he doesn't get any praise from anyone. It's a thankless job."

"You're right. I'm sorry." She thought of Kylie Hartford. The young woman had a whole team of investigators trying to solve her case, doing their best to bring her justice. Homicide detectives in big cities received intensive training in crime scene investigations. They didn't always have all the resources they needed, but they got a lot more help than cops in a small town like River Rock.

They had arrived at the cemetery. Everyone had left. He pulled into the empty space next to her car. "Don't look so down."

"You don't understand," she said. "I've worked hard to get where I am, and this might be my one chance to prove myself."

"I'm not sure how helpful Chief Schneider is going to be," he said as she unbuckled her seat belt and grabbed her bag.

Her fingers were wrapped around the door handle when she looked at him. "What about you? Will you help me?"

"Of course. You were always there for me when I needed a friend. Maybe now I can repay you for everything you did for me."

"I didn't do anything. You weren't the only one with problems. When everything fell apart at home and then Rebecca disappeared, I needed a friend too." She hopped out of the truck. "Thanks, Aspen. For everything."

He nodded. "I guess I'll see you around."

Sawyer waved as he drove off. Then she got behind the wheel of her car and returned Sean Palmer's call.

"This is Sawyer," she said when he answered. "What's going on?"

"I heard about the girl . . . Isabella. Homicide."

She lifted an eyebrow. "Word gets around quickly."

"It comes with the territory," he said. "I wanted to make sure you were okay."

"I'm fine," she said, wondering why he would worry but appreciating the call all the same.

"As a reporter," he said, "I always make sure I know things about the people I bring on to work closely with me."

How much did he know about her? she wondered, and why was he telling her this now?

"As a *crime* reporter," Palmer went on, "I also know a thing or two about criminals . . . killers. They don't like people like you or me meddling in their affairs."

He really was concerned. "Does that mean you'll give me more time so I can look into Isabella's murder?"

"I'm serious about the risk."

"I understand," she said.

"All and all, that whole speech you gave about not letting these girls be forgotten is about your friend Rebecca, isn't it?"

She thought about that for a moment. Maybe he was right. Rebecca had simply disappeared, and sometimes it seemed as if no one had cared. "Sure," she said. "It's about Rebecca. But it's also about Peggy, Avery, Isabella, and every young child out there who never got justice. They shouldn't be forgotten, Palmer. Isn't that part of why we do what we do? Report crimes so that people can protect their children, and the families of victims can get some closure?"

She heard an audible sigh come through the line.

"I'll give you until the end of next week. But that's it. I can't do any more than that."

"I appreciate it."

"You haven't worked one day for me yet, and I'm already having regrets."

"Nobody knows River Rock and its nuances better than me," Sawyer reminded him. "I grew up here. The people know me, and my parents are a big part of River Rock. The story will be important. I will see to it that our audience cares. Part crime reporting, part human-interest story. It'll be good for both of our careers."

He laughed at that. "Just get back here as soon as possible."

She took a breath. "Thank you."

"Too soon for that," he said.

"What about the Kylie Hartford case? Anything new?"

"They brought Kylie's boyfriend in for questioning yesterday. He's the number one suspect. They're talking about making an arrest."

"So soon? Do they have evidence?"

"Why do you sound surprised? You said yourself that he had the motivation—jealousy. Detectives talked to Kylie's neighbors, her coworkers, friends, and family. It doesn't look good for the boyfriend."

"Remember the picture I took of Kylie's apartment, the one of her living room?"

He didn't respond, so she went on. "I looked up the book and the author, and it turns out he had a book signing on the same day Kylie was murdered. I was hoping someone could find out if maybe Kylie met up with someone at the convention."

"I'll talk to Perez. See what he knows."

Sawyer was glad he was receptive to at least checking it out. "About Kylie's boyfriend . . . aren't you afraid they might be rushing to judgment?"

"It's not our call to make."

Something wasn't sitting well with Sawyer. Instinct and all that. Something about the look on his face and the whole situation that made her question whether he was guilty. She wondered if she would be able to talk to him when she returned to Sacramento.

"Most cases are solved within the first forty-eight hours," Palmer said. "The longer the case remains open, the more difficult the investigation becomes."

"Sure. But that doesn't make the boyfriend guilty."

"Listen," Palmer said. "I get it. You've wanted to be a crime reporter for a long time. You've worked hard. You're passionate about what you do, and this is your first official—"

"All true," she interrupted, "but nothing you said has anything to do with what I'm telling you. If the boyfriend is guilty, then he's guilty."

"You saw him in his truck, crying. You talked to neighbors, and you know he dated Kylie for five years. You're feeling a connection. But we don't know what evidence the police have found."

He was right. She needed to trust the authorities to do their job, just as she wanted Palmer to trust her.

"I'll see you next week," Palmer said. "Stay safe."

CHAPTER NINETEEN

Except for a gauzy stream of moonlight coming through the window, the room was dark. He lay in bed and wondered why he'd fought the urge to kill again for so long. Last night had blown him away.

Exhilarating.

He closed his eyes to relive the moment. There hadn't been any blood. Maybe a few scratches on her tender skin caused by the sharp bits of bark covering the tree. It was her face, her expression, the way her shiny, long hair stuck to the trunk of the tree, spread out like a fan around her face. The picture she made had been visually striking, intense, and unnerving all at once.

She had tried to fight him off, but once he had her restrained beneath the ropes, she'd grown quiet.

She was so beautiful.

He hadn't been able to resist her. It wasn't until he rested his mouth on hers that she started protesting again. That's when he realized how much he liked it when her brow furrowed and her nostrils flared. He also liked her body wriggling against his chest when he pressed his body on hers.

He inhaled, did his best to calm his racing heart.

Last night had been nothing like the others. He'd snuck up behind both girls and swung the hammer fast and swift, crushing their skulls.

So much blood. So fleeting and anticlimactic. Both times he'd felt nothing!

But that was then, and this was now.

He was calling the shots and making his own decisions.

A giggle escaped him. He clapped his hand over his mouth.

Killing the girl had been more than pleasing. Maybe because she had never, at least that he knew of, made fun of him or teased him like the other girls had.

"Isabella," he said aloud, feeling each consonant on the tip of his tongue.

When he'd finished touching and playing around with her, he'd wrapped his hands around her neck. The last thing he'd expected was to enjoy listening to her beg for her life. But that's exactly what had happened. Listening to the unsteady shrill of her voice while watching her fear bloom—slowly at first, like a seedling sprouting from the ground, and then shifting suddenly to full-blown horror—that's when he was brought to the very peak of sexual excitement.

A first for him.

He'd killed chickens and other animals to get off, but that was nothing compared to what he'd experienced less than twenty-four hours ago.

He smiled into the darkness.

Killing the girl had given him wings. He was taking flight; he could feel it, the lightness within and the breathlessness as joyful tears came to his eyes.

He would kill again. How could he not?

CHAPTER TWENTY

There was a knock at Aria's one-bedroom garage studio before the door swung open. She shut her laptop and stood, surprised to see Harper arrive with a pet carrier. She hurriedly scooped Mr. Baguette, her cockatiel, off her shoulder and put him in his cage before crossing the room to shut the door. "What's going on? Where did you get that carrier?"

"I went to the store. No way was I going to let Raccoon get his claws into me." Harper set it on the floor.

Aria made a face. "Raccoon?"

"Sawyer named him. Not me."

"Why can't he stay with you? You guys have a lot more room than I do. And Mr. Baguette won't be able to wander around outside of his cage."

"Nate is allergic. You should have seen his eyes this morning. They're puffy. He's practically blind, and his nose was red and super dry."

Aria knelt down to take a look at Raccoon. "I'll have to talk to Sawyer about this and see what she plans to do with him."

Aria loved animals. She'd been fostering dogs and cats and birds for years. She'd even taken in a pig for a few days, and a parrot. Mr. Baguette was one of the few foster animals she'd gone on to adopt. She was happy for the animals when they were adopted, but she always cried too when it came time to say goodbye.

The cat hissed at her when she put her hand on the side of the carrier. "You are a feisty raccoon, aren't you?"

Harper was in the kitchen, a super compact area that had everything most kitchens possessed. Nate had built it within an alcove at the far corner of the studio. Harper was opening and closing drawers.

"What are you doing?" Aria asked.

"Looking for latex gloves. This place is a mess."

"It's my mess. Leave it alone."

Harper's gaze was fixated on something Aria couldn't see. "Why do you have a gun sitting out in the open? What if Lennon or Ella had come over?"

"I had an early shooting practice, and I was going to clean it. It's not loaded, and I knew Ella would be at camp for a week and Lennon is with his dad."

Despite telling Harper to leave her mess alone, her sister was still piddling around in her kitchen, which was set off from the rest of the living space by a countertop and two high stools.

Aria sat down on one of the stools and watched her sister clean the dishes. She was used to it. She'd learned to keep her mouth shut when her sister went on one of her cleaning frenzies. But it wasn't easy, having a conversation while she scrubbed, her face and body tense. Harper's kids and husband had also learned to move around her as they went about their daily lives.

Aria loved her sister more than anything, but she worried about Harper. Once, she'd found Harper in her bedroom with all the curtains pulled shut, simply sitting in the dark, doing nothing. Those moments worried Aria the most.

When Harper finished with the dishes, she mixed vinegar with dish soap and then put the bristle end of a long-handled dish brush into the solution and swirled it around. "Leave the brush for about an hour and it'll be good as new."

"Great."

Harper peered into Aria's eyes. "You can talk to me, you know, if you ever need to get something off your chest."

Aria sighed. "Thanks, but no thanks." Harper was always wondering why she didn't go on dates or have many friends. Her issues with people were all connected to Uncle Theo and dozens of other shadowy faces, but she knew better than to tell that to Harper. Aria slid off the stool and went to Mr. Baguette's cage. The cockatiel began to whistle the theme from *Star Wars*.

"He's gotten that tune down," Harper said. She pointed at Aria's sleeve. "Looks like he pooped on you again."

Aria grabbed the tissue she kept tucked under her belt and cleaned it off.

"Have you talked to Sawyer since she left?" Harper asked.

"We've been playing phone tag for two days," Aria said. "She left a message, though, letting me know she was fine and planned to stay for a few more days."

"I still can't believe she would go anywhere near that place."

"I can."

Harper arched a brow.

"Sawyer's not like us," Aria said. "She might experience anxiety at times, but she's strong. She faces her fears head-on."

The truth was, Sawyer's return to River Rock had stirred up all kinds of shit from Aria's past. She had hardly slept last night. Anytime an image of a man from the past crept into her brain, she'd jumped out of bed, covered her ears, and started humming and jogging in place.

Maybe Raccoon would be the distraction she needed.

"I think Sawyer is too fearless," Harper said. "It's as if she's trying to prove to herself or maybe to us. She jumps into things too quickly, like moving in with Connor, a man she hardly knew. Never mind her new job as a crime reporter. Now she's back in River Rock. It's like she's drawn to death and destruction like a moth is attracted to flame." Harper shook her head. "Sometimes I wonder if she's lost all sense of self-preservation."

CHAPTER TWENTY-ONE

Sawyer's hands were full. She was carrying a bucket filled with cleansers, a mop, broom, dustpan, and a box of garbage bags.

"What are you doing?" her mom asked.

"I've had a change of plans. I need to stay in River Rock for a few more days, so I thought I'd move into Gramma's cottage if that's okay with you and Dad."

"It's dirty, cluttered."

"That's why I'm going to clean it." Sawyer used her chin to gesture at the doorknob. "Can you get the door for me?"

"I thought you were leaving after the weekend?"

Sawyer set everything on the floor. "I talked to my boss, and he's agreed to let me stay and cover the Estrada murder."

Mom's stony expression gave away her disappointment. "I don't understand you."

"You've never tried to get to know me. How could you possibly understand me?"

"Right there," Mom said. "The way you talk to me. All three of you were always disrespectful, running around like wild animals."

"You were never here. How would you know what we were doing?"

"I don't appreciate your tone."

"What don't you like exactly? That I'm being straightforward, or that I'm speaking the truth when I remind you that you and Dad weren't always there when we needed you? That you left a sexual preda- tor to look after us."

The upper half of her mom's body sagged. "It's been years since you left, and yet that's all you focus on."

"If I'm hurting inside, shouldn't *you*—my mother—be hurting too? I've had a chance to watch Harper with Lennon and Ella, your grand- children. She's an amazing mom, always there for them."

"I suppose she spoils them," Mom said with a shake of the head. "Parents give their children everything these days. Harper's children will never understand that life can be difficult and that you don't always get what you want."

Wow. Better to be neglected and abused than lathered with love. Sawyer wondered why she bothered. Her mother had never listened to her. Mom wore blinders. She'd always been married to her views. She was always right, unable or unwilling to bend. "Why didn't you believe me when I told you what Uncle Theo had done?"

"I never said I didn't believe you."

The truth had never felt so heavy, like a brick settling inside Sawyer's stomach, weighing her down. "So why would you allow him into this house?"

"He's your father's brother. He's family. He's done his time."

Chills ran through Sawyer's body. Harper had been right—Mom had known.

More than anything, Sawyer felt the urge to pack up and leave River Rock for good. Never look back. But she had a job to do, and her mom wasn't the only stubborn one standing in the room. Sawyer wasn't going to leave River Rock and mess with her career because of a woman who never gave two shits. She used her shoulder to give the door a push to get it to open. She scooped up the cleaning supplies, turned toward her mom, and said, "You never once told me you loved me."

"That's ridiculous."

"It's the truth." Sawyer stepped outside, didn't bother shutting the door before walking toward the cottage.

Sawyer dropped everything once she got to the cottage door. Her hands shook as she slipped the key into the lock and opened the door. *Breathe.*

She used to constantly make up stories in her head, telling herself her mom was human, and like most parents, she'd simply made mistakes. But that wasn't true. Mom had known what Uncle Theo had done, and she'd done nothing about it. She'd never reached out to offer emotional support, never held Sawyer in her arms or offered a kind or sympathetic word. Their relationship had always been fraught with tension.

Suddenly she understood why Harper had cut Mom out of her life. It had been the only way to preserve her sanity and save herself.

Sawyer's anger at Harper for leaving her behind had blinded her to her parents' faults. Determined to punish Harper, she'd thrown her parents in Harper's face, making them out to be good, decent people, which was far from the truth.

Standing beneath the doorframe, Sawyer's shoulders fell as she looked inside the cottage. The place was a wreck. She was a wreck.

The windows were dirty, and there were cobwebs in every corner of the room. The wastebasket was filled to the brim with used tissues and trash. Had Gramma been living in this filth?

There were no blankets on the bed. Just as Dad had said, the mattress was stained. Sawyer was no Harper when it came to cleanliness, but this was simply more abuse at the hands of her parents.

The floors creaked beneath the weight of her feet when she stepped inside. Holding her breath, she crossed the room and opened the window to get some air flowing through. A spider dropped onto the windowsill. She gasped. Its body was thick and round, and it crawled down the wall and skittered under the bed before she could try to capture it and put it outside.

Hands on hips, she looked around the room. Where to start? She didn't have a lot of time. She needed to get the place cleaned up and take a ride to town. She had a lot to get done in a minimal amount of time. Her phone buzzed. It was Aria. *Damn.* She'd forgotten to tell her she wasn't coming home. She picked up the call, said hello.

"Where are you?" Aria asked.

"I'm inside Gramma's cottage." She glanced at the bed and imagined Gramma Sally propped against pillows, warm beneath her quilt, telling one story or another in hopes of making Sawyer smile. She wondered where all Gramma's knickknacks and books had been taken.

"You're still in River Rock?" Aria asked.

"I meant to call earlier. I didn't want to say anything the other night, but I'm going to do a write-up about River Rock and the unsolved murders."

"Why would you do that?"

"Because somebody needs to dig a little deeper. Somebody needs to remember those girls."

"Well, that shouldn't take long, right?"

Silence.

"What's going on?" Aria asked.

There was no way to soften the truth, so she blurted it all out, quick and to the point. "There's been another murder—a young girl—and my boss wants me to stay to cover the story."

"You're fucking kidding me?"

"I'm not."

"Harper is not going to like this one bit. Can't they send somebody else to do the story?"

"Harper is not my guardian. And no, they can't send anyone else. I know this town inside and out, and that alone makes me the right person for the job."

A long pause. "You know I—we—only want the best for you."

"I get it," Sawyer said. She wanted to tell Aria everything . . . that Aria and Harper had been right and she never should have come to River Rock in the first place. Gramma was gone forever, and coming here wouldn't bring her back. She wanted to tell Aria how seeing Uncle Theo had been a jolt to her system. But she also wanted to stay in River Rock and prove to herself and to Sean Palmer that she had what it took to be a damn good reporter. "I'm fine," Sawyer said, as if to convince herself more than her sister.

"So how old was the victim this time?" Aria asked.

"Sixteen."

Aria said nothing. She didn't need to. She was thinking of the other girls—the unsolved murders.

"Did you know the other victims?" Sawyer asked. "Peggy and Avery?"

"Not the first girl . . . but when Avery James was killed, I was freaked out. Avery was in the class ahead of mine. We were all scared," Aria said. "The teachers watched us like hawks. Every day they reminded us to walk home in pairs. I was fourteen at the time, and I can still remember everyone in River Rock looking at each other as if they were a possible suspect." She paused. "Of course, Mom and Dad never seemed too affected by it all. With all the tourists coming in to pan for gold at the time, it was easy to blame the murder on some nebulous stranger. But it never made sense to me."

"What didn't make sense?" Sawyer asked.

"If it was a stranger, you know, an out-of-towner, why would the killer return to the same place to kill again? Wouldn't he go to Shasta or Yreka or some other town close by?"

Sawyer said nothing.

Aria asked, "Do you know if the newest victim had a chunk of her hair cut off?"

Sawyer already knew the answer, but she pulled up the digital pictures she'd taken yesterday, zoomed in to look at the missing clump of hair above Isabella's right brow. "Yes. She did."

"Don't you think there's a good chance it's the same killer?"

"It could be a copycat."

"The first girl was found in 1996. If this is the same guy, why would he come back to River Rock to kill again after all this time?"

"That's what I need to find out."

"It's not your job to solve the crime, Sawyer. If you go around asking too many questions, you could put yourself in danger."

"I'll be fine. I promise."

"You can't make promises like that. Besides, I thought you were working on a murder case in Sacramento."

"I am—I was. They have a whole team of people working that case. In fact, the police already have their eyes on someone they think might have killed the girl."

"That was fast."

"Yeah," Sawyer said wistfully. "I do wish I could talk to the guy."

"The killer?"

"Innocent until proven guilty," Sawyer reminded her.

"Why would you want to talk to him?"

"I don't know. It's the weirdest thing. The morning after the murder, I was called in to take pictures of the crime scene, and I saw him sitting in his truck, crying. It didn't look like remorse to me. It looked like a man who had lost someone he loved."

"Maybe he killed her in the heat of the moment and regretted what he did," Aria said. "If you could have talked to him, though, what would you have talked to him about?"

"Are you kidding me? Everything. Why was he sitting in the parking lot, crying? What the hell happened? Where was he when Kylie was strangled to death? The list goes on."

"You are passionate about what you do, aren't you?"

"I guess I am."

There was another pause before Aria said, "You need to call me."

"I'm talking to you right now."

"No. I mean every day to check in. Otherwise I'm going to worry, and Harper will go nuts. You know she will."

"Don't tell her. She's way too sensitive. Maybe if she didn't keep everything so bottled up inside, she wouldn't have to spend every minute cleaning."

Aria exhaled. "Are you still angry with Harper after all she's done for both of us?"

"What did she do for me?" Sawyer asked. "Besides leave me here to rot?"

"We've been over this before."

"I know. I know." Sawyer rubbed a hand over her face. "Harper is all screwed up in the head. But think about it all from my perspective. Harper knew what Uncle Theo was capable of, and yet she left town without me. How is she any better than Mom or Dad?"

"Harper turned eighteen a few days before she dragged me to the truck in the middle of the night," Aria said half-heartedly. "She was too young to be burdened with taking care of either one of us."

"So why you and not both of us?" Sawyer inwardly cringed at how pathetic she sounded. But it wasn't as if Harper had needed to choose one over the other. She could have saved them both.

Aria groaned. "Harper has spent years beating herself up over everything that happened when we were growing up. We weren't her responsibility, Sawyer. It was a horrible time for all of us. She did what she could, and she's been trying so hard to make up for leaving you behind. Why can't you cut her a break?"

Silence followed.

Aria said, "I'll talk to her tonight and tell her you'll be staying in River Rock for a while."

"Thanks."

"Before you go," Aria said, "what do you want me to do with the cat? Nate is allergic. They can't keep him. And poor Mr. Baguette is stuck in his cage until you figure out what to do with him."

"I don't want him to go to the pound," Sawyer said. "Can you find a kennel where he can stay until I get back?"

"You can't afford a kennel. I'll take care of him until you return, but you'll need to figure it all out then."

"Thanks. I owe you."

"Yeah. You do. Call or text tomorrow to check in," Aria said.

"I will."

"Love you."

"Ditto," Sawyer said before she hung up. She wasn't sure why she couldn't say those three little words, but something held her back every time. Expressing her feelings was just as difficult as touching and showing physical affection. It would take time, her therapist told her. The important thing was how she felt inside. She cared about her sisters and would do anything for either one of them.

Sawyer figured that was a good start.

CHAPTER
TWENTY-TWO

Sawyer used a paper towel to wipe sweat from her brow. She'd been cleaning for hours. Every cobweb was gone and the windows gleamed. She had swept the floor but still needed to shake out the area rug that she'd thrown outside. The door to the cottage was open, and her dad peeked his head in. "Mind if I come in?"

"Not at all." She waved him in. He didn't appear to be as tired and broken down as he'd seemed the first night she'd arrived.

"You've been working hard. The place is shaping up."

"Thanks." Sawyer walked to one side of the mattress, the side farthest from the door. "Mind helping me turn this over?"

He walked over to the other side, and it hardly took any effort for both of them to flip it. Compared with the dirty side, this side of the mattress looked brand new.

"You know where to find sheets and pillows," he said.

"Thanks for the help."

He scratched his whiskered jaw. "How are your sisters?"

First Mom, and now Dad. Had a bit of remorse finally crept into their souls? "I thought you and Aria kept in touch?"

"Small talk," he said. "She tells me she's fine. I say good. We hang up."

"You've always been a man of few words."

"That's no excuse. I should have tried harder to talk to you girls and get to know all of you."

"Yeah, well, that's life. Like Mom is always saying—today is a new day."

"You hate when she says that."

Sawyer was surprised he knew anything at all about what she liked or disliked. "I do despise it," she said. "Today is just another day. It doesn't make yesterday magically disappear forever."

Dad smiled.

Sawyer stared across the bed into his sea-green eyes. Who was this man, really? And why was he here now, talking to her? Was it an age thing? Had he been wallowing in some sort of come-to-Jesus soul searching? *Don't waste your time,* she wanted to say, but didn't. When she was young, she used to fantasize that Mr. and Mrs. Russell, the people who owned the bookstore, were her parents. She could have hoped and wished until her face turned blue, but Mom and Dad would never have been the sort of parents who raced her to the kitchen to get their hands dirty in a bowl of pancake batter or put the fear of God into her if she didn't get As or Bs on her report card. She couldn't remember either one of them ever feigning interest in what she was doing. So what did he want?

"What is it?" Sawyer asked. "Is there something you want to say to me?"

His eyes shimmered.

"Say it," she prodded.

But no words came forth. Instead, he bowed his head so that his gaze seemed to rest on the floor. He obviously wanted to get something off his chest, but she wasn't going to push him. She waited him out. Let the quiet strangle them both. Whether it was confessions or apologies or something else, she wasn't sure she wanted to hear it—not now, maybe not ever. "I've got to get to town," she finally said.

He lifted his head, watched her as she gathered her bag from the bedside table. "I heard you were reporting on the murder."

"I am." She didn't bother going into more detail than that. What would be the point? "Is it okay if I stay here in the cottage while I'm working on the story? I don't plan on being here long."

"It's fine," he said unconvincingly.

"I should go." She had intended to take a shower and change her clothes, but her sudden desire to get away overrode any need for cleanliness. As she walked past him to leave, he grabbed hold of her arm. Her instinct was to pull away, but she held still, waited. "Be careful," he said as he released his grasp.

"I always am." She stepped out of the cottage and walked the path through the side yard to the driveway. She climbed into her car, relieved when the engine started right up on the first try.

CHAPTER TWENTY-THREE

Aria read Sawyer's story about the snake at the birthday party online. The thought of losing someone so tragically caused a heaviness to settle in her chest. She then read about Kylie Hartford, another tragic story. A thumbnail picture revealed the authorities' number one suspect—Zach Jordan.

Aria sat up in her chair.

She knew Zach. For years he'd volunteered at the SPCA. He was one of her mentors, a genuinely nice guy. And for someone like Aria, who tended to avoid people, that was saying a lot.

Never judge a book by its cover. The thought hit her hard, stopping her from being too quick to assume someone like Zach would never kill his girlfriend. She knew firsthand what nice, kind-looking men could do.

It was the reason she carried a gun.

It was the reason she'd been seeing a therapist.

It was the reason she hardly slept at night.

But still.

She thought about what Sawyer had said she would do if she were here in Sacramento. She'd said she would talk to Zach and ask him questions.

Aria finished reading the article.

It didn't look good for Zach, mostly because he was the last person seen with Kylie. He'd been spending a lot of time at Kylie's apartment when she wasn't there. He worked in construction, so why wasn't he at work during the day? And why were Kylie's neighbors suspicious of him?

Aria put Zach's name into a popular search engine. His address popped right up. He lived on the outskirts of Curtis Park, less than ten minutes away. She looked at the time. It was six o'clock. She thought about giving Sawyer a call, then decided against it. What good would it do, worrying anyone?

She shut down her computer, opened Mr. Baguette's cage and dropped some millet in, then made sure there was still plenty of food and water for Raccoon. She grabbed a backpack from her closet, where she noticed Raccoon curled up in the corner. Slowly she reached out, hoping he'd sniff her or let her pet him, but instead he darted away and disappeared under the bed.

Poor thing. He was scared to death of people.

She and Raccoon had a lot in common.

Aria left the studio, then made her way to the house to let Harper know she wouldn't be joining them for dinner. She found Harper in the kitchen, making a salad to go with the lasagna she had in the oven.

"I don't know how you do it all," Aria said.

"And it's only just begun," Harper said wearily as she glided a hand over her stomach.

Aria's mouth fell open. "Are you pregnant?"

"Don't say anything. I haven't told anyone. Not even Nate."

"Why not?"

"I don't know how to tell him." Harper's shoulders fell. "This wasn't part of the plan. Nate's construction business is doing okay, but it's not like we're rolling in dough. The mood changes and headaches I was experiencing were too much, so I stopped taking the pill and made an appointment to get an IUD. I screwed up. Another child will definitely put more pressure on everyone."

"Hey," Lennon called out from the living room. "Look at this!"

Harper followed Aria into the family room, where Lennon was pointing a finger at the television. "That's Brad Vicente. He works for Zeon, one of the gaming giants. Vicente created my favorite game, *Total Diplomacy.*"

Two men appeared on the screen. The camera zoomed in close on the man on the left. "Brad Vicente, known for his creation of a popular video game, is in the hospital after having his penis cut off. A surgeon skilled in microsurgery was called in to reattach the appendage. Penile replantation is rare, but the doctors are hopeful that the surgery will be successful. It could be days before authorities are able to piece together what happened."

"Is he married?" Aria asked.

Lennon chuckled. "A little desperate, aren't you, Aunt Aria?"

Aria thumbed her nose at her nephew. "I don't want to date the guy. I'm just wondering who cut off his penis. I thought maybe it was his wife."

Harper crossed her arms. "Who cares? He probably deserved it."

"That's a little harsh, Mom. We don't even know what happened."

Harper went back to the kitchen to finish chopping vegetables.

"I've gotta go," Aria said as she made her way to the door. "I just wanted to let you know I won't be here for dinner."

"Why not?" Harper asked.

"Someone called in sick down at the shelter. They need me. Save me some lasagna, will you? Bye!" Aria left before Harper could interrogate her.

It took her only twelve minutes with traffic to get to Zach's house. It was a single story. Aria looked inside her backpack at her gun. Even if he *had* killed his girlfriend, surely he wouldn't risk killing her too. She decided not to load it. She'd use it to scare him if the need arose.

She shouldered her bag and climbed out of the car. Planter boxes filled with weeds lined the walkway. The place looked severely neglected. She heard noise inside the house. She rapped her knuckles hard against the wood door. The guy who answered was probably in his midtwenties, younger than Zach, who she guessed to be in his early thirties. "Is Zach Jordan here?" she asked.

"Zach," he yelled before walking away, leaving her standing there.

She peeked her head inside, watched the young man who had opened the door pick up a controller and take a seat on the couch next to another young man she didn't recognize. A sweet scent drifted from the room to where she stood.

"Zach!" the other guy yelled when he saw her looking in.

"What do you want?" Zach shouted back as he came into view. "Hey," he said when he spotted her at the door. "What are you doing here?"

"I'm Aria Brooks from the SPCA. We worked together for a while."

"I remember."

"I was wondering if we could talk," she said.

"What about?"

"I'd rather talk in private."

"Inside or out?"

The inside of his house was small and cluttered. Beer cans and trash covered most of the tables. A hookah pipe sat on a side table next to the couch.

"Out," she said.

He stepped outside and shut the door. She followed him to his truck, which was parked at the curb. He leaned against the tail end and said, "This is about as private as it gets around here."

"I heard about what happened to your girlfriend."

His head was down, his arms crossed over his chest. Aria's belief in the goodness of people had eroded over the years. Right now, her cynicism was on high alert. She couldn't think of one reason why she should beat around the bush. "It looks like you're the number one suspect."

He didn't move a muscle.

"My sister is a crime reporter. She works for the *Sacramento Independent*. She saw you the morning after the murder. You were sitting in your truck, and she thinks maybe you were crying."

When he finally looked up at her, his eyes were red and watery. "Maybe I was," he said. "What's it to you or your sister?"

"Where were you the night Kylie Hartford was murdered?"

"Are you with the police?" he asked. "Did they wire you and send you over here to talk to me?"

"No."

"You're a lawyer?"

She shook her head.

"Then why are you here?"

"For months I watched you work with animals, and I just thought you were a really kind human being. When I saw you were a suspect, I felt compelled to ask you all the questions my sister couldn't because she's out of town. So will you talk with me?"

He said nothing.

"If you're arrested, I might be the only person, other than a court-appointed lawyer, who's going to be able to tell your side of the story. Why are Kylie's neighbors pointing fingers at you?"

He took a breath and looked around before saying, "The night before she was found"—he closed his eyes, took a breath, then opened them again—"we argued. I yelled at her. She shouted back. I left and slammed the door on my way out. It probably sounded worse than it was, but there's no denying I was angry."

"What were you arguing about?"

"Matthew Westover, an anchorman at *Good Day Sacramento*, where Kylie worked."

Women adored Matthew Westover, but Aria didn't understand the appeal. "Can you elaborate?"

"I knew she was going out for drinks after work with her coworkers, and I knew Westover might be there, but until that night I had no idea she was still fucking him."

"She told you that?"

"Yes."

"You said 'still.' This had been going on for a while?"

He nodded. "Matthew Westover wasn't the first guy, and I knew he wouldn't be the last. But I never stopped hoping that I would be enough for her."

What the hell? Aria didn't understand people. "Why did you stay with her?"

His eyes pierced Aria's. "Because I loved her."

Aria had never experienced that sort of love, and she was fine with that. But nobody could convince her that Zach Jordan wasn't telling the truth. She could see the deep affection he'd had for Kylie in his eyes and scrawled into every line of his face. She asked one more question. She already knew the answer, but she asked anyway. "Did you kill Kylie?"

"No."

"Where were you the night she was killed?"

"I was hoping I could stay away from her, punish her by not texting or calling. I was still mad about her being with Westover. I'm not proud of it, but after she got off work, I followed her to a book signing at the Sacramento Convention Center. After she disappeared inside the building, I drove to Device Brewery in Midtown and drank my sorrows away. They had to kick me out when they closed. Somebody got me to my truck, where I passed out. The next morning, I drove straight to Kylie's apartment to tell her I loved her and couldn't stand being apart for even one more minute. I was the one who found her." He squeezed his eyes shut. "I ran out of there fast, jumped in my car, and called 9-1-1."

CHAPTER

TWENTY-FOUR

Sawyer pulled up behind a media van stationed outside the house where Isabella Estrada had grown up. The one-story ranch-style home appeared freshly painted. The yellow and pink rosebushes separating the house from the neighbors on both sides were in full bloom.

Walking toward the house, she heard the van door open and close behind her. Next thing she knew, a young woman with determination in her eyes was shoving a microphone in Sawyer's face.

"Did you know Isabella Estrada? Are you a friend of the family?"

"No and no," Sawyer said as she walked onward, never slowing.

The front door flew open before Sawyer could knock.

"Get off our property! I'm calling the police!" The man was big and broad and frightening. It took Sawyer a half second to realize he was talking to the woman standing next to her.

"Shit." She backed off and hurried back to the van.

His gaze settled on Sawyer. "Who are you?"

Be up front was Sean Palmer's mantra. She wondered how often he followed his own advice. "I'm Sawyer Brooks. My parents are Joyce and Dennis Brooks." Not a lie.

His big shoulders relaxed. "Listen," he said, "I don't mean to be rude, but my sister and brother-in-law are in a whole lot of pain right now. Unless you can tell us who might have killed my niece, I can't help you."

"I was hoping—"

"Let her in," came a male voice from inside the house. The man standing in front of Sawyer filled the doorway, making it impossible to see past him. He finally stepped aside. She recognized him at once. "Caden," she said, "I'm so sorry about your sister."

He nodded, said, "Let's go to the back."

She followed him through the house, caught sight of people in the living room. A dark-haired woman was talking in a calm, soothing voice to a middle-aged couple sitting on the couch. The woman on the couch was crying while the man next to her tried to comfort her.

Caden paused when they got to the kitchen, then waved her toward the side door leading to the backyard. She followed him outside, down three wooden steps, and across a rocky path, where he finally stopped at a pair of aluminum chairs with red padding faded by the sun.

"Sorry, but it's a little chaotic inside right now."

"Thanks for talking to me at all. How are you holding up?"

He shoved his hands in his pockets and shrugged. "It's pretty shocking. But I needed a break from all the craziness. Are you living in River Rock?" he asked.

"No. I left after graduating. I live in Sacramento, but I came back for my gramma's funeral."

"I'm sorry," he said.

She nodded. "I'm sorry for your loss too." She paused. "How about you? Do you live in River Rock?"

"No. I went to college in Oregon and ended up in Portland. I work in advertising." He smiled. "I'm engaged."

Sawyer could see that he was doing all he could to stay strong. "Congratulations on the engagement."

"Thanks."

An awkward moment passed before Sawyer asked, "Who was the woman inside, talking to your parents?"

"A grief counselor. My mom is on the brink of having a nervous breakdown, so Dad found someone to help them both through this ordeal. I came as fast as I could. I don't know how much help I'll be, but Dad asked me to come, so I did."

"Were you and Isabella close?"

"Not really. Thirteen years apart was a big gap. When I called home, we would talk. We spoke last week, in fact. She was stoked because she'd passed her driver's test and could finally drive without Mom and Dad in her face. Her words, not mine."

"So she had a car?"

He looked baffled. "Is this an interview?"

"I'm a journalist," she admitted. "I don't want Isabella to be another unsolved mystery in this town, so I thought I would find out as much as I could about what happened."

He shifted in his chair and then looked over his shoulder. "I shouldn't talk to you. Dad would be upset if he knew there was a reporter in the house, and that's the last thing he needs right now."

"Nothing you tell me is going to be in print today or tomorrow. Nobody has to know we talked. I want to help, Caden. I don't know about you, but I've never forgotten Peggy Myers and Avery James, the girls killed here when we were younger."

He said nothing, but he was listening.

"Do you remember Rebecca Johnson?"

He nodded.

"They never found her. I think about her almost every day."

He propped his elbows on his knees, his gaze directed downward.

"Peggy, Avery, and Rebecca had family members who cared about them: mothers, fathers, brothers, sisters, uncles. People forget that sometimes. If I do my job right, Isabella will not be forgotten. Nobody's life should be defined by murder."

Caden lifted his head. "Okay," he said. "What do you want to know?"

Over the next twenty minutes, he told her Isabella had been a happy kid, a people pleaser. He got teary-eyed when he talked about when he was living at home and how Isabella didn't like it if he was sad or had a bad day. She would bring him a sandwich she'd made herself, which was never appetizing. And oftentimes she would make funny faces for as long as it took to make him smile.

He also provided Sawyer with the particulars: Isabella drove a blue Honda Civic, she played the piano, she thought boys were silly, and she and her best friend, Amanda Harrington, were obsessed with Taylor Swift. Isabella also liked to run, which Caden told her was what she was doing when she was killed.

By the time Caden finished, both their moods had changed. Hearing all the little details about his sister made Sawyer think of her own sisters and how difficult it would be to lose either one of them so tragically. He walked her to the door and said goodbye.

On her way back to her car, Sawyer peered through the window of the blue Honda Civic parked in the driveway. A crystal dangled from the rearview mirror. There was a calculus workbook on the back seat and a binder. She looked over her shoulder toward the house and saw someone peeking through the curtains.

Was it Caden or his uncle? She couldn't tell.

As she continued on her path toward her car, the reporter stepped out of the van and tried to block Sawyer from walking past. "You must be a friend of the family," she said. "You were inside the house for quite a while. How is the family holding up?"

"Isabella Estrada was brutally murdered yesterday. How do you think they're doing?"

As Sawyer drove away, she thought about her job. Objectivity, accountability, fairness, and truth were the key ethical responsibilities of every journalist. But sometimes reporters—broadcasters, particularly—went for emotion when they interviewed the victim's family, throwing compassion and concern out the window, which only made things worse.

She glanced at the time. It was 4:00 p.m. She had a long list of people she wanted to talk to. Caden had mentioned Amanda Harrington as being one of Isabella's good friends. Sawyer also intended to talk to Chief Schneider and get the facts. For instance, who found Isabella? When, and what time? Were there any witnesses who might have seen someone in the vicinity around the time of the murder? Were there any suspects?

CHAPTER TWENTY-FIVE

From a few blocks away, he watched Sawyer disappear inside the Estrada home. It made sense that she'd go there first to get answers to her questions. But he couldn't lie. He was surprised they'd invited her inside their home less than forty-eight hours after their only daughter had been strangled and strapped to a tree.

If only he were a fly on the wall.

Who was she talking to? What sort of questions would she ask them? And what could they possibly tell her about Isabella that would enlighten her audience? Teenage girls were self-centered and only cared about themselves. He was doing the town a favor by getting rid of ones like Isabella, who were never held accountable for their actions. It was sickening to watch the way parents rushed in to save their darling daughters from the tiniest of problems.

He was the person Sawyer should be talking to.

The thought made him chuckle. Isabella was dead because she happened to have been in the wrong place at the wrong time. Any young girl would have worked. The only reason he'd killed her was to try to keep Sawyer Brooks in River Rock as long as possible. The funny part was that it had worked.

Seeing Sawyer again after all these years had jump-started something within, sparked the fire that he was certain had been building since the day he was born. He'd been obsessed with Sawyer since the first time they had met. He would do anything to keep her close. Someday he might find the courage to tell her how he felt.

Not today, though.

He needed to give her time to get to know him, show her he could be trusted, and that he was worthy of her love.

CHAPTER TWENTY-SIX

Before Sawyer got to the main road, she pulled onto the shoulder and used her cell to do a search to find an address for Amanda Harrington.

Derek Coleman's name and number popped up, since she'd talked to him recently. Should she give him a call and let him know she might be staying in River Rock longer than first planned?

No. It was Saturday. She didn't want to bother him on the weekend. But if she called him on Monday, she would be interrupting his work.

She was doing what she always did—overanalyzing. Without giving it another thought, she pressed the screen with her finger, put the phone to her ear, and wondered what she would say if he answered.

"Hello?"

Damn. It was him.

"Is that you, Sawyer?"

"Oh, hi, sorry. I was a little distracted. Obviously. I just wanted to let you know—"

She heard a voice in the background. A woman calling his name.

"Hold on," he said to Sawyer while he told whoever it was to go on without him and he'd be right there.

"Don't let me keep you from whatever you were doing," Sawyer said. "I can talk to you later." He was obviously with a woman. She sounded young and carefree, probably had zero anxiety, and was lovely inside and out. This was awkward. She never should have called.

"I'd rather talk to you than play badminton with my sister," Coleman said. "I'm at my parents' house."

She heard chatter and laughing in the background. "Are you having a family reunion?"

He chuckled. "You could call it that. Every time we get together, which is much too often, it's like a reunion. I have four sisters and two brothers. Between those six, I have fourteen nieces and nephews. Ten of those are females. The males are outnumbered."

"Females are the future," she said.

"So I've heard."

Stay on track, she reminded herself. "I called to let you know I might be staying in River Rock longer than planned."

"When will you be returning?"

"I'm not sure. A young woman was killed yesterday. Strangled," Sawyer told him. "Found naked and tied to a tree."

"Horrible. Did Palmer ask you to stay and cover the murder?"

"No. It was the other way around, actually."

"I guess I'm not too surprised."

"Why is that?"

"You've always made it clear that it's been your dream to work the beat."

Sawyer was taken aback. They had rarely talked about private matters over the years, and yet it seemed he was so tuned in to her.

"I'm being presumptuous."

"You're not," she said. "I asked you a question, and you answered it. And you're right on both accounts. I called to let you know because I didn't want you to think I wasn't interested."

"In me or in dinner?" he asked.

"Dinner," she said. "Of course."

He laughed. "Well, I'm happy to hear that. Now I'm left to assume that this means you *are* interested."

Her insides quivered. She couldn't let him spend the next week thinking she might be someone she wasn't. "I have to be honest with you."

"Please," he said.

"I feel a need to warn you that I'm sort of a mess. I was sexually abused, and I've been seeing a therapist for years, and we've pretty much gotten nowhere. I was living with a guy named Connor up until last week, when I caught him in bed with another woman. I don't know about you, but I find it strange that I haven't given him a first or second thought since. I have an aversion to being touched. I have panic attacks from time to time, I don't trust anyone, and I'm often paranoid. For instance, since arriving in River Rock, I'm certain I'm being watched." She rubbed a hand over her face. "I can't believe I'm telling you this. It's not that I try to hide who I am from people, but I don't usually just spout all my flaws on a whim." Her heart raced. She felt nauseated. "Jesus, I'm sorry. Get back to your family. I never should have called."

"Please don't hang up," he said.

How did he know she was about to do just that?

"I leave the toilet seat up more times than not," he told her. "I hardly ever finish a book once I've started. I've been known to make sound effects when I'm driving. I have a nervous twitch, and my leg bounces whenever I sit down for too long. I also talk to myself while cooking. I could go on, but then you'd never talk to me again, so I think I'll stop right there and leave it at that."

"Was that supposed to make me feel better?" she asked.

"Yes."

She didn't know whether to laugh or cry. "Well, thank you. Really. Can I hang up now?"

"Goodbye, Sawyer. We'll talk when you get back. Stay safe."

She was mortified by everything she'd just shared and considered apologizing again, but instead she said, "Goodbye." After disconnecting the call, she let out all the bad air in one long exhalation. How was it possible that she'd worked with the man for all those years and never once stopped to wonder about him? And why had she felt the need to share so much of herself with him?

A loud knock on her car window made her jump.

Shit.

It was Oliver. Make that Melanie. She pushed the button to open the window. She inwardly repeated her new name, not wanting to offend by calling her Oliver. Melanie wore thick eyeliner, and her hair was in a long fishtail braid that swept naturally over one shoulder.

"Sorry," Melanie said, leaning down so they were face-to-face. "I didn't mean to frighten you. I saw you sitting in your car for a while, and I wanted to make sure you weren't lost or anything."

"I'm not lost," Sawyer said, her heart still beating rapidly. "I was talking to someone on the phone."

Melanie straightened. Smiled. "Oh, good. Just making sure."

Before she could walk away, Sawyer said, "You wouldn't happen to know where I could find Amanda Harrington, would you?"

Her nose crinkled. "What in the world do you want with Amanda Harrington?" Melanie's eyes narrowed slightly. "Oh, this has something to do with Isabella Estrada and your job, doesn't it?"

Sawyer nodded. "I want to talk to people, see what I can find out about the murder."

"Well, then Amanda isn't the person you want to talk to. You need to go see her boyfriend."

"Isabella's brother told me she didn't have a boyfriend."

Melanie frowned. "The brother lives in another state, doesn't he?"

"Yes."

"Then he probably never knew what Isabella was up to. Secrets . . . ," Melanie said. "This town has more secrets than mosquitoes, and that's saying something."

An image of the tiny bites all over Isabella's pale skin came to mind. "Any idea how long Isabella had been seeing this person?"

Melanie appeared to think about it. "Close to a year is my guess."

"And she didn't tell her brother?"

"Probably because her boyfriend is—was—her math teacher."

"Oh, God," Sawyer said. She thought of Caden telling her that his sister thought boys were silly. Her insides flip-flopped. "Please don't tell me he's married with kids."

"Afraid so, on both accounts."

"How do you know this?"

"I've always been observant. Watching them make out in the back room of the bookstore was my first clue."

Sawyer squeezed her fingers tight around the steering wheel. "I hate this town. I bet you there's not one person living in River Rock who hasn't screwed someone over, literally or figuratively."

"I'm guessing the odds would be in your favor." Melanie lifted a perfectly shaped brow. "If you want, I can show you where he lives."

Sawyer perked up. "Yes, please. Get in."

Jonathan Lane was the math teacher's name. Like everyone in River Rock, he lived only a few miles from town. Not only did he have the allotted wife and two kids, he lived in one of the newer cookie-cutter homes—a two-story house with blue trim and a white picket fence. Jonathan Lane was over six feet tall and lean. Sawyer knew this because he was mowing the small patch of lawn in front when she parked at the curb and got out of the car.

Melanie asked her a question, but she hadn't heard what she'd said. Sawyer was on autopilot. All she could think about was the forty-year-old man taking advantage of a sixteen-year-old while his wife looked after his two young children. Thank God Nate was a good husband to Harper. From what Aria had told her, Nate had been the guy driving the truck the night Harper and Aria escaped River Rock. Sawyer should probably be just as angry with Nate as she was with Harper for leaving her there. But she hadn't known him, and a lot of the details of that night were still sketchy. Maybe Nate hadn't known at the time that Sawyer existed.

She walked up to Jonathan, as close as she could get without putting herself in danger of being run over by his push mower. The moment he saw her, he released his hold on the bar. The engine belched and died. "Hey there," he said in a friendly-dad-type voice.

"Jonathan Lane?" she asked.

"That's me."

He had little round eyes and a pointy noise. Everything about him said "creep." "I understand you were Isabella's math teacher. Is that right?"

He pulled a small towel from his pocket and wiped his brow. "That's correct." He looked over his shoulder toward the house. She didn't have to wonder what he was worried about. It was more than likely he was checking to see if his wife knew they had a visitor.

Sawyer heard a car door open and close. Out of the corner of her eye, she saw Melanie walk to the front of the car and lean against the hood, her arms crossed.

"I'm doing a story about Isabella," Sawyer told him. "I want my readers to get a clear picture of who she was and where she grew up."

"I see."

He didn't see a thing. His eyes were on Melanie. "I also grew up in River Rock."

He didn't look the least bit interested, but he shifted his weight from one foot to the other and said, "Listen. Isabella was a bright girl. Good grades. Good student. I was devastated when I heard what happened." He jumped when the front door clicked open behind him. "I've got work to do around the house and papers to grade," he said, his voice suddenly leaning toward authoritarian. "You'll have to talk to her friends if you want to know more about her."

"If you want to talk in private," Sawyer whispered, "I'd be happy to meet you at the school in, say . . . thirty minutes."

His face reddened. "I want you off my property."

"What's going on?" a woman asked as she approached. She wore jeans and a T-shirt. A thick headband pulled her brown, wavy hair away from her face. A small child, maybe five, peeked her head out the door.

"My name is Sawyer Brooks. Are you Mrs. Lane?"

"I am." She smiled. "Camilla," she offered.

Jonathan feigned a smile as he attempted to gain control of the situation. "Ms. Brooks is doing a story about Isabella," Jonathan explained to his wife.

"I see."

"Ms. Brooks was just leaving, since I told her it would make more sense if she talked to Isabella's friends instead of her math teacher."

"She was a sweet girl," Camilla said. "Very pretty. My husband did tutor Isabella on the weekends every once in a while. Isn't that right, honey?"

Jonathan didn't move a muscle.

"Were you home when that occurred?" Sawyer asked Camilla.

"No," she said. "They needed quiet, so the weekend tutoring only happened when I took the kids to visit with my parents."

"I think it's time for you to go," Jonathan said.

Sawyer felt a sudden pounding in her ears. Jonathan Lane had had his chance to talk and come clean. He should have taken her offer to talk in private, but he hadn't. The man had taken advantage of a young girl, and yet he thought he could just send Sawyer on her way and nobody ever needed to know what he'd done. The arrogant look on his face reminded her of every man who had ever used and abused her. "Tell your wife the truth right now, or I'm going to do it for you."

"I want you to leave," he said.

"The truth is," Sawyer told his wife, "I wanted to talk to Jonathan because I heard he was the person closest to Isabella."

The woman cocked her head, intensely curious.

"If what I heard is true," Sawyer continued, "that would mean Jonathan took advantage of Isabella. As her teacher, he had daily, unmonitored access to Isabella, a sixteen-year-old girl who was at an age where she was only just discovering her independence, her emotions, and more specifically, her body."

"Get off my property," Jonathan said, pointing a shaky finger toward her car.

Sawyer refused to back down. "You preyed on a young and innocent girl who was just learning to drive. A carefree girl who liked to make people smile and who spent hours listening to Taylor Swift. Her life was only just beginning, and you—"

"Get in the house," he ordered his wife.

She didn't budge.

Nothing was going to stop Sawyer from telling Mrs. Lane what she'd heard. This was one secret that would be told right here, right now. "Your husband is a pedophile. I suggest you both go to the police station and talk to Chief Schneider about your husband's relationship with Isabella before I do."

Jonathan's face was a shade of purple, his body shaking before he lunged for Sawyer. He'd caught her off guard, and they fell. Her head thumped against the ground where the lawn met with the sidewalk. He was on top of her, his hands wrapped around her throat. Sawyer struggled to get free, the side of her face scraped against cement. She couldn't get air into her lungs. She kicked her legs, hit him with her fists, but he wouldn't let go.

Adrenaline was on his side. He had more to lose.

Mrs. Lane pulled at his arm and shouted for Jonathan to stop.

He squeezed harder. "I'll get you for this, you little bitch."

As Sawyer's vision blurred, she saw Melanie swing an umbrella at Jonathan's head. He released his hold on Sawyer. She sucked in a breath, coughed, and sputtered as Melanie pulled her to her feet and ushered her to the car.

"Get out of here! You too, you freak," he shouted at Melanie.

Sawyer tried to free herself from Melanie's grasp so she could ram her head straight into his gut, knee him in the groin, and make him whimper. But Melanie held tight, her arms wrapped around Sawyer's waist as she forced Sawyer into the passenger seat.

More than one neighbor across the street had come out of their houses. They looked like cardboard cutouts, no one moving, merely watching the show as Melanie buckled her up. "He's not worth it," Melanie warned.

Melanie tossed the umbrella in the back, grabbed the box of tissues on the back seat, and handed it to Sawyer before walking around to the other side of the car.

Melanie was perfectly calm as she scooted in behind the wheel. The key was still in the ignition. Melanie started the engine, buckled up, and drove off, careful not to call more attention their way.

"He tried to kill me," Sawyer said, her voice hoarse.

"I've known that man my entire life," Melanie said. "Up until a few months ago, when he and Isabella were in the bookstore and I saw his hand slide down her backside, I thought he was a good guy. And even then, I didn't think the weasel was capable of being violent."

Sawyer struggled to swallow. She turned the rearview mirror so she could see the damage. The right side of her face was scraped, which made the scratches from Raccoon look like nothing. A couple of the areas were deep. Her throat was bruised. Her left eye was swollen half-way shut.

"Should I take you to the hospital?"

"No."

"The side of your face looks bad."

"Isabella was strangled to death," Sawyer said, hoping to change the subject since there was no way she was going to the hospital. "Do you think Jonathan Lane killed her?"

"I don't know," Melanie said. "The first person I thought of when I heard about Isabella was your uncle Theo."

Sawyer didn't know what to say. She hated Uncle Theo with a passion. He was a scum-of-the-earth rapist. Was he a killer too?

"Isn't he the reason your sisters left River Rock?" Melanie asked.

"Yes," Sawyer said. "He's also the reason I don't sleep well at night."

"Back when we spent long days at the bookstore, I knew something wasn't right with you. I figured your quirks and mannerisms had to do with your parents."

"Strange that you should say that," Sawyer said. "When I ran into Old Lady McGrady at the coffee shop, she told me she thought Gramma was afraid of my mom. I knew the two of them never got along, but afraid?"

"Hmm. I don't know about that. I only meant that your parents were gone a lot, and it was obvious you weren't happy, so I thought maybe you were lonely."

Sawyer noticed they were heading toward her parents' house. "Why don't you drive us to your car, and I can drive home from there?"

"You could be concussed and not realize it," Melanie said. "I'll take you home and walk from there. I like walking."

Sawyer looked Melanie's way and saw the anger on Jonathan Lane's face when he called Melanie a freak. "Have people in River Rock spoken to you like that before? The name-calling?"

"Oh, yeah," Melanie said. "That was nothing."

"Does everyone know about your hormone therapy and the surgery?"

Melanie laughed. "It's pretty obvious, don't you think?"

Sawyer smiled. "Stupid question."

"I told my mom and dad years ago. It took Dad a while to understand that I didn't want to just *look* like a girl—I wanted to *be* one."

"It takes courage to be your authentic self."

"I wouldn't call it courage. For me it wasn't a choice. And it's gotten better—easier—with each passing day, especially now that I'm handling things my way."

"So did you know back when we spent weekends in the bookstore, reading?"

"I've known since I was eight. When I would look in the mirror, I always saw a stranger looking back at me."

Sawyer didn't comment, just listened.

"The transition phase was hard. The structure of my muscles and the curvature of my spine changed. My feet are smaller, and I'm not as tall as I used to be. But it's all been worth it. At some point, I figured out I could either spend my life being unhappy, or I could do something about it. I'm not alone. A lot of people are going through similar transitions. I know that much."

Melanie drove up Sawyer's driveway and parked in front of the garage. She killed the engine and handed Sawyer the keys.

Sawyer's mom stepped outside, hands on hips, scowling.

"No wonder your gramma was scared," Melanie said.

Sawyer laughed. They both did.

"Thanks for everything."

"Anytime," Melanie said. "If you need any more help while you're here, you know where to find me."

They climbed out of the car at the same time and shut the doors. Sawyer made the climb up the stairs leading to the front door while Melanie hiked down the driveway.

"I just received a call from Fiona Dorman," Mom said. "She told me you and that boy attacked Jonathan Lane."

"Jonathan Lane attacked me, not the other way around. And Melanie is a girl, not a boy."

Mom followed her inside the house and to the kitchen, talking while Sawyer filled up a plastic ziplock bag with ice and held it to the side of her head. Sawyer's good eye fixated on her mom. There was so much bitterness carved into her tightly pinched expression.

"Why are you doing this?" Mom asked.

"Doing what?"

"Coming here after all this time and making trouble?"

"I loved Gramma Sally. That's why I came. I also thought it might be nice to see you and Dad."

"You didn't visit for nearly two years when my mother was alive, so why now?"

"I missed her. I wanted to say goodbye."

Her eyes narrowed suspiciously. "And yet you left the funeral early."

"I had already said my goodbyes to Gramma. There was no reason for me to stay and talk to your friends."

A silent standoff ensued.

Sawyer squared her shoulders as she dissected, analyzed, searched for something . . . anything that might tell her Mom cared even a little bit that she'd been hurt and might be in pain.

But there was nothing there. Not a kind word or an offer to help in any way. It surprised Sawyer that her mom's apathy bothered her at all. "Jonathan Lane came at me full throttle and slammed me to the ground," Sawyer explained anyway. "He strangled me. If Melanie hadn't intervened, I don't know what would have happened. And yet you blame me?"

"Fiona lives directly across the street from the Lanes. She saw everything."

"But I'm your daughter, your flesh and blood, and I'm standing here, telling you what happened."

"You have always been a drama queen," Mom said, waving away any concern with a flutter of her hand. "You and your sisters were always making up stories—you most of all. Anything to get attention."

"Everything I ever told you was the truth."

Long-buried animosity and frustration heated the air between them.

Mom lifted her chin. "I don't want you working on the Estrada case."

Sawyer should have known there was more to her mom's hostility. "I'm not working the case. I'm merely talking to people who knew Isabella so I can add context and depth to what would otherwise be like every other news story—just an account of events."

"You're intruding in people's lives, barging into their homes, and causing problems." Her voice wavered. "I live here. You don't. I'm asking you to stop."

Sawyer shook her head. "I can't think of one time in my life that you were supportive of anything I did." Sawyer adjusted her ice pack. Her throat felt raw. "Do you have any idea how long it has taken me to find an ounce of self-worth and value? You never had any emotional attachment to any of your daughters, did you? Was that because you and Gramma were never close? You didn't know how to have a mother-daughter relationship?"

Mom made an annoying *tsk*ing noise. "Gramma Sally was a lot like you. She saw the world through rose-colored glasses, thought she could make life's pains go away if she willed it to be. A kiss on a scraped knee. There, all better. But that's not how the world works. My father knew that. He knew that life wasn't always fair and that not everyone was rewarded for hard work. If he needed to use a belt to get his point across, that's what he would do. None of this pussyfooting around like most men do these days."

Sawyer had never met her grandfather, and Mom rarely mentioned him. "Your father beat you?"

Mom smirked. "He taught me about life. I could either adapt or break in half. I accepted my fate and dealt with it. It didn't mean I liked it. But I wasn't soft like you and your sisters, railing against the unfairness of it all. If you were smart, you would do what I did."

"And what's that?"

"Get over it. Put all those traumatic events, imagined or otherwise, behind you once and for all."

"Why did you hate Gramma so much?" Sawyer asked.

"When she married my father, she made a vow, and then she broke it. I didn't hate her. I just didn't respect her decisions. She was a coward."

Sawyer had nothing more to say. She turned toward the door and reached for the knob.

"If you drop the Estrada case, you may stay. Otherwise, it's best if you packed your things and left."

"I'm staying," Sawyer said flatly, her body and mind numb. Without another word spoken between them, she turned and slipped out the kitchen door. When she opened the door to the cottage and stepped inside, she released an appreciative sigh. Dad had made the bed for her. Although it wouldn't be dark for another hour and she'd hardly eaten, she dropped her purse onto the floor, left the bag of ice on the bedside table, and slid off her shoes. Then she climbed under the covers and dozed off.

CHAPTER TWENTY-SEVEN

It was past midnight when Malice finally got a chance to log on to the private group. The rest of The Crew had come and gone, posting their comments throughout the day. Apparently, Cleo's next-door neighbor was a nurse at the hospital where Brad Vicente had been taken, and Cleo was able to get some information. Doctors had reattached Brad Vicente's penis, but it would be another twenty-four hours before they would know if the penile reattachment was successful. Doctors worried the placement of the cut might have been too close to the base and therefore he could lose nerve function. When told the news, Brad grew extremely agitated and was now recuperating in the psych ward, where they could keep a close eye on him.

Cleo's update generated a heated debate about right and wrong and where The Crew went from here. Malice skimmed through the messages until the conversation turned to when would be an acceptable time to strike next.

PSYCHO: I, personally, don't give two shits about Brad Vicente. He's a monster who should be locked behind bars. He raped and tortured dozens of women. He even had the gall to video his violent acts so he could get off watching that shit whenever he felt the urge. Despite a few hiccups, we did our due diligence with the wigs and masks. The police have video footage of Brad and his penchant for violence. He'll be thrown in jail. I'm ready to move on to Otto Radley.

Malice sighed. She'd known from the start that Psycho could be impatient at times. Maybe it had been a mistake to plan for nearly a year before making their first move. Dealing with Brad had seemed to light a fire inside Psycho. Her yearning for justice had become a war cry.

CLEO: I don't disagree with you as to whether Brad deserved or didn't deserve what he got. But I do think it's best if we lie low for now. The police will be on the lookout for three women of various builds, all fitting our likenesses minus the wigs and masks. I vote that we wait a week or two before moving on.

PSYCHO: I never would have signed up for this if we hadn't all decided together to go after Otto once Brad was taken care of. One monster at a time. That was the deal. The sicko who held me captive for three years is being released tomorrow. I plan to follow him from the moment he walks through those prison gates. The warehouse where we originally planned to keep Brad is empty and ready to go. I see no reason not to make use of it. What I need to know is, who's in?

LILY: I am.

BUG: I agree with Cleo. Tomorrow is too early to make a move. We need to wait and see if Brad goes public with cries of being the victim despite the videos. If he does, we wait and find out what he knows about us, if anything. And what about the waiter? Would he be able to identify any one of us? He met Cleo at the restaurant. What if he comes forward?

CLEO: Besides the blonde wig I wore to dinner, I had on three-inch heels and plenty of makeup so that I wouldn't be recognized if I ran into anyone I knew. I also made sure there weren't any cameras inside or outside the restaurant before agreeing to have dinner with Brad.

PSYCHO: The waiter is scared. He's a little boy. I'm confident he'll play dumb if the police knock on his door.

BUG: But that's my point. You don't know what Brad or the waiter will do. A little patience will go a long way in this situation.

CLEO: Two of us want to wait and see how the Brad situation plays out, and two of us are ready to move forward, is that correct?

They all answered with a yes.

BUG: I guess Malice will be the deciding vote.

PSYCHO: I'll be waiting and watching Otto walk free. I'm not letting him out of my sight. If the opportunity arises, at any time, for me to get him into my car without being seen, I can't make any promises.

Malice rubbed her temples. Exhaustion was setting in. At moments like this, her passion for vengeance and justice waned. And yet all she had to do was close her eyes to relive the sexual abuse she'd endured as a young girl. Her life had been ruined because of one person. She was unable to go about completing simple tasks without intrusive and disturbing memories flashing through her mind. And for that reason, she needed to stay the course and finish what she'd started. They all needed closure, and if that meant taking risks and making mistakes along the way, so be it. She placed her fingers on the keyboard and began typing.

MALICE: I vote we move forward and make sure Otto Radley is punished accordingly. Once Psycho has him in her care, I'm ready to take care of business.

CHAPTER TWENTY-EIGHT

Sawyer sat up and listened.

Something had awakened her—a noise, a grunt.

She sat motionless, the beat of her heart drumming against her ribs. An owl hooted in the distance. She'd forgotten about her bruised face until her head began to throb. Another noise. Definitely human. Someone was outside the window.

A branch snapped.

Slowly, she moved the covers and slipped her legs over the side of the bed. Her feet touched the floor. She bent over, found her bag in the dark, and reached inside. Her fingers brushed against her wallet, a pen, the notebook she carried everywhere, and her keys. Careful not to make any noise, she held her keys in a fist and slowly pulled them out. She then removed the canister of pepper spray from the ring. It was no bigger than a tube of lipstick. She grabbed her phone too, then put the purse quietly back on the floor.

Both the window and the door were locked, but it wouldn't take much effort to break in. A forceful shove against the door would do the trick. She'd removed the curtain from the window, so it was bare. A shadow caught her eye. She lay back against the pillow and tossed the covers over her legs just as a bright beam of light shot into the room. Clamping her eyes shut, she feigned sleep as the light from the flashlight fell across her face.

She considered yelling to possibly scare him or her off, but she wanted to know who was prowling around in the middle of the night, so she waited. Beneath the covers she used her thumb to ready the nozzle on the pepper spray.

The room fell into darkness. She thought she heard the window being jiggled. Then all was quiet until a moment later when the doorknob turned to the right and left. Every muscle tensed as she waited for the door to be kicked open. Seconds turned to minutes. She didn't move. She just lay there, eyes wide open.

CHAPTER · TWENTY-NINE

Once again, Malice questioned her sanity. It was 3:30 a.m. on Sunday. It was dark except for a few random stars, and here she was, sitting behind the wheel of a cargo van, watching and waiting. She had no idea where Psycho had gotten the vehicle, and she didn't want to know.

The only sound was the hoot of an owl.

Malice wore the same black wig she'd had on when they'd dealt with Brad. She also had on a dark hoodie that she kept low over her face. The eye mask was in her backpack. If Otto Radley, the man who had kidnapped Psycho twenty years ago, showed up, she'd put it on.

But that was a big *if.*

What sort of moron would walk the streets late at night, mere hours after being released from prison?

Leaning forward, she narrowed her eyes to better see. And there was her answer.

Holy shit. It was *him.* Psycho had called it.

Otto Radley was back, and he was going straight for the bait, which was in the shapely form of their friend Cleo. This was the second time Cleo had volunteered to put herself at risk in the name of vengeance.

The run-down apartment where Otto was staying was a few blocks from a park in North Highlands. Cleo was sitting on a bench, leaning back, legs crossed, taking a hit from her cigarette.

Otto Radley was a giant, his arms like battering rams and his neck as big as a tree stump. His chest was round and thick, and even without seeing his face, he scared the shit out of her. He could easily break Cleo in two without any effort.

They were fucked.

Adrenaline pumping, Malice glanced to her right, where she could barely make out Psycho wearing all black and standing tall as she tried to meld into the trunk of one of the trees dotting the park. Behind her was a grassy field where people spent summer days throwing Frisbees and running after their kids.

Malice wrapped her fingers around the key, ready to turn on the ignition. Otto towered over Cleo like a skyscraper. He must have asked her for a cigarette because she was pulling a pack from the purse hanging from her shoulder.

No. No. No. Psycho had warned Cleo he wouldn't waste any time taking action. If he approached, Cleo was told to tase him. Immediately. Without hesitation. But she hadn't, and Otto was quicker than Malice imagined. Before Cleo knew what hit her, Otto had Cleo clutched tight to his chest, carrying her away. He stepped across the cement curb, taking her into the park, past the tree where Psycho was hiding.

Malice leaned forward, her heart beating fast.

Psycho stepped out of hiding and tased Otto in the back of the head.

Malice inhaled, turned on the ignition, and brought the van closer to the action where she could see three bodies rolling around on the ground. Through the open window she heard groans and grunts. Malice grabbed her pepper spray and slipped her wrist through the strap on her stun gun, jumped out of the van, and opened the back cargo doors. A dog barked in the distance as she approached three entwined bodies.

She saw Cleo break away. She was clutching her arm and wincing in pain. Psycho was fighting for her life. Apparently one hit of the Taser hadn't been enough. Otto was a beast.

Anger filled Malice as she brought the stun gun to his shoulder and held tight. He flinched but didn't go down as she'd hoped. His elbow came back hard. She grunted but kept her balance, put the Taser to his neck, and finally his chest, firing in short intervals.

Otto fell back, his head thumping hard against the ground.

Psycho used her legs to push away from the bulk of his frame. Malice wasn't taking any chances. She took the pepper spray and squirted it into his eyes, blinding him.

"Hurry," Psycho said as she jumped to her feet. "Let's get him out of sight."

It took all three of them to drag him to the curb and get him into the van. Psycho jumped into the back with him. Malice shut the cargo doors, ran back to the front, and slipped in behind the wheel. Cleo hardly had time to shut the passenger door before Malice took off.

"We have a problem," Psycho said. "Find an alleyway, any place dark, and stop the van."

Cleo held tight to her right arm as she looked over her left shoulder. "What's going on?"

Psycho growled. "He's wearing a fucking ankle monitor."

"Is he secure?" Before setting off earlier that evening, they had gone over their plan. Once Otto was inside the van, the first thing Psycho needed to do was use duct tape and rope to fasten his wrists to the metal bars under the two front seats. His legs would also be bound together, but there was nothing to secure his ankles to, which would leave Psycho susceptible to getting jabbed with a foot or knee if he had the strength. They would zap him multiple times with the Taser or stun gun if needed, but getting zapped too many times could kill him.

Malice glanced at Cleo. "Know anything about monitoring devices?"

"No."

"Neither do I. Call the others and see if anyone knows how they work."

Malice kept her eyes on the road and on the lookout for a decent spot to pull over.

"I have Bug on the line," Cleo said. "She wants to know if the strap on the device has any hooks—small plastic hooks."

"Yes," Psycho said. "There are hooks."

"You'll need a tool, maybe a screwdriver, to spread the strap apart until it breaks free. Be careful, though, because it will need to be put back together."

"Why?"

"If done fast enough, Bug says the base where the device is monitored will think it looked like a glitch, and it won't get reported."

"There's a screwdriver in the toolbox," Malice said.

"What else does she have?"

"If the strap around his ankle is loose, you might be able to use a lubricant like lotion to slide it off or use a lighter to heat the strap and make it expand."

Psycho cursed. "Nope. Too tight."

Malice drove into an old shopping center. The parking lot was empty. A couple of the buildings had sheets of plywood where windows used to be. She drove around to the back where a large metal dumpster overflowed with cardboard and trash. "You motherfucker!" Psycho shouted.

Malice put the van in park and looked behind her to see what was going on.

Otto had managed to knee Psycho in her side. Big mistake on his part. The ongoing electrical chatter coming from Psycho's Taser made Malice wince. It was much louder in a confined place. A minute or so later, Otto lay semi-unconscious, and Psycho quickly grabbed the scissors from the box of tools they'd brought and cut off his monitor.

"What are you doing?"

"I'm going to toss this thing and be done with it."

Cleo looked at Malice, the phone still at her ear. "Bug says she's right about that."

Malice got out of the van and opened the back doors to let Psycho out. Cleo and Malice watched as Psycho used her shirt to wipe prints off the monitor before shoving it into a dark crevice at the top of the dumpster. She then ran back and jumped into the cargo van.

Malice shut the back doors, slipped in behind the wheel, and resumed driving. "How's your arm?" Malice asked Cleo.

"It could be broken. I'll wait until morning to have it looked at."

"Step on it," Psycho told Malice. "The Taser hardly affects this guy, and we still need to drag him into the warehouse when we get there and make sure he's fastened good and tight to the steel pipes. It's not going to be easy with only two of us."

Cleo put her phone away. "You'll have plenty of help. Bug and Lily are going to meet us there."

CHAPTER THIRTY

The thought of a dark shadow looming over her jolted Sawyer awake. Her mouth was dry, her throat sore. She slipped on her shoes, grabbed the pepper spray that had rolled to the other side of the bed, and stepped outside. Despite being fully dressed in the same jeans and T-shirt from yesterday, the morning air chilled her.

Brittle leaves crunched beneath the soles of her shoes as she made her way around the side of the cottage where a row of blooming rosebushes greeted her. Directly beneath the window, a good portion of a rosebush suffered broken branches. Pink rose petals were scattered about the ground. She followed footprints in the weed-covered dirt around the cottage until leaves and debris from the trees made it difficult to track. One trail of footprints led toward the woods. Another trail led to the house, but she could be looking at her own footprints from yesterday. It was hard to tell.

She checked the cottage door for any signs of attempted entry. Nothing. Even though she'd only be here for a few days, she wondered if she should pick up a lock and chain. Easy enough to install.

Groggy from lack of sleep, she returned to the cottage to get a change of clothes. The cottage bathroom consisted of a toilet and a sink. If she wanted to take a shower, she'd have to go inside the main house.

The side door to the kitchen was locked. She used the key Dad had left her to get inside. There was a note on the kitchen counter next to a bowl of fruit. "Be back later—Dad."

Her stomach grumbled, prompting her to put her clothes and purse on the counter and open the refrigerator. There wasn't much inside. A half a loaf of bread. Some milk, ketchup, mustard, a block of cheddar cheese. She pulled out a glass dish. It was a casserole. She took a few bites before putting the casserole away and opting for a bruised banana instead.

On her way to the bathroom shower, she paused outside Dad's office. She reached out and rested her hand around the doorknob. Her heart raced. Seconds ticked by before she attempted to open the door.

It was locked.

Growing up, she and her sisters were never allowed inside his office. The only time she'd ever seen her dad get angry was when he'd found Sawyer and her friend Rebecca playing in his office. Rebecca had run from the room the second he walked in, but Sawyer had been hiding under his desk. The look on his face when he found her and dragged her out remained fresh in her mind: the bulging veins in his neck, the flared nostrils, and the whites of his eyes as he shook her so hard she'd thought he might accidentally break her in half.

Sawyer released her hold on the doorknob and continued on. Nothing about the home she'd grown up in brought her comfort. The walls felt as if they were closing in on her, every piece of furniture heavy with sorrow, the ceiling weighted down with grief, threatening to cave in at any moment.

In the bathroom, she set her things down and locked the door. As she waited for the shower water to heat up, she stripped down and caught her reflection in the mirror. She'd suffered much more than a bump to the head. Her left eye was bruised. She looked as if she'd gone a few rounds in the ring. A thick line of blood had dried on the side of her face. Her throat was dotted with bruises where Jonathan Lane's thumbs had pressed hardest.

Once again, she wondered if he'd killed Isabella. Had Isabella tried to end things between them and possibly pushed him over the edge?

She stepped into the shower. She was getting nowhere. Uncle Theo and Jonathan Lane were both on her list of suspects. Uncle Theo was a rapist who had been convicted and jailed. Jonathan Lane was a pedophile. Nobody could tell her otherwise. And he was violent.

Putting together a list of suspects wasn't easy.

There was a one-in-three chance that the police would never identify a victim's killer. She could have driven by the person who killed Isabella. Maybe they'd been at Gramma's funeral.

She needed to keep talking to people around town, which wouldn't be easy. People tended to clam up because they didn't want to get involved.

As hot water rushed over the top of her head, images of Kylie and Isabella floated around in her mind. Both dead. Eyes wide open, calling her forth, begging for help.

Sawyer had found an entry for Uncle Theo in her mom's address book tucked away in the kitchen drawer. He lived at 201 Glen Road. His home was a glorified shed, with a sagging porch and metal roof. The two windows, yellowed by time, looked jaundiced. The woodpile out front was covered with an old tarp. The grass and weeds obscured the pathway leading to the front door.

As Sawyer reached out to knock on the door, her hand began to tremble, and her heart skipped a beat. *No.* She couldn't handle an anxiety attack. Tips on how to handle her stress ran through her mind. She needed to relax before she could regain control of her thoughts.

She took a breath, then pulled out her phone and left a text message for Aria, letting her know where she was in case anything went wrong. Once that was done, she focused on inhaling and exhaling.

She was at Uncle Theo's house. He wasn't the same man he was all those years ago. He was frail and weak. She would be fine. Whatever she was feeling, it was temporary.

With that thought in mind, she knocked. It was still early. Uncle Theo was probably sleeping. She knocked again. As she waited, she launched the camera app on her cell phone and swiped across to video mode.

The door creaked open.

She aimed the screen in his direction and tapped the "Record" button.

Her phone was vibrating. Someone was calling her. She ignored it.

Uncle Theo rubbed his bony fingers over his face. His unwashed hair hung in limp strands over bloodshot eyes. "Are you recording me?"

She nodded.

"Why?"

She straightened her spine, thankful when her hands stopped shaking. "I have questions that I need you to answer."

His shoulders drooped. "You said you never wanted to talk to me again."

She kept the video rolling. "That was before you murdered Isabella Estrada."

He squinted. "I didn't murder anyone, and I've never heard of that person."

She had no idea whether or not Uncle Theo knew Isabella, let alone killed her, but after seeing him at her parents' house and then again at the funeral, she could tell he'd been worn down by the hardships of life and might easily break down and tell her if he was responsible in any way. His red face and broken blood vessels told her he'd most likely been using alcohol as a crutch. He looked thin and dehydrated, nothing like

175

the Uncle Theo she remembered. She nudged her way inside his place and looked around. "Why did you kill her?"

"You're crazy."

She knew all about the accusatory method that interrogators used to get a confession. Sawyer pivoted on her feet, circling in place, video rolling as she got a 360-degree view of his living space before landing back on his face. "You killed them all, didn't you?"

She kept her eyes on him. Watched his body language for any sign that he might be lying.

"What are you doing here?" he cried out.

"Explain it to me, Uncle Theo. After spending ten years locked up, they let your sorry ass out of jail, and one of the first things you did was commit murder?"

"I didn't kill anyone."

"For all those years you were locked up, there were no murders. But you're released, and another young girl is murdered. Coincidence?"

"I swear to you, I didn't do it. I'm on a new path."

It irked her that she actually believed him. But that wasn't going to stop her from poking and prodding. If he knew anything about Isabella's murder, she planned to make him talk. "Asking for forgiveness because you've found God is such a crock of shit," she said. "Guys like you can't just stop assaulting young girls. It's in your DNA. It's in your blood. It's what you do. So stop with the finding-God shit, okay?"

"I wish I could take back everything I ever did to you and your sister."

Sawyer narrowed her eyes. "But you can't."

"It doesn't go away," he said with a shake of his head. "I wish it did."

"What doesn't go away?" Sawyer asked. "I want to hear you say it."

"The urge to sin, to do the wrong thing and make bad choices. I got a lot of therapy inside, plenty of solitude to think about things I did. I would never harm another person."

"That's bullshit."

He shook his head adamantly. "No. It's the solemn truth. I mean it. Never again."

"Maybe you told yourself that you would never rape another innocent girl, but the urge was too great, so you killed Isabella instead."

"I don't know any Isabella. Please. Leave me alone. I said I was sorry." His head fell, chin to chest.

"You're good at this, aren't you, Uncle Theo? You've been at this game for a long time. Sexual predators know how to groom and manipulate people. It's what they do."

He didn't look at her. Uncle Theo had spent his entire life coercing victims. He was an actor. Oscar material. She left him standing in the middle of the room. The kitchen was easy enough to find. She began opening drawers and digging into his things. She wasn't sure what she was looking for, but she felt good about going through his belongings and causing him grief.

She found an old black-and-white photo of Uncle Theo with Sawyer, Aria, and Harper at a barbecue at her parents' house. Uncle Theo was all smiles. Sawyer took a close look at Harper. She was probably thirteen at the time, lean and long with freckles across her nose. Her jawline looked rigid, her eyes cold. Her disdain for the picture-taker was clear.

Aria's arm was draped around Sawyer. They looked neither happy nor sad.

Three young girls, and yet only one seemed to know what the future held. Sawyer ripped the photo to shreds and continued on.

"Please don't do this," he said. "I told you I was sorry, and I meant it."

She stopped and turned his way. "What about your friends? The men you sold me to that first night? Who were they?"

He shook his head. "I don't remember."

"I want names," Sawyer said. "Give me a name and I'll leave."

Uncle Theo's weakness emboldened her. When she was small, he'd made her cower, and now she would do the same to him, show him what it felt like to have no choice, no power. She entered the only bedroom in the house, opening drawers, rummaging through his things.

"How much money did you make that night?" she asked him as she tossed a pile of shirts out of her way. "Or any night, for that matter," she went on. "Aria told me they were called rape fantasy parties." She looked at him. "It has a nice ring to it. How did you advertise?"

He fidgeted, looked around, anywhere but at Sawyer.

"Look at me! How do you expect to ever garner forgiveness if you can't even look me in the eyes?"

His head came up. His watery eyes fixated on hers.

"How much money did you make?" She stepped closer to him, heat warming her face, making her head throb. "Tell me the name of one of your fucking friends!"

"They weren't my friends," he shouted back at her. "None of it was my idea."

He wasn't making sense. "What?"

He shook his head and said nothing.

"You said it wasn't your idea. I want to know whose idea it was to sell me and my sister to your friends?"

He was crying now, sobbing uncontrollably.

As far as Sawyer was concerned, he wasn't human. "It must suck to lose everything. You were living the high life, and you were so damn cocky, but then you got caught and look where you ended up? In a dump." She cocked her head. "Did you ever stop to think that someday one of your victims, like, say, me—your own niece—might come to visit you when you were old and useless, beaten down by your own depravity? Did you ever think about that?"

He said nothing.

She opened the closet door.

"Please don't," he begged.

"Oh, why not?" She tucked her phone into her waistband. "I'm getting warm, aren't I?" There were piles of worn shoes on the closet floor, a paper bag filled with aged *Playboy* magazines, and two plastic bins. She reached for the bins and slid them out. The top one was filled with odds and ends: cooking utensils, a dented tin pan, paintbrushes, a hammer and nails, a measuring tape, wood glue. She moved the bin aside.

Uncle Theo rushed forward when she pulled the lid off the bottom bin.

Stunned by what she saw, Sawyer began sifting through the pile of photos, dozens of them. Little girls in compromising positions, aged two to twelve was her guess, all of them naked and scared. Her heart thudded dully in her chest. "You're disgusting. I was right about you. Your depraved soul has no limits."

She focused on one particular photo, picked it up, and stared at the little girl, who was looking into the lens of the camera. Long-buried emotions flooded through Sawyer and exploded in fury. Uncontrollable tremors racked her body. Her head pounded.

Facing her uncle again, she put the photo up close to his face. "Are you going to search for this little girl, Uncle Theo, and ask for her forgiveness? Maybe when you find her, you can tell her all about your therapy and how you found peace in the solitude of your cell. I'm sure she'll understand."

He grabbed the photo, put it in the bin, and placed the lid on tight. When he was done, he stood silently, rubbing his hands over his face as if trying to scrub off all the layers of immorality.

"It was you, wasn't it?" she asked. "You were the one prowling around the cottage last night?"

He looked at her then, his eyes suddenly round and bright, as if he was scared for both of them. "It wasn't me. I swear it. If you were smart, you would pack up and leave River Rock for good and never return." He shook his head violently, as if possessed. "It wasn't me," he said again. "The devil is close. You better run."

CHAPTER THIRTY-ONE

It was noon on Sunday by the time Malice was able to get back to the warehouse off Power Inn Road. Getting Otto Radley set up inside hadn't been easy, even with four of them helping. They had cleaned up the warehouse weeks ago, thinking they would use the building for Brad. They had brought two cots, camping chairs, Coleman lanterns, and a mini camp stove to make coffee or tea.

Home away from home.

She parked next to the cargo van, grabbed the soft-pack cooler from the passenger seat, climbed out, and took a look around. The closest building was miles away. But still, they were taking a big risk. It had taken months for The Crew to decide where they would keep the men they brought to justice. They had considered the Sacramento rail yard, where lots of trains were rusting away, but then the city finally decided to do something about the eyesore. And besides, much of the rail yard was guarded.

This abandoned warehouse was by far their best bet. But after the long search, she couldn't drive by a shipyard container or a dumpster without thinking someone might be trapped inside.

Malice walked around the side of the building to the back, where they had found a door that wasn't locked. The front of the building was secure with metal bars.

How would her sisters feel if they knew what she was up to? Shocked? Amused? Angry? She couldn't think about that now. "One predator at a time," she said under her breath before knocking on the metal door.

She heard the chain they had fastened around the handles being lifted before Lily opened the door. Five foot six, blue eyes and golden hair, she was wearing a mask and a black wig. The outdoor adventure shop where she worked sold gear for every occasion. She grew up hunting with her dad and had provided them with the coffee maker, camping chairs, and a rifle.

Malice had never shot a gun before, and she wasn't about to start now. Although hunting was definitely a thing where she grew up, guns had never been in her life. They scared her. Last night, every member of The Crew except Cleo had been shown how to load and unload the weapon. Once loaded, Lily easily swung the barrel back into place, cocked the hammer, and pretended to fire. Every time the sequence was repeated, Malice had gritted her teeth and held her breath.

Guns had never been part of their plan.

But neither had cutting off a man's penis.

"What have you got there?" Psycho asked excitedly as Malice stepped inside.

Malice handed her the soft cooler. "There are sandwiches, dried fruit, pretzels, nuts."

Psycho smiled. "Great."

Malice looked around. Their prisoner was in the far corner, which was good because she didn't want to have to look at him too closely when she was here. They had fastened Otto's arms and legs to old metal piping that might have once been used for bringing in water. "Can he hear us?"

"Just keep your voice down." Psycho shrugged. "We're using aliases, and there's not much we can do about it since I want him right where I can see him at all times."

"Hey," Malice said to Bug. "Has anyone heard from Cleo?"

"I did," Lily said. "Her arm is sprained, not broken. She's wearing a sling and taking the rest of the day off."

Bug was sitting in one of the camping chairs. She had her computer on her lap. "I'm going to take off in a few minutes," she said. "But it looks like our man Brad is denying that he's the guy in the videos we left for authorities to find."

"That's no surprise," Psycho said.

"No," Bug said, "but what's weird is that people on social media seem to be siding with him."

"That's bullshit," Lily said. "I thought you posted the videos. Can't people see what he's doing to these women—torturing and raping them for days and getting away with it? Why would anyone side with a monster like that?"

"Because like most predators," Malice said, "he knows how to charm people. I saw him this morning on TV. His story has already gone nationwide. He's doing interviews right out of his hospital room."

Bug nodded in agreement. "He's convinced a large group of followers that his profile in sections of the video has been photoshopped, and he's been set up by an angry mob of females who weren't happy after he dumped them."

"He's been at this for a while," Malice went on. "Brad knows what he's doing. He used to focus on one woman, pouring on the charm, grooming, and manipulating until he had her right where he wanted her. He's still doing the same thing, but with the public."

Lily turned to Bug. "I want all those videos, even mine. Two can play at this game."

"It gets worse," Bug said.

"What do you mean?" Lily asked.

"All the favorable press toward Brad has given our waiter friend the confidence to come forward and tell his story. They have some blurry footage of Cleo in her blonde wig inside the restaurant, but that's it. Even so, the waiter told investigators and reporters that she seemed to be having the time of her life with Brad."

"I'm going to kill him," Psycho said, pacing the room. "I warned the little asshole, and now he's going to pay."

Malice held up a hand. "One predator at a time. Take a breath. Calm yourself. We need you here."

"I should have known it was you," Otto said from the corner of the room. "The wig can't hide those scars you wear so well. I remember every slice I made with the blade."

Bug looked that way. They all did. One eye was uncovered. "I thought we covered his eyes," Bug said.

"You did," Otto said. He made a slurping noise. "A little saliva goes a long way. I'll get out of these chains too." His laugh came out as a bark. "Did you get my letters, Christina?"

They all looked at Psycho, who'd visibly stiffened at his words. Nobody had known Psycho's birth name until that moment. Psycho had never mentioned getting any letters from Otto, but judging by her body language, she had received correspondence from the sicko while he was in prison.

"I knew you would come for me," he said. "I just didn't know you would come so soon. I taught you well."

"I should have killed you the second you walked past me in the park."

"Why didn't you?"

Psycho walked up to him and kicked him hard in the gut, making him grunt. Kneeling down, she reached out and used a box cutter to slice through the side of his face, starting at the hairline and ending an inch past his ear.

Malice was about to tell her to stop, but Lily raised a hand and shook her head at Malice.

Otto hardly flinched when Psycho cut him. Maybe because he'd been ready for it. Blood ran down his face and dripped onto his pants.

"That felt good," Otto said. "Aren't you going lick it up like I used to do?"

Psycho spit in his face, found a roll of duct tape, and wrapped it around his head and face, covering everything except his nose and mouth.

Malice didn't want to watch. She pulled off her wig and mask and busied herself with helping Bug gather her things so she could walk her to her car.

"He knows Psycho's identity," Malice told Bug as they walked outside. "We're fucked. Completely and royally fucked."

"We'll figure something out."

"Like what?"

"I don't know, but you need to calm down. Whatever happens in the end, nobody is going to believe that monster over the woman he kept chained and locked underground."

"What was the point of all that planning, then?" She threw her arms wide. "Slicing and dicing him was never discussed."

Bug found her key and opened the trunk of her car, where she carefully placed her things. "I guess you could think of all that planning as an outline, a first draft. The end product rarely resembles the original idea."

The thing about revenge, Malice thought, was that it all sounded so glorious—making someone pay for what they did. They were going to teach these guys a lesson, scare them, make them sweat. But cutting him open? "So you're good with what you saw happening in there?"

Bug slammed the trunk closed. "I guess I don't see it like you do. For three years—" She stopped midsentence as if to collect herself and started over. "For three years Psycho was kept underground, in the middle of a wooded area where nobody could find her. Psycho is obviously more fucked up than any of us imagined. But if that had been *me* alone in the dark for one thousand and ninety-five days, being sliced and diced and fucked eight ways to Sunday, I would be leaning toward crazy too."

Malice watched Bug open her car door, then pause and turn back toward her. "My advice to you," Bug said, "is to stop looking at everything as black or white. There is no right and wrong with what we're doing. I went into this whole thing knowing that it was dangerous and illegal."

Malice said nothing.

Bug wasn't finished. "For me, revenge is about retaliation and not about restoring justice. For years, I trivialized what happened to me. It was the only way I could try to forget about it and move on. But that's bullshit. Those football players knew exactly what they were doing when they spiked my drink and carried me behind the school. I had no say. And I had no control." She swallowed. "I want them to feel what I felt. I want them to pay for what they did to me."

Malice watched Bug climb into the car and drive away, gravel popping beneath the tires.

Bug was right. She needed to calm down and get her head on straight, remember why she'd gotten involved with The Crew in the first place.

Every sexual predator out there needed to pay for what they had done, including her father.

CHAPTER THIRTY-TWO

After leaving her uncle's house, Sawyer drove to the area of the woods where Isabella Estrada had been found. She turned off the engine and stared straight ahead. Yellow crime scene tape still encircled the area around the tree.

She stayed seated in the car and thought about Uncle Theo, wondered if he could have been responsible for Isabella's murder. She despised the man, and yet she didn't think he was capable of murder. It was an instinctive feeling based on her past knowledge and experience of her uncle. Although she'd gone to his house with fire and conviction, she hadn't expected to find anything. The pictures had been a surprise. And yet they shouldn't have been. Maybe she was in the wrong line of work, after all. Or maybe she was blind to his faults because he was a family member. Her therapist had once told her that abuse and betrayal by someone you once trusted was often too much for the soul to bear, and so you tended to ignore it or pretend it didn't happen. Just because she didn't think he murdered Isabella, didn't mean she didn't think he should be locked up.

Sawyer pulled out her notebook and pen and wrote at the top of the first page: *Who killed Isabella?* She jotted down names: Uncle Theo,

Jonathan Lane, a member of the Estrada family, a stranger. She put a star next to Jonathan Lane. He seemed like the obvious suspect. And he was definitely violent.

If the same person who had killed Peggy Myers and Avery James killed Isabella Estrada, it had to be someone who had lived in River Rock all these years. Or maybe they had moved away and come back.

She snorted. Everyone in River Rock could be a potential killer. For now, she would concentrate on people who lived here in town.

Many murderers, especially serial killers, had mental challenges. They had been wrongly treated by their parents or bullied in school. For that reason alone, she added Aspen Burke and Melanie Quinn to the list. As she stared at the names, her chest tightened.

Tapping her pen to her mouth, she continued to stare at the names, repeating them in her head as she thought about each person. She drew a line across Uncle Theo's name. He was a shell of the man he used to be. He didn't have the physical or the mental strength to commit murder. She crossed off Aspen's name, and Melanie's too. If she was going to keep them on the list, she might as well add Old Lady McGrady, Erika, and her husband, Bob, to the list too.

Frustrated, she ripped the list of suspects out of her notepad, crumpled it, and tossed it to the floor.

She needed to be smart. And patient. She needed to interview more people, talk to everyone in the whole damn town if she had to. Bob came to mind. She definitely wanted to have a chat with him. Maybe she would see if Melanie wanted to come along for the ride.

Tomorrow she hoped to have a chat with Chief Schneider, see if he could give her any details about the case. She also planned to fill out a report against Jonathan Lane. She was about to climb out of her car to have a look around when her cell phone buzzed. It was Aria. "Hey there," Sawyer said.

"Oh, my God! You're okay!"

It took Sawyer a second to remember leaving Aria a text message before she knocked on Uncle Theo's door.

"Why didn't you pick up my call or at least text me after you left Uncle Theo's house?"

"I got distracted. I'm sorry."

"Where are you?"

"I'm sitting in my car, staring at the tree where Isabella Estrada was found."

"Oh, shit. I never asked you who was killed. I didn't realize it was Caden's sister."

"Did you know her?"

"No, but I knew Caden. My friend liked him, and we hung out at his house a few times. He was a momma's boy back then, and he wasn't happy to learn his mom was going to have another baby."

"When I talked to him, he came across as genuinely upset about her death."

"I'm sure he was. I mean, that was sixteen years ago," Aria said.

"He was in my class," Sawyer said. "I just remember him being shy."

"I think he was a sophomore when I was a senior in high school," Aria told her. "I never told my friend, but he used to follow me from class to class. I have no idea how he got to his own classes on time."

"Hmm. He's living in Oregon. He's engaged, and he wasn't in town when his sister was killed."

"Did Isabella have a boyfriend?"

"Yeah, a forty-year-old married man with two kids."

"Dang."

"I went to his house to talk to him," Sawyer said. "He refused to talk to me in private and didn't like me telling the truth in front of his wife, so he lunged at me and tried to strangle me."

"What the fuck? Are you okay? Has he been arrested?"

"I'll be fine, but no, he wasn't arrested." Sawyer took a look in the rearview mirror and brushed her fingers across the purplish dots around her throat. "Even Mom blames me for bothering him and his wife and intruding on their lives."

"And yet after all that, you're still in River Rock," Aria reminded her.

"Yeah, I'm still here. Once I get the details from Chief Schneider and talk to a few more people, I'll have no choice but to wrap this up and come home."

"The sooner the better," Aria said.

Sawyer sensed something in her sister's voice. "Are you okay?"

"You have so much going on that I shouldn't bother you with this, but Harper has been acting strange, and I'm worried about her."

"Strange in what way?"

"You know how she always cleans, eats right, and makes time for yoga and meditation?"

"Yes. Go on."

"She's been leaving the house at odd times. Her yoga mat hasn't moved from the basket in the family room. There's never fresh fruit or anything to eat. When she is home, she looks exhausted, like she doesn't sleep anymore. This morning I went over there, and the kitchen sink was piled high with dishes. That's a first."

Sawyer couldn't help but smile. She'd only been gone a few days. "I'm sure Harper is fine."

"Damn! I have more to tell you, but I have another call coming in from work. I've got to go."

After she hung up, Sawyer got out of the car and walked toward the tree. Isabella Estrada.

Why had she been out here in the middle of nowhere?

Sawyer walked back to the area where she'd gone to last time. She'd completely forgotten about the tiny bit of fabric she'd found until now. She stuck her fingers into the back pocket of her jeans and remembered she'd been wearing her nicer slacks for the funeral. She'd have to search for it later.

Twigs crunched beneath her sneakers, and light struggled to reach the forest floor, instead tossing shadows all around her, making her nervous. The flattened area was still there. Nothing had changed.

Continuing on, shrubs and trees wherever she looked, she noticed one shrub that had distinctly broken branches. She walked that way. There were footprints, hardly any fallen leaves. Someone had been in this exact spot for a while. Maybe hours. Waiting. Watching. She crouched down until she could see right through a hole that had been made through the brush. She stared, tried to figure out what someone might have been looking at or for. Past a grouping of trees, she saw what looked like a path. She jumped back to her feet and slowly headed that way, taking note of broken branches and flattened earth where someone had stepped. Her heart hammered against her chest. She was following Isabella's attacker's same path. She was sure of it. She stopped when she reached a narrow trail. She knelt down where both sides of the trail had obviously been disturbed. There were divots in the earth where Sawyer imagined Isabella had tried to crawl away, grasping for a hold and finding none.

Who did this?

On her feet again, Sawyer decided to follow the path. She could go left, which would take her back toward the crime scene, or she could go right.

She went right.

Walking at a good, clipped pace, she kept her gaze on the meandering footpath ahead, looking for anything abnormal. The earth below her feet was damp and devoid of leaves. She'd been walking for at least five minutes when she heard the snap of a branch.

She stopped and listened.

A woodpecker sounded in the distance. A flutter of leaves fell to the ground to her left. Twigs and forest debris crunched nearby. She held her breath as she turned toward the sound and reached into her front pocket for her pepper spray. "Who's there?"

Nothing.

She couldn't stand there forever, so she took another three steps. This time when she heard the crunch of leaves somewhere behind her, she kept walking, quickened her pace, her thumb on the nozzle of pepper spray. Her heart raced. The footfalls became loud and pronounced, gaining ground. She stopped and turned around in time to see someone dart off and disappear behind a row of tall pines.

What the hell?

Something brushed up against her.

She screamed.

Shit! It was a dog. A golden retriever with floppy ears and a wagging tail. She was trying to read the tags when a line of people appeared on the trail ahead. She recognized the man in front as the gentleman who had spoken at Gramma's funeral, the guy in the plaid suit who had talked about aging and how important it was to get moving.

She knelt down and gave the dog a proper greeting, rubbing the fur on his back and neck. "Good dog."

"We heard a scream," the leader of the pack said as he approached. "Did Frodo scare you?"

"It wasn't the dog's fault," Sawyer said. "I was feeling a little skittish."

"Understandable." He looked around as the four men and women behind him came to a stop. "You probably shouldn't be out here alone, especially after what happened to that young girl."

"You're right. If you don't mind, I'll follow you back toward my car," she said, pointing. "It's parked back that way in the direction you're headed."

He nodded.

She gestured toward the path behind him and his friends. "Does the path lead to the park?"

"Yessiree. Next time you want to go for a walk, come with us. We meet in front of the bear statue at nine thirty every day."

"Ten thirty a.m. on Sundays," someone in the group corrected.

"That's right. Join us anytime," he said. "We need to keep moving." He made a twirling motion with his finger to let her know it was time for her to turn around and get going.

Ten minutes later, Sawyer climbed in behind the wheel, made sure all the doors were locked, and then buckled up. She gave a quick wave to the men and women waiting to see her safely off, then pulled away.

As she drove along the dirt path back toward the main road, she peered into the woods. Somebody was still out there. She could sense it. Even now, someone was watching her.

She'd only talked to a few people about Isabella. She couldn't imagine the math teacher being let out of his wife's sight. And what about Uncle Theo? It would have been almost impossible for him to get to the woods before her. And he had no idea where she was off to when she'd left his house.

As she merged onto the main road, she thought about what Uncle Theo had said. "They weren't my friends," he'd told her.

What had he been talking about? Was he trying to tell her that the rape fantasy parties weren't his idea? Had someone put him up to it?

And what about the fearful look in his eyes when she'd asked him if he'd been prowling around the cottage last night? He'd adamantly denied being there.

Uncle Theo knew something.

She never should have let him off the hook so easily. She was going back to see him. If he broke down and cried, she'd wait him out, make him tell her what he knew.

He owed her that much.

CHAPTER THIRTY-THREE

Aria was waiting for the next customer in line to tell her his order when she noticed Harper across the street, walking at a brisk pace.

She took off her apron, told her manager it was an emergency and she would be right back. A wave of stifling-hot air hit her the moment she stepped outside. She rushed to the curb and glanced across the street as Harper was stepping into a deli. As soon as traffic allowed, she crossed the two-lane road. What the hell was Harper up to?

Midtown was busy this time of day, and she weaved through a throng of people to get to where she'd seen Harper disappear. Pulling the door to the deli open, she didn't take a breath until she saw Harper in line at the take-out register.

She came up behind her and said, "There you are!"

Harper let out a gasp as she turned around, obviously surprised to see Aria.

"You weren't at the house this morning," Aria said, stating the obvious. "You've been sneaking off a lot lately."

"Are you keeping tabs on me?"

"Maybe I am. You're not having an affair or something stupid like that, are you?"

She shook her head. "Of course not."

"You want to know why I believe you?"

"Why?"

"Because you look like shit. Nobody ever looks like shit when they're having an affair." Aria wrinkled her nose. "Have you taken a shower lately?"

Harper huffed. "It's not easy, taking care of two kids and a husband. I can't remember the last time I had a day off to do whatever I pleased. After I leave here, I think I might treat myself to a mani and pedi."

"Your kitchen sink was filled to the brim with dirty dishes. I'm not judging, but that's simply not something you've ever been okay with. Something's going on."

Harper was up next.

Aria watched as four twelve-inch sandwiches and napkins were put inside a plastic bag and handed over the counter for Harper to take. She'd obviously called in the order because she took the bag and headed for the door.

Aria stayed at her heels. "You're going to eat all that?"

Harper said nothing as she pushed her way through the door and weaved through the crowd as if she could so easily brush her little sister off.

"Come on," Aria said, loud enough for anyone to hear. "It's me, your sister. Tell me what's going on here."

Harper stepped into a small alcove out of the way of other pedestrians. She exhaled. "I didn't want to tell anyone because it's private, but I'm going to tell you so you'll get off my back. And then you're going to promise me you won't tell anyone, and that includes Nate, the kids, and Sawyer. Promise?"

"I promise," Aria said. "Unless you're seeing another man . . . then my promise is null and void."

Harper rolled her eyes. "I'm writing a book."

That was the absolute last thing Aria expected to come out of her sister's mouth. "You're shitting me."

"If you mean to ask if I'm serious, I am."

Aria narrowed her eyes. "I never once in my lifetime heard you talk about wanting to write a book."

"Because I didn't want anyone telling me it was a stupid idea."

Aria lifted her chin. "What are you writing about?"

"It's going to be a memoir."

"Who are those sandwiches for?"

"My critique partners."

"You have critique partners?"

"Yes. We've been helping one another for over a year."

Aria wasn't convinced. "Helping each other in what way?"

"Like helping each other learn to narrow our focus and use elements of fiction to tell our stories." Harper sighed. "I need to get going. I'll talk to you more about it later, okay?"

Something wasn't right, but Aria nodded. "Fine. We'll talk about it later. You're sure you're okay?"

"I'm good."

"And what about the baby?"

Harper stiffened. "The baby is good too."

Aria continued to scrutinize her. Harper might look like a wreck, but she also appeared to be less tense. Her mouth wasn't pinched. She wasn't exactly glowing, but she looked . . . satisfied.

"For the first time in my life, I'm doing something for me," Harper added.

Aria stepped forward and hugged her sister. Sawyer wasn't the only one who seemed to have a difficult time showing affection. Harper and Sawyer were as different as they were alike. All three of them had never had their emotional needs met, leaving them to grow up in a world full of fear. But it wasn't the physical, observable signs of problems that worried Aria. It was the things she couldn't see inside her sisters.

Aria watched Harper run off. Despite the inspiring speech about finally doing something for herself, Aria wasn't falling for it. Something wasn't adding up. But right now, Aria felt the need to focus on Sawyer. If Sawyer wasn't back by the end of the week, she was going to River Rock to bring her home.

CHAPTER

THIRTY-FOUR

Sawyer pulled up in front of her uncle's house for the second time, glad to see that his truck was still in the driveway. On the way there she'd been thinking about what she wanted to say to him. Instead of using verbal darts, she decided she would use a kinder, gentler approach. She wondered if she could pull it off. It was clear that all the built-up anger she'd been harboring inside for so long hurt her more than it hurt him, but she couldn't seem to turn it off.

Her therapist often reminded her of something Martin Luther King Jr. had once said: "Darkness cannot drive out darkness, only light can do that. Hate cannot drive out hate . . . only love can do that."

As she walked up the path leading to the door, she repeated those words over and over, but she still felt the anger bubbling inside.

Uncle Theo didn't come to the door after she knocked. He'd probably seen her drive up and was hiding, hoping she would go away. She reached for the doorknob, surprised when it turned and she was able to open the door and walk inside. "Uncle Theo. I know you're here. I didn't come back to yell at you. I just want to talk."

Silence.

She exhaled as she walked across the living area to the kitchen. The picture she'd ripped to pieces was still scattered across the linoleum. "I need you to tell me what you know," she said, walking slowly, afraid she might scare him into sneaking out the window. "You said something about the parties you threw not being your idea. Whose idea were they, Uncle Theo? I need to know." She stopped beneath the doorframe leading into his bedroom.

Her stomach clenched.

Uncle Theo hung from the ceiling fan by a thick cord. His face was swollen, eyes bulging from their sockets. His feet dangled a few feet from the ground. It was easy to surmise that he'd pushed the mattress aside and used the bins Sawyer had pulled from the closet earlier to reach the ceiling fan before kicking them aside.

A dull ache settled in her chest as she walked toward him and placed her fingertips around his wrist to see if there was any chance she could save him. There was no pulse.

She felt hollow inside. Not because he was dead, but because she didn't care that he was dead. He was everything wrong with the world. Mostly, he was a coward. He could have helped her by telling her what he knew, but instead he'd taken the easy way out.

She walked outside and called 9-1-1.

Sawyer sat on the front stoop of Uncle Theo's house, answering Chief Schneider's questions. She'd already told him about her early-morning visit and finding the bin filled with child pornography. She'd also told the chief she had returned to Uncle Theo's house because she still had so many questions that only her uncle could answer.

The emergency lights from the chief's police vehicle had been left on. Sawyer turned a few inches to her left to shield her eyes from the swirling glare.

The chief was five foot nine with a bulging gut. He'd grown another chin since she'd seen him last. He still had kind glass-green eyes beneath crinkled eyelids. His hair was mostly silver and gray like his mustache, and she wondered how many more years he had before retirement. He looked weighed down by his belt with its heavy flashlight, security holster and pistol, magazine clip, and baton.

"So what was your uncle's state of mind when you left the first time?" the chief asked her.

"When Uncle Theo let me inside, he looked beat up by life. And then when I found his stash of pornography, he freaked out." Sawyer decided to leave out the part about accusing Uncle Theo of murder, since she had a feeling the chief wouldn't appreciate her overstepping any boundaries when it came to his investigation.

"Freaked out?"

"Got a crazed look in his eyes," Sawyer said. "Uncle Theo looked suddenly possessed. He told me the devil was close and that I'd better run."

The chief made a note on his little pad of paper he'd pulled from his shirt pocket. "I'm still not clear on why you returned since you'd already had your say."

Aspen came out of the house then, glanced from Sawyer to the chief, and said, "We've got him bagged up and ready to go."

"Good. Now block off the house with caution tape," Chief Schneider told him.

Aspen got to work.

"So, what sort of questions did you plan on asking Theodore the second time around?"

She was tired of beating around the bush. Maybe the chief could answer a few questions. "I wanted to know more about the rape fantasy parties he used to take Aria and me to."

Chief Schneider cleared his throat.

"When I brought it up this morning, Uncle Theo said the parties weren't his idea. He acted as if he'd had no choice in the matter. When I questioned him on that, he started sobbing."

"Why didn't you mention all that earlier?"

"Because it isn't easy to talk about being raped by your uncle and his friends. I wanted to keep it private, sort of like how you don't want to go around talking about your drinking problem."

His eyes hardened. "Watch yourself. You know, I always worried about you girls, but I never heard of any party like you're talking about, and although I do appreciate your candor, I don't appreciate your insinuation."

He scratched his jaw as he inhaled, looking around as if to pull himself back together. When he turned back her way, he met her gaze straight on, daring her to look away. "I get the point you're trying to make, so I'm going to let it go this time."

She held his gaze, didn't blink. She was fired up, and yet she knew she needed to calm down. Too much whiskey or not, Chief Schneider was one of the good guys. "Thanks," she said without much feeling.

"Anything else you'd like to add?" Chief Schneider asked.

"Yes, there is. I'm doing a human-interest story on Isabella Estrada, and I was wondering if it would be possible to see the police report."

He shook his head. "Not a chance."

"Why not?"

"Because we don't disclose investigatory records."

"Chief, you know the law, and you know those records need to be made available to me upon request. Otherwise, I'm going to report that you denied me access."

"What are you trying to prove?" he asked.

"Nothing. And I'm not trying to be disrespectful. I'm just doing my job like you and attempting to report a crime so people in the community won't be in the dark about what's going on. That's all."

"I received a call from Mr. Estrada," the chief said. "He didn't appreciate you coming by to talk to his son. I gave your mom a call this morning. It would be best, Sawyer, if you left the investigation to me and my team."

Sawyer came to her feet and dusted herself off. "Answer me this, Chief. Did you ever talk to anyone in this godforsaken town when Peggy Myers and Avery James were murdered? Or did you turn the other way and pretend it never happened, like everyone else in River Rock?"

"Clearly you're upset about your uncle. We'll talk another time." The chief started walking away.

"I want to know when you're going to bring in Jonathan Lane for questioning. You know, the forty-year-old married man who was fucking his sixteen-year-old math student?"

The chief's face reddened. "Jonathan Lane is my brother-in-law. My sister told me everything. Sounded to me like you were trespassing, but if you feel the need to fill out a report, I'll file it away with the others."

"Are you fucking kidding me?" She gestured at her throat. "He strangled me."

"You better watch your tongue."

Aspen appeared out of nowhere and ushered her away before Sawyer could respond.

Sawyer gritted her teeth. She didn't like having his hands on her. "Let me go," she said. "What are you doing?"

"What am I doing? I'm saving you from being locked in a tiny cell downtown."

"The chief can't lock me up for being rude."

"You're being naive. People are taken in all the time for mouthing off. They call it disorderly conduct. So what were you thinking back there?"

He brought her to her car and said, "Go home."

"I don't want to go home."

"You sound like a three-year-old. You can't go around pointing fingers and accusing people of murder. I've never seen anyone cause more trouble in such a short amount of time."

"Don't you see it, Aspen?"

"See what?"

"Nobody cares what happens in River Rock. Isabella Estrada was murdered and strung to a tree, and nobody gives a shit!"

"That's not true."

"What about Peggy and Avery? Nobody wants to talk about them. Is that what's going to happen with Isabella?"

"You're starting to sound like a broken record, Sawyer. And you're not being fair to Chief Schneider. There is protocol to be followed. The state police will be called in shortly. Everything doesn't happen in a day."

She started to speak, but he cut her off. "You seem to have forgotten that you can catch more flies with honey than vinegar."

She looked at him then. He was serious. She laughed.

"What?"

Being nice and following the rules rarely got results. "You sound like an old man."

"I gotta get back to work," he said angrily.

She took a breath. He had no business pulling her away from the chief, but he'd wanted to calm her down, and his little trick had worked. Her heart was no longer beating against her ribs. She climbed in behind the wheel of her car and drove off. She would talk to the chief another time.

Five minutes later, she pulled up the driveway to her parents' house, parked the car, and got out. The front door was unlocked. She walked in, hoping to sneak down the hall and through the kitchen to the cottage.

"Sawyer, is that you?" came her father's voice from the room her mother called the salon. Sawyer never went into the salon, because when she did, all she could see were those men's faces, the ones who had paid Uncle Theo to do as they pleased with her—a small, defenseless child.

She sucked in a breath and headed that way. Until this very moment she hadn't had a second to think about the implications of Uncle Theo's death. How would Mom and Dad take the news? She recalled the chief telling her he'd called Mom this morning. Her chest tightened. They knew everything.

She walked into the salon. Her gaze fell on her father. He was sitting in his favorite chair.

Mom was standing in the corner near the floor-to-ceiling built-in bookshelf. She carefully slid a book with a leather spine back into place and then took a seat on a cushioned Queen Anne armchair.

They were both quiet . . . both watching her.

The air enveloping them was electric in a hauntingly eerie sense— thick with an energy that sizzled and sparked.

Dad gestured toward the Empire side chair that appeared to have been set in the middle of the room, facing them both, for just this purpose. They were going to have a chat.

Sawyer walked over to the chair, mindful of the squeaky sound her shoes made against the polished hardwood floor. She took a seat, kept her hands folded in her lap, and looked from one parent to the other.

For the first time in her life, she had their full attention.

And she didn't want it.

Life was funny that way. Giving you what you craved most when you no longer wanted it.

The chief had definitely called Mom about Uncle Theo. Her face looked as if it had been chiseled from stone. "You killed Theodore."

Dad raised a hand as if to either stop Mom from talking or buffer the blame coming from her statement. *Silly man.* Dad could light up the room with an impressive display of fireworks, and it wouldn't do any good. Nothing would stop Mother Dearest from having her say. Mom's opinions on all things were all that mattered. Mom loved to listen to the sound of her own voice. She was the ruler, the queen of her household, of her husband, and of her sorry little life.

"I asked you to leave it alone and mind your own business," Mom told Sawyer, talking to her as if she were a child. "But you couldn't do it."

"I went to Uncle Theo's house to talk to him. That's all."

"You accused him of murder."

"Did Uncle Theo call you after I left?" Sawyer asked.

Mom hissed. "Of course he called me. He was extremely upset."

"Why would he call you and not his brother?" Sawyer asked. "Why call you at all, considering he was the one badgering me to talk to him and forgive him?"

Nobody had an answer.

"For the record," Sawyer said, looking from Mom to Dad, "I didn't kill Uncle Theo. He found a good, strong cord and hung himself from the ceiling fan in his bedroom without any help from me."

Mom looked at Dad. "I warned you about her. I told you that if she came to Sally's funeral, she would cause trouble, but you wouldn't listen."

Dad sighed, his eyes fixating on Sawyer. "I'm going to have to ask you to leave. I know you don't like to drive when it's dark, so you can pack your things tonight and set off at first light. Your mother and I have things to do at the store in the morning, so we'll have to say our goodbyes now."

Sawyer felt a strange mix of emotions. Not sad. Not relieved. Nothing she could put her finger on. But she found it strange to think she might never see her parents again. That thought alone emboldened her further. "I went to see Uncle Theo for the second time, because I needed to know the truth."

"The truth?" Dad asked.

Sawyer nodded. "Uncle Theo implied that someone else was responsible for selling me and Aria to rich old men. He said the rape parties were not his idea."

"Here we go again," Mom said in her usual dramatic fashion. "If a young girl tells herself over and over again that she's been sexually abused, she begins to see it as the truth." Mom's face softened. "You were never raped, Sawyer. It was all in your head. Uncle Theo used to give you girls sleeping pills to calm you down. You were all energetic children, too much for one man to handle while we were away. Unfortunately, one of the symptoms of the drug he gave you was hallucinations."

More lies. "What's the name of the drug?" Sawyer asked.

Mom's smirk dripped with disdain. "That's not important. The only thing that matters is that now you know why you and your sister Aria have been so confused. When you go back to Sacramento, you can tell Aria what you've learned, and maybe together you girls can move on to bigger and better things."

Sawyer stared at her mom as she thought back to those years after her sisters left. Mom had always scolded her for mistakes she'd made. Mistakes Sawyer had acknowledged. Mom never took into account how courageous Sawyer had been to speak the truth. Always criticizing. Never a proud moment.

Sawyer turned toward her dad. "Is she speaking the truth?"

He said nothing.

She didn't really expect an answer. Her dad had no spine. "What choice do you have but to believe whatever the queen tells you?" Sawyer asked him. "Everyone in this shitty little town has something to hide. River Rock was built on secrets."

Mom came to her feet. "That's enough."

Sawyer also stood. "I guess this is goodbye." Sawyer kept her gaze fixated on her mom a moment longer. "It's hard to believe Gramma gave birth to someone like you. She was so caring and sweet, and I was lucky to have her in my life, which makes me wonder, what the hell happened to you?"

Sawyer walked out of the room, made her way through the kitchen, where she grabbed a piece of fruit and headed for the cottage to pack.

CHAPTER
THIRTY-FIVE

Malice opened her eyes and pushed herself to a sitting position. She'd slept on a thin pad she'd taken from one of the cots. She preferred to sleep level with the ground. She didn't feel well. Her head pounded against her skull—thump, thump, thump.

Psycho's cot was empty, but Malice only had to look toward the darkest corner of the warehouse to see her silhouette. Other than a quick bathroom break outside every so often, Psycho refused to leave Otto's side. She'd spent most of her time sitting on the hard ground a few feet away from him, her back against the wall, watching him and saying nothing.

Everyone in The Crew had agreed that they would take turns sleeping in the warehouse, making sure Otto didn't escape. Psycho stayed every night, regardless of who else was here with her.

Malice wondered if what Psycho was doing, staring at the man day and night, was therapeutic, or if it was merely causing her further turmoil. It was difficult for Malice to wrap her mind around the fact that Otto Radley had repeatedly cut through Psycho's flesh and then crudely sewn her up using fishing wire.

The man who had used Psycho's body as his own personal plaything for all those days and nights was sitting right there after all this time, chained and at his victim's mercy.

What was going through Psycho's head? The plan had been to scare the man, but after twenty years in prison, this guy wasn't afraid of anything.

Malice looked around for the gun, panicked when she didn't see the rifle leaning against the wall.

She pushed herself to her feet.

The weapon had been moved. It now leaned against the wall closer to the door.

Malice took a breath to try to calm herself.

The door was shut and locked in place with a metal bar that slid through two metal hooks. There were enough crevices and cracks in the place for Malice to see that it was still dark outside. She glanced at her watch. Five thirty a.m.

Every joint was stiff and sore as she walked toward their designated cooking area. She needed coffee. One of the women had brought a cooler filled with hard-boiled eggs and cheese and crackers. The sandwiches she'd brought yesterday were long gone.

Using a jug of water, she began the process of making a pot of coffee. She'd never been camping before, but she was a quick learner.

As she went about gathering whatever she needed, she wondered how she would feel if that was *her* father tied to the metal pipes.

Imp-like glee shot through her.

It always seemed strange that physically her father was miles away, and yet mentally he was right here, right now.

Always.

A day didn't go by that she didn't think of him and wish him dead.

Back then, in the light of day, even when he wasn't sneaking into her room, she would catch him looking at her, his yearning palpable.

Such a secretive man, like a shadow, gloomy and haunting, a dark presence in her life. Nothing had changed. He still troubled her dreams.

Oftentimes she would find herself in another dimension, reliving the horror of feeling her father's fleshy, hairy body moving, grinding, his breath in her ear, panting and groaning as he fucked his own daughter.

Suffocation—unable to get enough air—Malice had experienced it every day from age six to eighteen. More often than not, his thick body pressed heavily on her, the pressure so much she'd wished he would accidentally smother her.

She never fought him.

Not once.

They had a deal.

A blood-curdling roar tore through the ugly memories and filled the warehouse. Malice dropped the can of coffee. It clanged against the cement floor, rattling along as it rolled out of sight.

Across the room she saw Psycho sitting on the ground, bent over Otto.

"What are you doing?" Malice asked, the words catching in her throat.

"What does it look like, or should I say sound like?" Psycho had to shout to be heard over Otto's screams and cursing.

"Payback is a bitch," Psycho shouted. "Isn't it, Otto?"

Malice walked to the corner of the warehouse where Psycho hovered over Otto. She stopped when she was a foot away.

Her stomach turned.

Psycho's hands were covered in blood. She had sliced through Otto's pants and the flesh of his left thigh and was now using a fishhook and wire to sew him up, not bothering to move the denim out of her way as she worked. Sewing the whole thing up, flesh and fabric, just like that.

Had Psycho's plan always been to torture the man? Sick to her stomach, Malice rushed to the exit, pulled the bar loose, pushed on the creaky metal door, and ran outside. The rage. The blood. The craziness of it all was too much. She got as far as a spindly pine tree before she dropped to her knees and dry heaved. Her stomach was empty, but that didn't stop her from retching.

It was a while before Malice felt good enough to come to her feet. She wasn't sure how long she'd been outside. But the screams had stopped, and her stomach was no longer roiling, so she decided it was time to make her way back inside. She glanced at her watch as she headed back. Lily would be here in a few hours to relieve her.

Malice stepped through the warehouse door. It was much cooler inside than outside. Thinking her eyes were playing tricks on her, she froze in place, didn't move a muscle.

Psycho had taken up where Malice had left off and was making a pot of coffee.

And Otto, ever so quietly, was creeping her way.

How could that be? They had chained him to the pipe. The answer was in his hand. He must have broken through the pipe while he was screaming. No wonder he'd been so loud. He'd been covering up his attempt at escaping.

Her heart raced as she reached for the rifle, careful that the butt was up against the crevice of her shoulder and her nonshooting elbow was directly below the barrel. She had to focus. She had no choice. She pushed the bolt forward and down and set her sight on her target.

Both Psycho and Otto must have heard the noise, because they pivoted so that they were looking right at her.

The only difference was that Psycho dropped to the floor.

Malice pulled the trigger. The blow sent her stumbling backward into the wall. Her ears were ringing, her eyes gritty. She looked ahead, wasn't sure what she was seeing through blurry eyes.

The gun held at her side, she stepped forward, trying to see, her body tense as she worried Otto would attack at any moment.

As her vision cleared and the ringing in her ears lessened, she saw Otto facedown on the ground. Only that wasn't the ground. Psycho grunted as she pulled and clawed her way out from under the man.

Malice wanted to help her, but she was afraid to set the gun down. She had no idea if the rifle held more than one bullet, since she couldn't remember what Lily had said about loading the weapon. She waited for Psycho to crawl out from under the man. "Is he dead?" Malice asked.

Psycho came to her feet, pushed the hair out of her face, and reached for Otto's wrist. After a moment, she let go. His lifeless arm thumped against the ground. "He's dead."

Relief and dread flooded through Malice.

"Put that thing away, will you?"

Malice leaned the weapon against the wall, then came back to where Psycho was examining Otto's head. "A clean shot right through the skull," Psycho pointed out.

"I'm a murderer," Malice said.

"You saved my life," Psycho said as she pulled her cell phone from her back pocket, pushed a button, and held it to her ear.

"Who are you calling?"

"Lily," Psycho said. "We need you to bring a shovel or two. Yes, right away. Okay. See you soon."

Malice looked at Psycho as if the woman had grown two heads, which she might as well have, considering she was covered in blood like something out of a horror movie. "Shovels?"

Psycho nodded. "We're going to need to bury him."

"We're not going to call the police?"

"Are you nuts?"

Yes, Malice thought. *I just killed a man. I am definitely nuts.*

CHAPTER THIRTY-SIX

Early Monday morning, Sawyer lay in bed, thinking about Uncle Theo. Seeing him like that had been shocking. Over the years, she'd envisioned Uncle Theo dying in hundreds of gruesome scenarios. But for some reason she was still scared. Afraid he would find a way to get her.

She heard the sound of gravel popping under tires as a car drove off. She sat up and looked around. It took a second to realize she'd left her bag along with her cell phone in her car. She slipped on her shoes, made her way outside and through the side yard to the front of the house.

Her purse was still sitting on the passenger seat. She grabbed it and walked back to the cottage, her arms covered in goose bumps. The mornings in River Rock were chilly, shaded by trees, everything crackling with icy morning dew.

Back inside the cottage, she pulled out her phone. It was dead. She plugged it in to let it charge as she went about collecting her things and using the bathroom. She grabbed the key to the main house and headed that way. The kitchen door was locked. She unlocked it and stepped inside. Everything was neat and tidy, as usual. You wouldn't know anyone was living in the house.

She left the key on the counter where her parents would see it.

Wanting to give her phone time to charge, she exited the kitchen and walked down the hall and into the room where her parents had sat her down to talk. The chair in the middle of the room had been tucked back under a beautiful Revival-style card table. Her mom did have a gift for collecting unusual antiques.

She would never set foot in this house again, and for that she was glad.

She thought of Gramma, and her friend Rebecca, and Isabella. She would still write a story, but it would be as much about Isabella as it would be about all the other lost souls of River Rock. She would turn this little town on its back and expose the sad, disgusting underbelly that floated through the air and moved through underground pipes like poison.

Sawyer walked around the room, brushed her fingers over an old settee with its sloping, upholstered arms. She touched the wall and a table too, realizing she had no connection to anything in the house. It was a weird feeling, knowing she'd spent half of her life within these walls and felt nothing but sadness and grief.

She inhaled. She was no longer that little girl. She was older and wiser and stronger. She would leave River Rock. This house, this place, these people would not win. She would tell the truth and break free of this place once and for all. The whole town was covering up, keeping secrets. Chief Schneider might not be the good guy she thought he was. His sister was married to Jonathan Lane. Nobody seemed surprised about there being a relationship between the math teacher and his young student. The mention of rape fantasy parties hardly made the chief flinch.

Inside a small porcelain bowl within an open rolltop desk was an old skeleton key. She picked it up, examined it closer, and felt compelled, driven by curiosity, to see if it would unlock the door to Dad's office. With the skeleton key in hand, she moved through the darkened hallway quietly, as if her parents were asleep in the other room.

Click.

The door opened. She walked inside the forbidden room. The vintage mahogany desk sat front and center. An antique leather chair was tucked in close on the other side. Floor-to-ceiling shelves took up the wall to the right. To the left was a fireplace set in brick.

She was twenty-nine years old, and yet she'd only been inside the room one other time. The space felt small and insignificant compared with her memories of it. She'd always imagined this secretive room where her dad spent much of his time being majestic. Magical. But it was just a room with a fireplace and a small window, curtains drawn. A Persian rug covered much of the old wood floors.

She went to the desk, brushed her fingers over the wood, trying to get a sense of a man she really didn't know. There was a calendar, a stack of books, a notepad and pen, and a hand-carved wooden in-box filled with mail. Close to the bottom, sticking halfway out, was an envelope that she pulled free. "Dennis" was written in long, cursive letters that looked like Harper's handwriting. She opened the envelope and pulled out a handwritten letter.

Why would Harper write Dad a letter?

There was no date in the margin or at the top of the letter, but the postmark on the envelope showed that it was sent days after Harper and Aria had disappeared.

Confused, she began to read:

To the man who gave me life,

I will never refer to you as my father or Dad. Never. Not after all the suffering you've caused me. I hate you. I cringe when I think of you kissing and fondling me. The smell of your sour breath on my face makes me gag to think of it.

Each night that you snuck into my room, I wanted to kill you. Did you know that I used to keep a sharp knife under my pillow? As you plunged yourself into me, I wanted to plunge the sharp end of the blade into you.

But I couldn't do it.

I was a coward.

The only reason I didn't kill myself was because I was afraid you would move on to Aria and then Sawyer.

My self-worth was reduced to nothing because of you. I can't sleep through the night without worrying you will creep into my room and rape me all over again.

You may have ruined me, but you did not destroy me.

If your wife reads this, I hope she knows she is just as much to blame. I once saw her peeking through the door. She didn't want your filthy hands on her, so she let you have your way with me, your sweet, precious firstborn.

The last time you came into my bedroom, you cried and told me you wanted to stop. I am writing today to remind you that we had a deal. I expect you to keep your promise.

Sawyer is too young to understand; otherwise she would be here with me now. She doesn't know that you bleed darkness. If you ever touch her, I will kill you.

—Harper

Sawyer used her forearm to wipe tears from her face. Her knees wobbled, and her chest ached.

Harper.

Dad was no better than his brother—two immoral; obscene brothers. But Harper had suffered the abuse by her own father, in her own house, night after night?

Poor Harper. All the signs of abuse were there. It broke her heart to think of Harper suffering for so long. She thought of the picture she'd seen at Uncle Theo's house. Harper standing straight and tall, so heroic, so sad.

The image of Mom peeking in . . . watching her daughter's abuse and doing nothing about it, made Sawyer's stomach clench. The room began to spin. Her chest tightened. This was truly a house of horrors. Sadness quickly boiled over into anger, dripping through her veins and making every muscle quiver.

Harper and Dad had a deal? What did Harper mean by that?

The wood floor in the hallway creaked. Sawyer ran toward the window, unlatched it, then—

"What are you doing in here?"

Sawyer whipped around. The letter was still in her hand.

Mom stood in the doorway, looking affronted.

Sawyer felt as if she were seeing her mom stripped down to the bone without any blinders on for the first time.

Harper was right.

Mom was no better than the two brothers she protected. "Dad raped Harper, his own daughter," Sawyer said in a steady voice. "Over and over again while you were telling me that my sister was out of control and a slut. You knew the truth, and you did nothing."

Mom pointed a shaky finger toward the exit. "Get out of my house."

"You," Sawyer said flatly, "are going down. So say goodbye to your little cozy life."

Dad appeared from behind Mom. He scooted her inside so he could enter his office and see what was going on.

Sawyer pointed at him. "I'm going to the police." She tucked the letter into her back pocket. "I'm going to tell Chief Schneider everything. If he refuses to do anything about it, it won't matter because

I'm going to rip the cloud of secrecy off this town like a kid opening a fucking Christmas present."

Mom looked at Dad, panic in her eyes. "I told you to burn that letter, but you wouldn't listen. What are we going to do?"

Dad put his hand on her shoulder.

She tried to shake him off as she always did, but his fingers held tight. "We're going to do what we should have done a long time ago," he said. "We're going to call Chief Schneider, invite him to the house, and tell him everything in person."

Mom's face reddened. Her nose and eyes crinkled. "You stupid, stupid man. I have given up everything for you." She stabbed him in the chest with her finger. "I lied for you."

Dad suddenly reminded her of Uncle Theo, so pathetically weak, standing next to Goliath.

Mom's face morphed into spittle and fire, reminding Sawyer of what Uncle Theo had said about the devil being close.

"I killed for you," Mom said, her voice dripping with venom. "And now you think because this little crybaby can't mind her own business that we're going to let her ruin our lives?"

Killed for you? Sawyer didn't move, hardly breathed.

"I should have gotten help for both of us," Dad said to Mom as he shook his head solemnly. "There were so many times I could have reached out for help to save us both."

Mom continued talking to Sawyer's dad as if Sawyer wasn't in the room with them. "I won't let you ruin my reputation because you couldn't keep your little wriggly worm in your pants."

"It's over, Joyce," Dad said.

Sawyer looked from her parents to the exit.

She needed to get away, get help. She took two steps before Mom pointed a finger at her.

"Stay right where you are, Sawyer. You're not going anywhere."

Dad's shoulders dropped. "Let her go, Joyce."

"Let her go, Joyce," Mom mimicked in a tinny voice.

Chills washed over Sawyer. The scene before her was unreal. Dad, a puddle of remorse and grief, seemingly oblivious to the other monster in the room, the all-powerful one, who for all these years had controlled him like a puppeteer controls his wooden dolls.

"This is all going to end right now," Dad said. "I'm not hiding from the truth any longer."

"It's not over, you foolish man. Not even close." Mom took a step backward, reached behind her for the fireplace poker, and swung the iron tool with amazing strength and dexterity.

Blood spurted from the center of Dad's forehead. Somehow he remained standing. His eyes looked overly bright as he reached out and grabbed hold of the poker still in her hands.

They both held tightly to the iron rod.

Mom was taller and stronger. Her eyes were alert, her jaw set as she fought for control.

The veins in Dad's neck began to bulge, his arms shaking from exertion, the blood running down his face nearly blinding him.

Sawyer's head was fuzzy. She couldn't think. Didn't know what to do.

It was as if the two of them were walking a tightrope—two steps to the left and then one to the right.

Suddenly Mom let go and watched him stumble backward.

Confusion filled Dad's eyes right before he hit the wall and collapsed to the floor, his body upright, his back against the wall. Mom walked toward him, leaned over, and took the poker from his grasp.

"No more," Dad said, his voice emotional.

You better run, is what Uncle Theo had said. Mom was insane.

Mom turned toward Sawyer.

Sawyer rushed forward and pushed her hard, watched her topple sideways into the wall and fall to her knees.

Sawyer ran out of the office and down the hallway, heading for the front door before remembering her keys to the car were in the cottage.

She stopped, turned back the other way, heard footfalls coming her way. Quietly, she opened the door to her left, stepped inside, shut the door softly, and took slow, careful steps down the stairs leading into the basement.

"Sawyer!" Mom called. "Where are you? I only want to talk for a minute before you head home. Dad is fine."

Sawyer could hear her walking around the salon where Sawyer had found the key. Sawyer's gaze darted about the room. It was cold and musty. Every wall was lined with boxes and bins and old discarded furniture. She was about to get down low between some bins when the door at the top of the stairs creaked open. Instead, Sawyer headed for the door in the far corner, the one that led into a crawl space. She and Rebecca used to hide inside sometimes when Mom would throw one of her tantrums. They would belly-crawl their way through the tight space to the vent leading outside and escape into the woods.

Her sisters used to tease them about going into the crawl space, telling them there were rats and every sort of insect known to man.

Sawyer squeezed her way through the door, a tighter squeeze than she remembered. There was no way her mom would be able to get through that opening, so Sawyer worked her way far enough inside where she could hide beneath a slope of dirt and wood beam. She would be well hidden if Mom took a look inside.

Mom called her name again.

The small door creaked open. The crawl space filled with light.

Sawyer didn't dare breathe. She kept her nose to the dirt and held perfectly still.

"It would be silly of you to hide in there. This is your last chance, Sawyer. Come out, or I'll have no choice but to lock you in there."

Sawyer said nothing. She could hear Mom breathing right before the tiny door clicked shut.

The crawl space was dark again.

Another noise pricked her ears. It sounded as if Mom was fiddling with the padlock on the other side of the opening. She could hear metal scrape against wood and then another click.

She tried not to panic. *Stay calm. Breathe.*

After the sound of Mom's footfalls moving up the stairs disappeared completely, Sawyer crawled back to the door. It wouldn't budge. She yanked harder, her heart racing. Mom had purposely locked her inside.

She'd said she had killed before. At the time, Sawyer had considered that maybe she was being overly dramatic, but now a different woman began to form in her mind. A dark, sinister woman who protected her husband even when she knew what he was doing behind closed doors. The woman was insane.

Keeping her head low, she inched her way around through clods of dirt until she found a spot big enough where she could turn in a half circle and attempt to make her way to the far side of the crawl space.

Something fell on her head and skittered about. Squirming and cursing, she swiped at the top of her head again and again until whatever it was darted away. She spit dirt from her mouth. The thought of spiders and rats had never scared her when she was small. But they terrified her now.

She made her way back to the slope of dirt.

Something was wrong.

The crawl space was too dark. She'd never been overly frightened there when she was younger because she'd always been able to see. Where was the light that used to come in through the vent?

Her chest tightened.

She fought the urge to scream.

Mom would hear her. She knew that because when she used to hide down here, she could hear people talking and walking around upstairs.

It wouldn't do her any good to scream. Even if Dad hadn't been seriously injured, Mom would find a way to stop him from saving her. She had no choice but to blindly continue onward, find the vent, and see what was stopping the light from shining through.

Chapter Thirty-Seven

Less than a block away from home, Harper could see Aria's car parked at the curb.

Her heart dropped to her stomach. She pulled to the side of the road to catch her breath. What was she doing? After all she'd been through, it had come to this? Who was she?

Her two lives were never supposed to overlap. It was too dangerous.

Unable to shut her mind down, she kept seeing images, like a movie reel in her head: the police cuffing her and leading her away as Nate, Lennon, and Ella watch with confusion in their eyes.

Her insides twisted and turned. *Get a grip,* she inwardly scolded. *Do what you've always done, Harper!*

Put it away, she scolded. *Bundle it all up—the thoughts, the images, the fear of being found out, and then shove it down deep inside and leave it alone.*

She didn't need to glance in the rearview mirror to know she looked like a crazed person—someone who had shot a man and then watched him bleed out.

She looked in the mirror anyway. Didn't like what she saw. It was Malice's face looking back at her. Fucking scary.

Go away, Malice.

She closed her eyes, rested her forehead on the steering wheel. A minute later, she lifted her head, smoothed her hands over her head, pulled a twig from her hair, and sat up taller.

Better. She could do this.

Her wig and mask were tucked into a zippered compartment in her purse.

Good.

She looked around for any clue that might tell someone she'd spent hours digging through rock-hard dirt to make a hole big enough to fit a humongous man.

There was nothing. The interior of her car was as clean as the day she drove it off the car lot. She replayed what had happened one more time, checking off boxes, making sure she hadn't missed anything.

After The Crew had finished digging, Psycho had stripped Otto Radley bare, and they had rolled him into his grave and covered him with dirt. They'd washed the shovels, scrubbed the floors, and removed any sign that anyone had ever set foot inside the warehouse. Next, they had gathered outside in a semicircle, stripped down, and washed their hair and bodies, using soap and water Lily had brought for that purpose.

Everything would be okay. Her hands were no longer trembling.

Harper was back, and she was ready.

She merged back onto the road. It was 3:15 p.m. Tuesday. The last time she'd seen Aria was Sunday at the deli. She pulled into the driveway and turned off the ignition.

Harper didn't make it far before Aria opened the door to her garage studio. Hands on hips. "Where the hell have you been?"

"With my critique group. We stayed at one of the ladies' houses and worked day and night."

"Bullshit."

"It's the truth," Harper said.

"Let me see your book. You know, all the pages you wrote, all that hard work."

"It's private."

"Why do you look like you've been hiking through the woods?"

"I drank too much. Way too much, ended up jumping in Christine's pool. I'm embarrassed enough. Leave it alone."

Aria crossed her arms.

"What?"

"I don't believe you. You would never drink while pregnant."

Harper said nothing.

"Is whatever you're hiding worth lying about?" Aria shook her head sadly. "All you had to do was call or text so I would know you were alive."

Struggling to find her voice, Harper said, "I'm sorry."

Aria huffed and disappeared back inside her place. She left the door open. Harper peeked inside, saw her sister toss something into a suitcase lying on the couch.

"Going somewhere?"

"As a matter of fact, I am."

Harper waited, and when Aria didn't expand on what she was up to, Harper asked, "Where are you going?"

"Why should I tell you? You and Sawyer can't even answer your phones. I don't know why I bother caring about either of you. It's stupid. I'm going to get an ulcer from worrying before I hit thirty-five."

Harper's stomach turned. "Sawyer's not answering her phone?"

"Ahh," Aria said with a wag of her finger. "It's not fun worrying about someone you care about, is it?"

Harper exhaled. "I said I was sorry, and I meant it."

Aria looked at Harper. Her shoulders dropped. "I'm glad you're okay. But Sawyer promised me she would check in every day. I haven't talked to her since Sunday morning before I saw you at the deli. It's been forty-eight hours, and when I call, I'm taken directly to her voice mail. I'm going to River Rock."

"Did you call Joyce or Dennis?"

"Yes. I called the house phone too. No answer." Aria shoved a few more items into her suitcase before she zipped it up and rolled it closer to the door. She shouldered her purse and said, "The cat is hiding under my bed. He'll be fine until I get back. I left plenty of food and water for the bird and the cat. I'll call you when I get there."

"No, you won't."

"Yeah, I will. I'm the dependable sister."

Harper thought about Sawyer. Her little sister was in trouble. She'd warned Sawyer not to return to River Rock, but she'd been too stubborn to listen.

The thought of seeing Joyce and Dennis sent chills up Harper's spine. But in her mind, she had no choice but to go with Aria. And this time, she wouldn't leave without Sawyer.

"I'm going with you," Harper said. "Give me five minutes to change my clothes and brush my teeth."

"You might as well take a shower too. You smell. But I'm not waiting long. I'm done waiting."

CHAPTER THIRTY-EIGHT

Sawyer woke to the sound of wood scraping against wood above her head. Mom or Dad was at it again. Moving furniture while their youngest daughter was held captive in the crawl space below the floors?

It had taken her a while, possibly hours, to make her way to the vents, only to find that they had been sealed off with cement. She'd had to crawl with her belly pressed into dirt. It was a tight squeeze and had required a lot of digging and moving moldy clods of dirt to get there. Once she was back where she started, she'd pounded on the door and screamed at the top of her lungs, begging for Mom to let her out.

It was no use.

At some point she'd fallen asleep from exhaustion. Her throat was still raw from yelling.

Sawyer still had enough wits about her to know she'd been inside the crawl space for at least twenty-four hours. She reached out and touched the door. Her knuckles were red and sore from knocking on the door and walls. She needed to find a loose board or a piece of pipe, anything hard enough to bang against the ceiling of the crawl space. Maybe then her dad would hear the noise and come to the basement to investigate. She was hungry and thirsty.

Instead of following the straight line she'd made getting to the vent, she veered to her right, trying not to think about the critters who'd made this their home as she dug her fingers into the clumps of dirt and cement.

As she moved along, inch by inch, making sure to stay close to the outside wall, she wondered if Mom would give in and let her out. Even as the thought came to mind, she knew it was wishful thinking on her part. Mom had protected Dad all these years. There was no way she would free Sawyer and give her a chance to go to the police.

The tips of Sawyer's fingers brushed against something hard. She began digging around the object before she found another one. It felt like two long, thin wooden or plastic poles.

Blindly, she continued to feel around, moving clumps of dirt until her fingers touched something round.

She was on her stomach, hardly enough room to lift her chin more than a few inches off the ground, but she took her time, digging with her fingers until the object came loose. There were two holes. It took another second or two for her to realize it was a skull.

She dropped it and pushed her hands against the ground, trying to get away. Her head hit a wood beam. *Shit! Get ahold of yourself!*

She held still for a moment, breathing, trying to collect herself. Her mom's words came to mind: *I killed for you.*

What was going on?

Had Mom killed Peggy Myers and Avery James? If so, their bodies had been found. But then who did these bones—

Sawyer's stomach turned. Rebecca—her best friend. The bones were small. Sawyer had graduated with degrees in criminal justice and biology. She knew enough about the human skeleton to know that these belonged to someone close to the size Rebecca was when she'd disappeared.

All this time, she'd been buried under the house?

Her skin tingled. Sawyer had never come here after her friend disappeared. Why would she? Her head fell forward in defeat. Images of Rebecca trapped down here. Had Rebecca been alive when she was locked inside?

When were the vents sealed? Mom or Dad could have done that while she was at school. She'd been so distraught after her friend disappeared, she'd never noticed. Even if she had, she probably wouldn't have thought much about it.

It sickened her to think she might have been able to help. *If only I had thought to look. I might have been able to save you.*

A doorbell sounded.

Sawyer didn't make a sound. She hardly breathed.

The sounds of her mom's footfalls as she walked to the front entry were directly above her head, which meant Sawyer had to be close enough to the front door that somebody might hear her if she could make enough noise.

Think, Sawyer. Think.

The door opened.

She heard voices.

She knew that voice. It used to be much deeper. It was Melanie.

"Melanie," she cried out in a pathetic squeak of a voice. This might be her only chance to let someone know she was here. She reached for Rebecca, grabbed the thickest bone, the femur, and used it to bang against the ceiling.

The chattering above stopped.

"Sawyer, is that you?"

Melanie was calling her name! She knew something wasn't right, and she'd come looking for her.

Sawyer banged against the ceiling again. Three times.

"Where are you?" Melanie shouted.

"Basement," Sawyer yelled as loud as possible, but her cry for help was drowned out by a crash and then a heavy thump as something collided with the ground.

Sawyer knocked on the ceiling.

Nothing.

No. No. No.

Next, she heard a swishing sound and the occasional creak of the floor as something was being dragged away.

Melanie.

Had Mom killed her?

There was a thickness in her throat as guilt and regret for befriending Melanie and getting her into this mess seeped into her bones. If Melanie were okay, she would be calling her name, but all was quiet.

The bone was still clutched within her grasp as she let her head fall to the ground. Without food or water, she had no idea how much longer she would last.

CHAPTER THIRTY-NINE

Harper opened her eyes and straightened in the passenger seat. Her neck ached from the position she'd slept in for the past few hours. It was dark outside. She shivered as they drove past the WELCOME TO RIVER ROCK sign, well lit by a streetlight. "What if Joyce and Dennis aren't home?" Harper asked.

Aria didn't answer her. She had insisted on driving. For the first two hours of their ride, she had grilled Harper about her make-believe book. Harper's lie was so far-fetched she'd given up answering Aria's questions and simply fallen asleep, leaving Aria alone to stew in her frustrations.

Harper looked at her sister. "Don't be mad at me."

"You promised we would never lie to one another. What's going to happen if I tell Nate that you were always out while he was away and that you didn't come home last night?"

"Please don't."

Silence.

"Can we focus on Sawyer for now?" Harper asked.

"Sure," Aria said. "And to answer your question, if Mom and Dad aren't home, I'm going to break into the house and have a look around."

"How do you intend to do that?"

"I don't know. I guess I'll figure that out when I get there."

"Did you try ringing Sawyer's cell again?"

"Yep. Dozens of times. This isn't good. She never should have gone to Gramma's funeral."

"It's my fault," Harper said.

"Everything that happens to us isn't your fault just because you're the oldest."

Harper had never wanted her sisters to know the truth, but she couldn't keep it to herself any longer. "There are things you and Sawyer don't know about me. In fact, I've made an appointment with a therapist."

"Jesus. It's about time. Sawyer and I have always known that you didn't escape River Rock unscathed. We figured Uncle Theo must have gotten to you too. You can't hold that shit in, Harper. It eats away at you and makes you crazy."

"It wasn't Uncle Theo," Harper said.

"Who, then?"

There was a long pause before she finally said it. "Dennis." Naming her father as her sexual abuser, saying it out loud, didn't change anything. Her body wanted to shut down. But she was stronger than that. She'd let that man take control of her body for too long. She wouldn't collapse now. Not ever. She wouldn't give him the power.

"Dad? What are you saying?"

"I'm telling you that he used to come into my room at night," Harper said. She swallowed. She'd never told anyone what had happened before. Even if she'd wanted to, she couldn't. It was as if the abuse was trapped, stuck deep down inside her. Her husband knew something had happened, and he knew she'd been traumatized, but even he didn't know it was her father who had abused her.

Strangely, killing a man had freed something inside her. She wasn't proud of it, but there it was. She wasn't sure any therapist could get it all out of her, let alone help her in any meaningful way. But killing a man had freed her, and she knew it was time to at least try to rid herself of the bile before she burst.

"Go on," Aria said as she followed the navigator's instructions on how to get to the house where they were raised. "What did he do to you?"

"He raped me," Harper said. "I was six the first time he touched me."

Aria growled. "I want to kill him."

"I did too, but I couldn't do it. I think I was thirteen when he began to visit on a regular basis. That's when I made a deal with him. He could have me. I wouldn't fight him. But if he dared touch you or Sawyer, I would make sure everyone in River Rock knew what he'd done."

There were few cars on the road. Aria pulled to the side, put the car in park, and looked at Harper. Aria simply sat there, shaking her head, her eyes filled with tears. "No wonder you're so fucked up."

"I appreciate that."

"Oh, Harper." Aria fell across the middle divider and threw her arms awkwardly around her.

They sat there for a few minutes, Harper's head resting against Aria's. Their arms twisted around each other.

After they moved away from each other, Aria pushed her hair out of her eyes. "This is a lot to take in. I am so sorry."

"Don't," Harper said. This was even harder to talk about than she thought it would be. An ounce of relief mixed with pounds of angst. "I don't know how to say this, but I don't think I can stand the thought of you feeling sorry for me."

"That's okay," Aria said. "I get it. I also understand why you always called him by his first name." Aria looked deep in thought before she asked, "Was there a reason you called Mom by her first name, or was it guilt by association?"

"She knew," Harper said. "I saw her watching."

"Son of a bitch. Fucking cunt and whore."

"Yeah, you could say that."

Aria took the car out of park and merged onto the road, and Harper was thankful to be moving on. Opening up like that was making it difficult for her to breathe. She used a tissue to wipe at her eyes.

Two minutes later, they passed the driveway, where they both took note of Sawyer's car. Not a good sign. Aria drove ahead, and once they were far enough away from the house, they both climbed out.

"Wait five minutes before you approach the house and knock on the door," Aria instructed. "I'm going to head up the hill and make my way to the cottage where Sawyer told me she was staying."

"What do you want me to do?" Harper asked.

"If Mom or Dad are home and they let you inside, play it cool. Tell them you're older and wiser now, and you wanted to talk to them. Make up something."

"Like what?"

"Tell her about the book you're writing."

"Very funny."

"What?" Aria sighed. "Talk about anything that comes to mind, but keep her occupied long enough for me to get to the cottage."

Aria started to walk away. She stopped, turned back, and said, "Do you have a weapon? Anything to protect yourself with?"

Harper pulled a stun gun from one pocket and pepper spray from the other.

"Nice."

"What about you?" Harper asked.

"I've got it covered. See you soon."

"Be careful," Harper said.

"You too."

Aria made sure her gun was snug in her waistband. She'd bought the gun when she'd turned eighteen. Keeping low, she crept through the woodsy area of the property.

The second Harper was out of sight, Aria sucked in air and fell to her knees. She looked up to the sky and inwardly screamed. How was it possible she never knew Dad was sneaking into Harper's room?

And Mom knew?

Uncle Theo wasn't the only monster in the family, it seemed. The whole thing felt surreal, and yet everything about her sister suddenly made sense. She'd never understood why Harper acted out in disturbing ways. Before they escaped River Rock, Harper had taken everything she did right to the edge of the cliff. Too much partying, drinking, and drugs. Too much dancing and flirting.

It all made sense now. Everything Harper had done was her attempt at escaping. Aria shivered at the thought of Sawyer being left alone with Mom, Dad, and Uncle Theo for all those years.

And now here they were, all three of them, back in River Rock.

Full circle.

Her fingers rolled into tight fists.

She forced herself to breathe. *Pull yourself together.* Pushing to her feet, Aria kept her focus on Sawyer. Their little sister was in trouble and needed them. Maybe now more than ever.

Aria looked around and took note of the path up the hill that would lead her to the side yard. Some of the trees had filled in, and the fence was new, but for the most part, everything looked as she remembered.

The leaves crunched beneath her feet as she hiked upward. A minute later she was at the gate. Standing on tiptoe, she reached over, relieved when her fingers brushed across the old familiar wire. She pulled on it. The wire lifted the metal fastener on the other side, and she was able to push the gate open and enter the backyard. She could see the cottage from where she stood. There were no lights on inside. To her right she saw the main house and the side door leading into the kitchen, where a dim light had been left on. There were also two bedroom lights on.

She walked quietly around to the back of the cottage where she could peer through the window, her hands cupped around her eyes and her nose pressed close to the glass. The moonlight put off enough light for her to see that nobody was inside. The bed was neatly made. No sign of Sawyer's things. As she crept toward the door leading into the kitchen, she wondered whether or not Harper had made her way inside the house.

She stopped at the door to listen. Heard voices. She recognized Harper's voice at once. The other voice belonged to a female, whom she assumed was Mom.

Dad must be in the bedroom, but wouldn't he have heard the doorbell and gone out to see who Mom was talking to?

Her stomach quivered. Her instincts on high alert.

She made her way quietly around the house, peeking inside windows and jiggling them to see if she could get in that way. When she got to her dad's old office, she was surprised when she jiggled the window and found it unlocked. The curtains were pulled tight, and there were no lamps or lights on inside the room. She shook the window, sliding it upward an inch at a time, until there was enough room to pull herself up and then use her feet to push her way through the opening. She rolled down onto the floor, hands first and then tucking her head under, without making much noise. The room smelled. Moldy and stale with neglect, and possibly something else she couldn't place.

On her feet again, Aria took two steps before she knocked into something and came to a halt. She bent down to her knees and reached out, held back a scream. She pulled out her cell and used the flashlight on it to take a closer look.

Dad!

His back was up against the wall, his head tilting to the right, his face gray and covered with blood. A letter opener was sticking out of his chest.

She felt for a pulse. Nothing. He was dead, and after hearing what Harper had to say, she wasn't sure how she felt about that.

A noise coming from across the room prompted her to jump to her feet. She pointed the cell phone that way. The beam of light fell on a young woman in the corner of the room. Her ankles and wrists had been fastened with zip ties. Her mouth covered with duct tape.

What the hell was going on?

Aria worried about Harper as she went to the woman and knelt at her side. She needed to hurry. She took a corner of the duct tape covering the woman's mouth and ripped it off without mercy.

The woman cursed under her breath and said, "If she hears us, she'll kill us."

"Who are you?"

"Melanie Quinn. I'm a friend of Sawyer's. Who are you?"

"I'm Aria, Sawyer's sister."

"I know you," she said. "I mean, I know *of* you."

Aria rummaged around the desk for scissors as Melanie talked.

"Your mom knocked me over the head with a vase when I came looking for Sawyer earlier," Melanie said. "When I was standing in the foyer, I heard Sawyer yelling for help. I'm not sure where she was. I swear it sounded as if her cries for help were coming up through the floorboards."

"Under the house," Aria said, her heart racing. "She's in the crawl space."

Aria cut the ties from around Melanie's wrists and handed the scissors to her. "Here," Aria said. "Call the police. I've got to go." Where was Harper? Her mind was swirling with speculation. The thought of either of her sisters being harmed made her sick to her stomach. She needed to hurry.

The door squeaked as Aria pushed it open. She looked both ways before stepping into the hallway and making her way toward the front entry. Nobody was there. Aria pivoted on her feet and walked into the salon where Mom and Dad used to greet visitors. Harper was on the ground, her hand on her head, blood trickling down across her fingers.

Her heart felt as if it might leap out of her chest. "Let me find something to stop the bleeding."

"No!" Harper said. "We're sticking together. That woman is insane. Caught me completely off guard when she grabbed a bronzed statue from that table over there and swung hard, as if her life depended on it. If I hadn't ducked, it would have been much more than a graze. I pretended to be unconscious."

"She killed Dad and left him to rot in his office. Which way did Mom go?"

"I don't know," Harper said. "She walked away, muttering something about how she should have taken care of the problem from the start."

"I think Sawyer is in the basement," Aria said. "We need to get to her before Mom does." Aria helped Harper to her feet, and together they rushed to the stairs leading to the basement. She flipped on the light and headed downward. Harper followed close behind.

Aria called Sawyer's name.

A knock sounded from inside the crawl space.

Harper went to the door leading inside the crawl space and tried to unfasten the padlock. "We need a key."

Aria stood at Harper's side and knocked. "Sawyer, are you in there?" She put her ear flat against the door.

The answer came in the form of a faint cry for help, followed by three distant knocks.

"I'm going upstairs," Harper said. "I think I know where she might keep the key."

"We need to find the key to get you out of here," Aria told Sawyer.

Another knock.

"This is perfect," Mom said from the top of the stairs. "So much easier to have you both in the same room." She took one stair at a time. Grasped within her right hand was a pistol aimed at Harper, who had gotten as far as the first step.

Aria could see the upper half of her mom above the railing. Her cheekbones were still a prominent feature, but her porcelain skin was now ashen. Dark shadows circled eyes that held no warmth. She'd always appeared tall, almost regal, to Aria, but now she looked shrunken, her shoulders slumped forward.

"You killed Dad," Aria said, hoping to throw her off her game and get her attention off Harper. "Why?"

"I spent my entire life covering up for his mistakes," Mom said, closing in on Harper. "I wasn't going to let him ruin everything because of a momentary lapse in judgment."

"What are you going to do with his body?"

"None of your concern."

Mom pulled a leather cord with the key from around her neck and tossed it over the stair rail to the floor. It landed in front of Aria's feet. The hand with the gun remained steady.

The room was small—nothing more than four cement walls. There wasn't any place for Harper or Aria to run to.

Aria bent over and picked up the key. Her own gun was tucked away in her waistband, but she couldn't risk having Mom fire her gun in a panic.

"Open the door and get inside the crawl space," Mom ordered.

"You don't think people will wonder what happened to Dad?" Aria asked.

Mom snorted. "The people of River Rock will believe whatever I tell them." She gestured for Aria to get moving.

"You can't kill us all," Aria told her as she inserted the key and purposely failed to open the lock. "Harper's husband and all our friends know where we are. They'll call the police and come looking for us. Turn yourself in before it's too late."

Mom reached the landing and jabbed Harper with the gun. "Get inside the crawl space with your sister."

Harper walked toward Aria.

Aria turned the key again. This time the lock came free, and she opened the crawl space door. She poked her head inside and saw Sawyer scooting her way. "She'll never let us out," Sawyer said, her voice hoarse.

Aria knew that was true. She'd seen what Mom was capable of. She had killed her own husband, the person who had stood by her side for forty years.

If she and Harper climbed inside, they would all die.

Before Aria straightened again, she reached into her waistband for her gun. Then she pivoted on her feet, weapon aimed at her mom. She really did hope that Mom would listen and do as she said. Nobody should have to kill their own mother, but she would do it if she had to. She'd seen the pain someone like Joyce Brooks could cause. Justice would be served, one way or another. "Put your gun down or I'll shoot."

Mom didn't flinch. "You'll never pull the—"

Aria pulled the trigger.

The sound was deafening.

Mom's eyes grew round with surprise. A tiny gasp escaped her before she toppled to the ground. The gun hit the floor and rattled around. Harper grabbed it, kept it pointed at Mom's chest. Harper's gaze met Aria's. "It's okay," Harper said. "It's okay."

Aria turned toward the tiny opening to help Sawyer out of the crawl space.

They were all alive. Maybe Harper was right. Maybe it was okay. It might be a while before she knew for sure, but right now, she needed to do what she would have done if Uncle Theo hadn't drugged her all those years ago . . . she needed to help her little sister.

Sawyer could hardly stand, her legs wobbly like a newborn foal. She was caked with dirt. The side of her face was badly bruised. Her hair was tangled and matted. Pale and seemingly in shock, she asked in a raspy voice, "How did you know to come?"

"You didn't check in like you promised," Aria said.

Aria couldn't take her eyes off Sawyer. A row of reddish-purple bruises circled Sawyer's neck. She remembered the story Sawyer had told her about how the math teacher had attempted to strangle her to death.

"What happened to your voice?"

Sawyer held on to the wall for support while she found her balance. "I've been screaming for nearly two days. Where's Melanie?"

"Your friend is going to be okay," Aria said.

"I'm right here." Melanie came halfway down the stairs, stopping when she saw their mother in a heap on the ground. Melanie didn't look much better than anyone else standing in the cramped basement. "I called for help," she said.

Sirens sounded.

"Come on," Aria said. "Let's get out of here."

"What about her?" Melanie asked, pointing at Mom.

The bullet had struck her front and center, where limp hands still rested and blood seeped through long pale fingers.

Harper felt for a pulse, then said, "Joyce is dead."

CHAPTER FORTY

Sawyer, Harper, Aria, and Melanie had sat in the salon while Chief Schneider, Aspen, and another police officer Sawyer didn't recognize made their way methodically through the house, careful not to touch anything as pictures were taken and an official account of what happened was pieced together and recorded.

Melanie and Harper were attended to on-site while Chief Schneider took in both of their accounts, one at a time and in separate rooms, before they were taken to the hospital. After that, he'd talked to Aria and then Sawyer while his men gathered evidence and took pictures.

A blanket covered Sawyer's shoulders, stopping her from trembling as she sipped water. She was dehydrated, and her throat was still raw from crying out for help.

Aria sat across from her, fidgeting in her chair. "Will I be arrested?"

"No. Absolutely not. We were all there, Aria. You fired in self-defense."

"I hardly gave her a chance. I was so angry at her after finding out about Harper and knowing she did nothing to stop it from happening."

"You did the right thing. She would have killed Harper. If there was ever any goodness in her, it was gone. She'd fallen off the cliff long before you were forced to raise your gun. You saved our lives."

Chief Schneider walked into the salon, a stony expression on his face and dark circles around his eyes. "We're almost done here. Aspen is gathering the bones from the crawl space. It'll be a while before we know who they belong to." He looked at Aria. "We'll be keeping your gun for now, but no arrests will be made."

Aria's shoulders fell in relief.

The chief looked to Sawyer next. "You're leaving in the morning?"

She nodded. "If that's okay?"

"That's fine. I'm going to finish polishing everyone's account of what happened. Don't leave here until I come by to get signatures."

"We won't. Thank you, Chief."

Aspen and the other policeman showed up to let the chief know they had everything they needed.

The house was quiet again.

Harper returned home an hour later with twelve stitches at the back of her head. Melanie, Harper told them, had needed fifteen stiches across her forehead and was thinking about changing her name to Frankenstein.

While Harper made makeshift beds for everyone to sleep in, Sawyer updated her sisters on everything that had happened during her visit, ending with her being in Dad's office when Mom and Dad found her.

They were all exhausted.

"There," Harper said, hands on hips. "It'll be one big slumber party."

Harper had pulled in padding from the lounge chairs outside and then found every blanket and pillow in the house to make three beds.

Sawyer took the bed on the end, surprised by how comfortable it was.

Aria took the bed on the other end, leaving Harper with no choice but to sleep between them.

They all lay there quietly in the dark until Aria broke the silence. "I knew Mom was crazy, but I never would have guessed she was capable of murder."

"She killed my best friend," Sawyer said softly. "But I can't wrap my mind around why she would have done such a thing."

"I don't know," Aria said. "But if Harper hadn't recorded our conversation with Joyce when we were in the basement, I don't know if

Chief Schneider would have believed us. Joyce cast a strange spell over this entire town."

Sawyer was only half listening. She couldn't stop thinking about Rebecca being trapped in the crawl space. She had talked to Aspen when he arrived with the chief. She'd made sure he knew where Rebecca's bones were. Thirty minutes ago, he'd texted her to let her know the bones were being taken to the lab. It would be up to forensics to figure out whether or not it was Rebecca who had died there.

"If Mom killed Rebecca, it would seem logical that she probably killed those other girls, including Isabella Estrada," Harper said.

"Do you think she was covering up for Dad?" Aria asked. "Had he touched them inappropriately at some point?"

"I was eleven or twelve," Harper chimed in, "when Peggy Myers was murdered. She used to come over to help me with my homework."

"What about Avery James?" Sawyer asked.

Sawyer could hear Harper crying. "Are you okay?"

"Yes," Harper finally answered. "Avery came to the house too. Mom and Dad weren't supposed to be home. But they were. I was only fifteen, but Dad asked me, begged me, to run something to the post office. Avery said she would do homework while she waited for me to return. When I came back, Avery was gone. Dad told me she'd gotten antsy and left. Avery treated me differently after that. She went out of her way to avoid me, but I never connected the dots until now. Dad must have taken advantage of her. That's why he wanted me to go to the post office. He wanted to be alone with Avery."

"But you said Mom was home," Aria said.

"Mom did what she did best," Harper said. "She turned the other way."

"And then she killed both girls to keep them quiet," Aria said.

"Even if that's true," Sawyer said, "we'll never know for sure now that Mom's gone."

Quiet fell around them. "We're lucky we survived," Aria said.

"I read the letter you sent to Dad," Sawyer told Harper. "I had no idea. I am sorry I've been so hard on you."

"We've all had a tough go of it," Harper said.

"It makes me sick," Aria told Sawyer, "to think of you here all those years with Mom and Dad and Uncle Theo."

"If you had just stayed put and not run from the truck," Harper said, her voice wistful.

Sawyer had no idea what Harper was talking about. "Are you talking to me?"

"Yes," Harper said. "If you hadn't jumped out of the truck and run back to the house as Uncle Theo was driving toward us, I might have had enough time to make you understand and convince you to come with us."

Sawyer swallowed a lump in her throat. "What are you talking about?"

"The night Aria and I left River Rock," Harper said.

"I was in the truck with you and Aria the night you escaped?"

"You don't remember?" Harper asked. "I never planned to leave without you. I kept you right there with me. Nate came as quickly as he could, but by the time he got there, we only had minutes to escape. I put you in the back seat of the truck, and then Nate had to help me get Aria from the house since Uncle Theo had drugged her. Earlier, before Uncle Theo left the house, I had to play it cool and pretend all was good; otherwise he might not have left. When we returned to the truck with Aria, you were crying and screaming, telling me you didn't want to leave Mom and Dad. I told you it wasn't safe at home, but you were furious. You started hitting Nate on the back of the head, so he put on the brakes. You jumped out and ran up the driveway, back to the house at the same time a car turned onto our road. Nate took off, and once I saw that it was Uncle Theo's car, there was nothing I could do. If he'd caught sight of Nate or gotten his license plate number, game over. The police would have been called, and we would have been dragged back home."

Sawyer's insides turned. She looked at Aria. "Why didn't you ever tell me this?"

"I was drugged," Aria said. "I don't remember any of it."

"I thought you knew," Harper told Sawyer, "because you were there. I carried you from the house to the truck. I held you in my arms and told you how important it was for all of us to leave River Rock. You told me you didn't want to leave Mom and Dad. You wanted to stay in River Rock, in your own home."

Sawyer swallowed a knot in her throat. "I have no memory of being in Nate's truck. I only remember standing on the porch outside the front door and watching the truck disappear, knowing you were both inside. I never saw Uncle Theo pull into our driveway."

Aria spoke up then. "He never parked in front of the house because Mom yelled at him whenever his car got in the way of the garage. He'd made a habit of parking around back."

"He drove right past us that night," Harper said. "I had ducked down the minute I saw headlights, and Aria was sprawled out on the back seat. Uncle Theo didn't know Nate, and therefore he had no idea we were inside the truck."

Shivers coursed over Sawyer. "As I stood there on the porch," she said, remembering, "Uncle Theo came up behind me. He wanted to know where everyone was. I said I didn't know. And that was the truth. His fingers dug into my shoulder, and he made me come inside, led me into the salon where four men I had never met were waiting. That's the night I was put on the market. I went numb after the first man led me to my bedroom and raped me. I don't know how long that night lasted. A day? A week? I do know that I forgot everything except standing on the porch and watching you leave me."

Harper reached for Sawyer and pulled her tight, holding her there for a long while. "I'm sorry I didn't come back for you. I didn't know how to convince you to come with me, and I was worried they would find Aria."

Aria crawled over and joined in the hug.

That's how they fell asleep. Three sisters holding each other close. Sawyer never wanted to let go.

CHAPTER FORTY-ONE

Sawyer was the first to awaken the next morning at six. She slipped on a clean T-shirt and the slacks she'd worn to Gramma's funeral, since her jeans needed to be washed. She made enough coffee for all three of them. By the time it was ready to drink, Aria and Harper were up. Together they folded the blankets and put everything away. Nobody mentioned Mom and Dad. There would be time to talk about what to do with the house later.

"Chief Schneider said he would be coming by this morning," Sawyer said. "He has more questions and wants to make sure he has all the correct contact information before we go."

Sawyer looked at the clock. It was seven thirty. "I have to say goodbye to Melanie and Aspen. It shouldn't take long. I'll be back before the chief arrives. I promise."

Aria didn't look pleased.

"Don't worry," Sawyer told her. "I'll be right back." She grabbed her coffee and keys and headed off. Outside, she breathed in the cool air. It took a couple of tries to start the car. She gave the engine a minute to warm up before driving away.

Something niggled at her as Sawyer thought of Isabella Estrada tied around the tree. She knew Mom was capable of murder. Mom might be petite and fragile in appearance, but she'd had the strength to swing an iron poker with enough force to kill her father. She'd also taken out Melanie and Harper. Every time, though, Mom had had the element of surprise on her side and was able to catch her victims off guard.

But did Mom have the strength and stamina to keep up with Isabella during one of her runs and then strangle her before or after tying her to a tree?

She'd read enough true crime to know it wasn't easy to strangle someone to death. Isabella was young and strong. She would have been able to fight back and ultimately get away.

And what about the day Sawyer went to the crime scene to take a look around? Had Mom been the one hiding in the woods watching her?

It all seemed doubtful.

She pulled up to the bookstore just as Melanie was unlocking the door. Sawyer tooted the horn to catch her attention. Melanie opened the passenger door. "What are you doing here?"

"I wanted to come say goodbye and tell you thank you before I head back to Sacramento."

Melanie smiled. "You're welcome." There was a crumpled paper on the seat that she picked up before taking a seat.

"How's your head feeling?" Sawyer wanted to know.

"Great. I think that whack from your mom actually knocked some sense into me." She frowned. "I shouldn't talk about your mom under the circumstances."

"It's okay," Sawyer said, stiffening when she saw the piece of paper Melanie had flattened between her palms and was now reading.

"Who killed Isabella?" Melanie read aloud before proceeding to name everyone on Sawyer's list. "I'm on your list of suspects?"

Sawyer inwardly scolded herself for not being more careful. "Not anymore," Sawyer said.

"Well, duh." Melanie shook the piece of paper. "You thought I was a possible murderer?"

"No. Of course not. I crossed you off the list." Sawyer pointed to the line where she'd scribbled through Melanie's name. "See?"

"Oh, great. I feel so much better."

Sawyer sighed. "You had a troubled life, so I added your name to the list. It was stupid."

"You had a troubled life too," Melanie pointed out. "Why didn't you put your name on the list?"

"Because I was the one doing the investigation. I would know if I was the killer."

Melanie rolled her eyes. "I was kidding."

"I really am sorry," Sawyer said. "I didn't come here to offend you. I came to say goodbye. Are you angry?"

"Me? No. I don't like it, but life is way too short to be mad about that."

"I didn't only come here to say goodbye," Sawyer said. "I also wanted to invite you to come visit me—us—me and my sisters in Sacramento if you ever get a chance. Maybe get out of River Rock for a while."

"I'll think about it, okay?"

"Okay."

Melanie slid out of the car, shut the door, and headed into the bookstore.

Sawyer knew she'd hurt Melanie's feelings. She could see it in her eyes, but there was nothing she could do about that now. Once she got settled in Sacramento again, she'd give Melanie a call and check up on her, see how she was doing.

Sawyer plugged Aspen's address into her navigation system and merged onto the main road. He lived only a minute away. Everyone in this town lived a minute away.

When she pulled up to his house, she was taken aback by the picture-perfect front yard. When his mom was alive, the place had been severely neglected, peeling paint and overgrown weeds. It was 8:00 a.m. He was probably getting ready for work. Since she only planned on being a few minutes, she left her purse and her keys on the passenger seat. She'd only knocked twice when he opened the door. He looked as if he'd just showered and shaved. His hair was still damp, his jaw smooth.

"Wow, look at you!" she said. "Snazzy."

He rubbed a hand over his chin. "I have been told I clean up pretty well."

She smiled. "Mind if I come in?"

"Please do." He opened the door wide, then shut it behind her as she made her way farther inside, stunned by everything he'd done to the place. Gleaming hardwood floors, stone fireplace, and fresh paint. No more sagging old couch or broken windows. The place looked like a model home. "This is amazing," she said. "Did you hire a decorator?"

"Nope. I did it all myself."

"Impressive," Sawyer said. "I came by this morning because I wanted to say goodbye properly this time."

His eyes widened. "Goodbye?"

She nodded. "I'm heading back home this morning."

"I thought you were going to stay and work on solving the Estrada murder?"

"I've changed my mind," she told him. "With everything that's happened, I'm sure you understand why I need to get away from here."

He rubbed a hand over his face. For a second there she thought he might be about to cry, but he collected himself. "Yeah, I guess that makes sense. But I was hoping we could hang out before you left."

"I'm sorry."

"How about some tea?" he asked. "The water is still hot."

She didn't like tea. Never had. What she really wanted to do was go back to the house, sign the police report, and get the hell out of River Rock. But judging by the reaction he'd had to her leaving sooner than planned, she said, "That would be great."

While he was in the kitchen, she walked around the living room, admiring the coaching plaques on the wall. She had no idea he'd become so involved at the school, coaching track and field and basketball.

He brought her a mug of hot tea. "It's still steeping, but I think you'll like it. I added a little honey to it."

She took a sip. "It's perfect."

He smiled, then snapped his fingers. "Let me get you a scone I picked up from the bakery yesterday. You're going to love them."

"You really don't need to."

"I know, but you need to eat something before your long drive." He pointed a finger at her. "Give me a minute. I'll be right back."

She continued to roam, took another sip of the tea. She peeked into a guest room, again taken aback by how perfectly neat everything was. Even Harper would have been impressed. The door to a second room was locked.

She moseyed back into the main room and wondered what he was doing. He'd installed beautiful stone around the fireplace. On the hearth was an iron ash holder with a small shovel and gloves. Her insides did a somersault as she set her mug on the mantel and reached for the gloves. She turned them over in her hands. The left glove had a jagged hole in it.

A knot formed in her belly.

Reaching into her back pocket, she pulled out the piece of fabric she'd found the day of Gramma's funeral when she'd driven with Aspen to the crime scene.

The piece of fabric was a perfect match.

Chief Schneider, she recalled, had looked surprised to see Aspen pull up in his truck that day. Aspen had told the chief he'd heard about the homicide on the scanner.

But that wasn't true.

She'd been with Aspen at the cemetery when he'd walked to his truck. He hadn't been wearing a radio, and the scanner inside Aspen's truck was never turned on when she'd driven with him from the cemetery to the scene of the crime.

How had he known where to go?

Aspen returned with a plate full of scones. He stopped when he saw the gloves in her hands. "What are you doing?" he asked.

She quickly dropped the gloves back where she'd found them. With false bravado she said, "Just admiring the beautiful stone." Her heart raced as she walked slowly back to the coaching plaques she'd seen earlier.

She needed to get out of here. If she ran, could she make it to her car before he caught up to her?

Her gaze wandered to the picture of Aspen with the team. Isabella stood front and center. Hadn't he told her he didn't really know Isabella?

She turned and saw that he'd put down the plate of scones. The torn scrap of glove now rested in his palm. "What is this?" he asked.

Her chest tightened. "I don't know," she said. "What is it?"

"Don't play games with me, Sawyer."

She took a step toward the front door and nearly fell over. The room was spinning.

He glanced into her mug, and that's when it dawned on her that he'd drugged her tea.

"You killed Isabella," she said.

"I did it for you."

He wasn't making sense. "For me?"

"For us."

Her vision blurred. It was as if everything was happening in slow motion as he swept her into his arms and carried her down the hallway and into a bedroom. She wanted to fight him, but her arms wouldn't move.

He put his face close to her head and breathed in the scent of her before placing her gently on the bed. He hovered over her. The tips of his fingers rested on his chin as he appeared to contemplate his next move.

Fear threatened to take control. She had to stay calm if she wanted to get out of here alive. When he left the room, she was relieved to find she could bend her legs and wiggle her toes. Her right arm wouldn't budge, but her left arm was mobile.

She'd only had a few sips of tea. Whatever he'd given her explained why he'd taken so long to get the scones. He wanted enough time to pass for the drug to take effect. If it was Rohypnol he'd put in her tea, she would lose muscle control and then experience confusion and drowsiness. She'd lost some muscle control, but her vision was already clearing. The adrenaline pumping through her veins took care of any drowsiness.

How long before such a small amount would wear off?

She inwardly counted to ten to try to calm her racing heart.

He returned to the bedside with scissors and a plastic bag. He looked down at her lovingly and stroked her hair. "Please. We need to talk," she said.

He shook his head at her as if she were a naughty child. "I can't hear you. You're going to have to speak up."

Her heart rate accelerated as he swept up a handful of her hair above her left eye and cut it off in one clean snip.

He was going to kill her. She thought of her sisters and wished she could tell them she was sorry for causing them so much grief.

She concentrated on breathing. It was as if she were outside her body, watching as he stuffed his nose into the lock of hair and inhaled, long and deep. He then carefully slid her hair into a plastic bag and set both the scissors and the bag on the bedside table. "There," he said. "You have no idea how long I've dreamed about this moment."

The mattress sank lower when he slid onto the bed next to her and pulled her awkwardly into his arms.

She felt a twitch in her right arm. A good sign.

Her face was pressed against his shoulder and neck. She could smell his aftershave.

"I've been saving myself for you."

She said nothing. Maybe her voice had left her again, she wasn't sure.

"I did kill Isabella," he admitted. "Mostly because I knew it might be my only chance at keeping you here in River Rock. As it turned out, I discovered how exciting it is to kill someone." His eyes widened. "It was a high." He bent his head, chin to chest, in an attempt to look deep into her eyes. "I never would have known I enjoyed killing at all if your mom hadn't asked me to kill Peggy and Avery."

Ridiculous. Why would Mom do that? She tried to ask him, but the words came out garbled.

"It must be a lot for you to take in, I know. Don't frown," he said. "Yes, I was young, but I hated those girls. Your mom told me that I needed to punish them for humiliating me. She was right. I was slow, and I had a stutter back then, remember? They made fun of me. I was big for my age. Peggy was a tiny thing, fourteen and skinny as a string bean. She was standing by the river's edge, and I just walked right up to her and bashed her head in with a hammer. Four years later, I did it again."

Her mom was insane. How could Sawyer not have seen what she was capable of before now? She tried to move. *Impossible.* She screamed, but a tiny squeak was all that came forth.

Aspen shrugged. "No big deal. I guess your dad was no better than Uncle Theo. Whenever Harper had friends over, he couldn't keep his hands to himself, so your poor mom had to cover all the bases." He stopped talking long enough to brush a hand over her face. "Such smooth, pretty skin."

A chill crept up her spine. *Aspen killed those girls?* He'd had a learning disability back then, and she'd witnessed him being bullied. He'd been bigger than the other kids but hadn't known how to use his size to keep the bullies away. She'd felt sorry for him.

Sawyer's jaw tightened. How long before she would regain movement? Five minutes? Ten?

He shimmied downward across the mattress so that he didn't need to crook his neck while he looked her in the eye, their noses touching. She pretended to be loopier than she felt. She wanted to bite him, dig her teeth into his flesh and make him bleed. But it wouldn't be enough, so she lay still.

"I love you," he said. "I always have. You were always so kind. I think your mom knew I liked you and used it against me." He smiled. "I didn't mind, though. I fixed up this house for you. For the longest time I didn't know how I was going to get you here, but when an idea finally struck, it was like an explosion of fireworks going off inside my head. I knew Gramma Sally needed to die. I still wonder why it took me so long to think of it."

His hand came to rest on her backside, slid slowly over her, shaking slightly from nerves. "You're so beautiful." His lips touched her forehead.

Her stomach churned. There was nothing she could do to stop him. He was in full control, and he knew it. "Don't feel bad about Gramma Sally," he said. "She was ready. I swear she looked relieved when I picked up the pillow and put it against her face. Hardly took any time at all. It was a peaceful death."

It was all too much. He'd killed Gramma Sally in hopes she would come back, and she'd fallen right into his trap. He had caused so much pain.

"Don't worry. I won't torture you like I did Isabella. I care too much about you." He sighed. "If you would have just spent a little time with me, I know things would have turned out so much differently. I would have spent a lifetime worshipping you."

She couldn't listen to any more of his bullshit. A rush of adrenaline swept through her, giving her the strength to pull her knees upward and use her legs to shove him to the floor.

Scrambling off the bed, she wobbled on her feet, grabbed the lamp from the bedside table, and slammed it against his head.

He fell back with a groan, but it wasn't enough. He was still moving. Dazed, he pushed himself to his knees.

She had gotten as far as the bedroom door when she felt his fingers curl around her ankle. She pushed the door forward then yanked it back, slamming it into his head.

He released his hold along with a horrified scream.

She ran through the kitchen, heard him thrashing about, shouting for her to stop, telling her she could never leave him.

Stumbling along, she made it out the door, didn't dare look back. In the car, her right arm refused to cooperate. She had no choice but to use her left hand to put the key in the ignition and turn it. The engine rattled and died. *No. No. No. Not now!*

She turned the key again. Nothing.

Aspen flew out of the house, his face bloodied. He took the three steps leading from the door to the walkway in one leap.

She turned the key for the third time.

The engine roared. Aspen's truck was parked in front of her car. She put the car in reverse and slammed her foot on the gas pedal. Aspen dodged the wheels and reached for the back door. She sped forward and rammed into the back of his truck.

Fuck!

She hadn't meant to put that much speed into it. She hurried and locked the doors right before he grabbed the passenger door handle and jiggled it, the veins in his neck straining as he punched at the windows with his bare knuckles.

She backed up again, went too far, slammed into a neighbor's car, jerked forward.

Aspen stood in front of her car looking at her through the windshield. He wasn't giving up. The determination in his eyes was frightening.

He would never stop.

She would spend a lifetime looking over her shoulder.

She thought of Gramma Sally, Peggy, Avery, and Isabella as she revved the engine. Letting out a guttural roar, she pressed her foot down hard on the gas and sped forward. She hit him straight on, pinned him between her car and his truck.

His eyes remained fixated on hers.

The tires were spinning, the undercarriage creaking from the stress as acrid smoke filled the air around them.

Blood trickled from his nose. He was still alive. How was that possible?

A minute passed before his head and upper body fell forward onto the hood of her car. When she backed up, his body sank to the ground. Breathless, she covered her mouth with a trembling hand. She pulled her cell from her purse and called the chief. "It's Sawyer."

"I'm at your parents' house with your sisters," the chief said. "Where are you?"

"You need to come to Aspen's house." Her voice was hoarse as she said, "He's responsible for the murder of Peggy Myers, Avery James, Gramma Sally, and Isabella Estrada. Aspen is dead."

The car engine sputtered and spit, then died.

Sawyer disconnected the call. Didn't move. Just sat there behind the wheel, her eyes on Aspen. Although she'd told the chief he was dead, she wasn't 100 percent sure. And she wasn't going to check. Her ears were pounding, her brain scrambling for something to hold on to as images of pushing Rebecca on the swings came to her. The sound of Rebecca's laughter made the corners of Sawyer's mouth turn upward. "Higher," Rebecca said. "I want to go higher."

It was less than ten minutes later when Chief Schneider pulled up in a police vehicle with Aria and Harper right behind him.

The chief went straight to Aspen, placed his fingers on his neck. A minute later he headed inside the house.

Aria and Harper knocked on Sawyer's car window and had to convince her that it was okay to come out. Aspen was dead, they told her. She could unlock the door.

When Sawyer climbed out, Aria's gaze fixated on her hair where Aspen had cut it. "He was going to kill you," she said in disbelief.

Sawyer nodded. Her body was still weak, so she used her car to keep herself propped up. "He said he killed Peggy, and later Avery, because Mom convinced him they needed to be punished for humiliating him."

"She didn't want anyone to know he was a sexual predator," Harper said.

"What about Isabella and Rebecca?" Aria asked.

"Aspen said he killed Isabella in hopes of keeping me in River Rock. If he's to be believed, Rebecca was Mom's doing. He also killed Gramma Sally."

"I always thought he was weird," Aria said. "But I never pegged him as a killer."

Sawyer's head still wasn't right, but she was finally able to move her right arm. "For all those years, the people I trusted to keep me safe were the ones I needed to be wary of. What sort of world are we living in? How am I supposed to make sense of any of this?"

"You won't ever make sense of what happened," Harper said. "None of us will."

They were all exhausted by the time Chief Schneider was done interviewing the three of them. Sawyer's interview took an hour. Aspen's body had been taken away in an ambulance. According to the chief, Aspen's trophy room was the same one Sawyer had tried to look into but couldn't because the door was locked. For years Aspen had been collecting mementos: hair clippings, newspaper articles, and pictures and drawings of the victims and the murder scenes.

Sawyer wondered how long it would be before she'd stop seeing the dark, empty look on Aspen's face when he'd cut her hair. For some reason, that one particular act had scared her the most. The thought of it made her stomach churn.

"Are we done here?" Aria asked the chief.

"I'm going to let the three of you go for now. I've got your numbers and your address in Sacramento if something pops up."

They all nodded.

"Take care," he said before he walked back toward the house.

Sawyer frowned. "My car is dead, like everything else in this town," she told Aria. "Mind giving me a lift?"

"Not a problem," Aria said.

The three of them walked across the street, arm in arm, a human wall of sisterhood.

The Brooks sisters, Sawyer thought.

As horrible as their childhoods had been, as shockingly evil as Mom and Dad turned out to be, Aria and Harper were the greatest gifts life had given her. Having them here at her side filled her with hope.

CHAPTER FORTY-TWO

Sawyer and her sisters had returned from River Rock two days ago. For the second day in a row, Sawyer found a quiet table inside the Sacramento Public Library on I Street where she could work.

She hadn't asked for time off, but Sean Palmer had insisted. Today was Friday. She would return to work on Monday.

The story about Isabella and River Rock was turning out much differently than she'd originally planned. When she first sat down to write it, she'd thought her fury over everything that had come to light would be her muse. But that wasn't the case.

There was a lot to process.

So many feelings.

Forget about Uncle Theo—Mom was a killer, and Dad was a rapist. And they were all dead. She needed to double up on her therapy appointments.

Yesterday, she'd written five pages, a condensed version about growing up in River Rock. This morning, she'd deleted most of it. How do you tell the story without telling the whole truth and nothing but the truth?

She couldn't handle the truth, let alone wrap her head around it.

It was that simple.

She was still in shock. It swam through her veins like blood.

She also felt so damn naive. How had she not seen Mom and Dad for what they were? How do you live with people like that and hardly glimpse what's hiding inside them?

Sawyer felt scared one moment, and ashamed and angry the next.

But she kept on writing, one word, one sentence, one paragraph.

It was noon when Sawyer's phone buzzed. It was Aria. She asked Sawyer to meet her at the coffee shop where she worked. There was something she'd forgotten to tell her. She said it was important.

Sawyer packed up her notebooks and pens along with her computer and headed off.

When Sawyer arrived, Aria was behind the counter. She took off her apron, grabbed two to-go cups from the counter, and ushered Sawyer outside.

They both took a seat.

"I have a fifteen-minute break," Aria said, "so I'm going to get right to it."

Sawyer said, "Okay."

"Remember when you talked to me about the Kylie Hartford murder and you said you wished you could talk to the guy you saw in the truck?"

Sawyer nodded.

"I talked to him."

"What?"

"Just listen. His name is Zach Jordan. He used to volunteer at the animal shelter where I work. He taught me a lot about how to handle animals that were scared and needed special attention."

Aria swished her hands through the air as if to clear the slate and start over. "None of that is important. Anyway, I went to his house over in the Curtis Park area. He didn't kill Kylie Hartford."

Sawyer appreciated her sister's attempt to help her out, but Aria had no experience with this sort of thing. There was no way she would have asked all the right questions, let alone be able to come to a conclusion as to whether or not he was innocent. "Why do Kylie's neighbors think otherwise?" Sawyer asked.

Aria's eyes widened. "Because the night before she was murdered, Zach and Kylie had an argument. They both raised their voices. He slammed the door on his way out."

"What were they fighting about?"

Aria snapped her fingers. "That guy who reports shit on *Good Day Sacramento*. You know—the one who thinks he's all that?"

"Matthew Westover?"

"Yes, that's him! I guess Kylie went out with her coworkers and hooked up with Westover. It wasn't the first time that has happened."

"Zach said that?"

Aria nodded. "He said something about Westover not being the first guy, and probably wouldn't have been the last."

Sawyer straightened in her seat, interested. "What else?"

"He's not proud of it, but the next day Zach followed Kylie after work. He said he watched her disappear inside the Convention Center right around the corner . . . She was attending a book signing or something."

"Waylan Gage," Sawyer said. "That's the author's name. I saw his book on the floor of Kylie's apartment when I was there."

"Oh, wow. Creepy."

Sawyer nodded.

Aria slumped forward. "I guess that's it. I thought you would be a little more excited."

"I am excited. It's just been a little crazy, trying to write the River Rock story."

"I can imagine. Or maybe I can't."

"So did Zach have an alibi?"

"Yes and no."

Sawyer made a face.

"It depends on Kylie's time of death, but he told me that after watching Kylie walk into the Convention Center, he drove around for a while before ending up at Device Brewery, which isn't too far from here. He said he was there until closing. Someone helped him to his car, where he passed out. They left his keys under the seat."

Sawyer jumped up. That was it! The missing link—time of death. If she could prove that Zach was at the brewery when Kylie was murdered, then he was innocent.

"What is it?" Aria asked.

"You are amazing."

Aria looked confused. "Me?"

"Yeah. You. I've got to go, but I'll see you tonight." Sawyer grabbed her coffee. "Thanks for this."

Aria was already putting on her apron. "You're welcome."

Chapter Forty-Three

Sweat pooled under Sawyer's arms by the time she locked up her bike and entered the brewery on R Street in Midtown. Although she wanted to work on her story about River Rock, the information Aria had gathered was too good to push aside.

When she'd talked to Palmer on her way home, she'd felt deflated to learn of Zach Jordan's arrest. Palmer was adamant that she let it be. It wasn't her place to get in the way of their investigation.

But how could she ever live with herself if she didn't do due diligence and at least talk to a few people? She asked the guy behind the counter if the manager was in. Ace, according to his name tag, was friendly and didn't ask her what this was all about. He just disappeared for a minute and returned with a big, burly guy.

"I'm Travis. What can I do for you?"

Sawyer had already pulled up a picture of Zach. Because of his connection to Kylie's murder, his face was all over the media outlets at the moment. "My name is Sawyer Brooks. I work for the *Sacramento Independent*, and I was hoping you could answer a few questions."

"Sure."

"I've been told that this man, Zach Jordan, was here last week. He stayed until closing, and someone who works here helped him to his car and left his keys under the driver's seat."

"That was me," Ace said.

"Mind if I let you two talk and I cut out?" Travis asked.

"That's fine," Sawyer said. "Thanks for your help."

"Not a problem."

Sawyer turned her attention back to Ace. "Any chance you recall what time Zach Jordan arrived at the brewery that day?"

"My shift started at six p.m. that night, and that guy there," he said, pointing at the picture on her phone, "was already sitting at that stool right there." He pointed to the middle of the bar.

"Did he leave and come back?"

"No."

"You sound certain about that."

"I am. It wasn't a busy night," Ace said. "I didn't take a break. And neither did that Zach guy. He threw back a lot of beers and never left that seat. We have cameras that would show him coming and leaving if that would help."

She wondered why she hadn't thought of that before. "You're a saint."

Ace chuckled. "Yeah, tell that to my wife." He gestured toward the back. "I better go get Travis. He's the one you'll need to talk to about getting video footage."

By the time Sawyer left the brewery, her adrenaline was soaring. It had taken Travis only ten minutes to find the video from the night of Kylie Hartford's murder. Although he wasn't allowed to give Sawyer a copy, he didn't mind her sitting in his office next to him while he ran through the footage.

Zach Jordan had arrived at Device Brewery in Midtown at 5:45 p.m. and been ushered out by Ace five minutes after midnight. Sawyer thanked Travis once again, stepped out of his office, and called Sean Palmer to ask him if he knew Kylie Hartford's official time of death.

Palmer said he'd had no reason to request the forensics report, but if it would help her sleep at night, he'd give Detective Perez a call and get back to her, which he did twenty minutes later, just as she arrived back at her sister's house.

Kylie Hartford's official time of death had been 10:30 p.m.

They had arrested the wrong man.

Sean Palmer wanted to know what was going on. It was Friday, though, and she had more work to do before she talked to him. He wasn't happy about it, but he agreed to meet her at 5:00 p.m. in his office.

———

At 3:42 p.m., Sawyer pulled the car she'd borrowed from Harper to a stop in front of the giant arm, an electronic device used to keep cars from moving on until the driver checked in. She was at *Good Day Sacramento* in West Sacramento, where Kylie Hartford used to work.

Sawyer leaned out the window and pushed a button, told security she had an appointment with Matthew Westover. After a few seconds, they buzzed her in. Once the chain-link gate slid open, she drove through, made a right, and parked close to the front of a brick building. As she walked toward the main entrance, she saw a CBS sign and a TV tower.

A security guard wearing a standard white button-down shirt and dark pants and shoes handed her a clipboard and asked her to sign in. Again, she was buzzed inside and asked to wait in the lobby.

Matthew Westover appeared shortly after. He was one of the main anchors on the morning show. He sported a French Crop hairstyle and wore a moss-green, fitted suit. A key card and ID hung from his belt.

They shook hands.

"Is there a private room where we could talk?" Sawyer asked. "It won't take long."

"Sure. This way."

He led her down a wide hall, opened the first door to the right, and flipped on the light. Three of the four walls were lined with boxes, but there was a table with chairs. And it was private.

He shut the door, gestured for her to have a seat. "Like I told you on the phone, I only have a few minutes."

"I'll get right to it, then. I heard from Kylie Hartford's neighbor that you and Kylie were dating."

He smiled. "Dating is a nice way of putting it, but sure, Kylie and I were seeing each other. Not on a regular basis, but if we happened to go out for a drink after work and things worked out, we usually ended up at my place or hers."

"Were you with Kylie the night of her murder?"

"No. We hadn't been on a 'date' in months. And I hate to be rude. She is dead, so it doesn't feel right talking about her this way, but since you're asking, you should know that I wasn't the only one she slept with."

"She had a boyfriend," Sawyer stated.

"Yeah, but that's not who I'm referring to. I hate to be blunt, but the clock is ticking. Kylie liked sex. All sorts of sex. With lots of different people."

"Orgies?"

"Not that I know of, but now that I think of it, she'd probably have been up for it. I'm merely telling you that she got around."

"So she was promiscuous."

He chuckled. "Sure. Promiscuous. And her boyfriend knew what she was doing."

Sawyer looked up from her notes. Aria had mentioned the same thing. "How can you be so sure he knew?"

Matthew smirked. "I was right there, naked as a jaybird, when he walked into her apartment and found us in a compromising position. If I'd known she had a boyfriend with a key to her apartment, I would have brought her to my place."

"What did her boyfriend do?"

"They argued, and then he stormed out. I never saw him again. Kylie told me not to worry. Said he didn't like her sleeping with other men, but he'd resigned himself to it."

"Interesting."

He nodded. "Anything else?"

"Did the police talk to you about Kylie's murder?"

"Yes," he said. "Detective Perez talked to a few of us."

"And you told him the same story you just told me?"

"Yes." He looked at his watch. "I've got to go." He stood.

Sawyer shoved her notebook and pen inside her purse and came to her feet. Again, they shook hands. His gaze roamed over her face and neck. "Looks like you have a dangerous job."

She smiled. "I can handle it."

"I'm sure you can." Sawyer watched him walk away and then went to the front desk to sign out. Westover had said Zach was resigned to Kylie sleeping around. It wasn't Sawyer's place to judge. And it fit what Aria said Zach had told her about Kylie sleeping with other men. Had Zach hit a breaking point? she wondered as she walked across the parking lot. Was his alibi as solid as it sounded?

A woman called out to her.

Sawyer turned that way.

The woman was heavyset and had lots of brown hair rolled into a messy bun at the top of her head. She wore a turquoise blouse over colorful leggings.

"Are you the reporter from the *Sacramento Independent*?" she asked.

"I am."

"My name is Brianne." She caught her breath. "I wasn't here when the detective talked to everyone, but Matthew told me you were coming to talk to him, so I thought I'd tell you what I know."

Sawyer waited.

"When I read the write-up in the paper about Kylie's murder and her boyfriend's arrest, it surprised me that nobody mentioned Waylan Gage."

"The author of the Jacqueline Carter series," Sawyer said.

"Yes! Kylie was absolutely obsessed with Waylan Gage. Since learning about Kylie's death, I haven't been able to sleep. I can't get what she said about the author out of my mind."

"What did Kylie say?"

"That she was going to get into Waylan Gage's pants, even if it killed her."

CHAPTER FORTY-FOUR

After leaving *Good Day Sacramento*, Sawyer had gone back to the library to research Waylan Gage and hit the jackpot.

At 5:00 p.m. on the dot, Sawyer sat across from Sean Palmer.

Palmer was leaning back in his chair, his feet propped on his desk. "You do recall my asking you to leave the Kylie Hartford investigation alone?"

"I do."

"And you realize there is a standard probation period?"

"I do." She frowned. "Why didn't you tell me that forensics found unidentified DNA in Kylie's apartment?"

"Because it happens all the time—could be the landlord, the plumber, a friend who stopped by," Palmer said. "So what do you have for me that couldn't wait until Monday?"

Sawyer proceeded to tell him everything she knew about what Zach was doing the night Kylie was murdered, including seeing footage of Zach walking in and out of the brewery, proving that he couldn't have murdered Kylie.

Before he could respond, Sawyer said, "And that's not all. I think I know who the killer is."

Palmer lifted a curious brow.

After leaving *Good Day Sacramento*, Sawyer had gone to the Copy Cat to make print copies of the digital pictures she'd taken at Kylie's apartment. She slid an eight-by-ten glossy of Kylie's apartment across Palmer's desk.

"Kylie Hartford was at Waylan Gage's book signing the day of her murder."

"So you've said."

"When I walked into the apartment, the book was on the floor, wide open. It had been signed by Waylan Gage."

"Yes," Palmer said. "I've seen the picture. Kylie could have had the book for a while," he suggested. "This doesn't prove that she went to the book signing."

He folded his hands. She could see that he was getting impatient.

Sawyer shook her head. "That's exactly what it proves. The book in question wasn't released to the public until the day of the signing, which means Kylie met Waylan Gage in person on the same day she was killed."

"Listen," Palmer said. "You're not a cop. You are a rookie reporter with very little experience. But," he added with emphasis, "after I talked to you on the phone when you were in River Rock, I made a few calls myself. It turns out the author sold over three hundred and fifty hardbacks that day. He wouldn't have had time to give much individual attention to his fans, but somehow you want me to believe that they hooked up after he finished signing books for the day?"

"I do," Sawyer said. "I met with Matthew Westover at *Good Day Sacramento*, where she worked."

He said nothing.

"Matthew Westover is the same man who Kylie's neighbors told police Kylie was 'dating.'" Sawyer used her fingers to make air quotes. "Matthew has known Kylie for a while now, and he didn't deny hooking up with Kylie. He also told me that her boyfriend knew everything."

"Maybe Matthew Westover is the man we need to concentrate on," Palmer said. "Maybe he's trying to throw you off his scent." He raised a hand. "For the record, I'm not serious about concentrating on Matthew Westover or anyone else, for that matter. I'm trying to help you see that we could theorize until we turn blue, but we'd be wasting our time."

She shook her head. "Matthew Westover is a playboy. He's a popular anchorman, so it's not a big secret that he gets around."

Palmer crossed his arms over his chest. "Okay, so tell me again. Out of all his fans that day, why did Gage choose Kylie Hartford to go after?"

"She was an easy target. She liked sex. And she was obsessed with Waylan Gage. Besides Matthew Westover, I talked to a friend of Kylie's at *Good Day Sacramento*. She wasn't there the day investigators questioned Kylie's coworkers, but she said Kylie told her flat out that she was going to that book signing, and she was going to get into Waylan Gage's pants, even if it killed her."

"You have the woman's name and number?"

"I do." She raised her hand. "If you'll let me add one more tiny thing."

"Go ahead."

"After I left *Good Day Sacramento*," Sawyer said, "I did some research on Waylan Gage. He releases one book every two years, and after each release, he tours the United States. Three years ago, he was in San Francisco. That same night a woman named Kathy Pollard was killed. Her murder was never solved."

"And she was a fan of Waylan Gage?"

She nodded. "It gets weirder. A lot weirder."

Palmer frowned. "You said you had 'one tiny thing' to add."

She ignored him. "The only reason I know that Kathy Pollard was a fan is because of her obituary. In it, her family mentions her love of reading and how ecstatic she was to have met Waylan Gage that day." Sawyer leaned closer, her gaze fixated on Palmer's as she tapped her finger against his desk. "The family even buried her with his auto-graphed book."

"So your theory is that not only did Waylan Gage kill Kylie Hartford—he also killed Kathy Pollard."

"And who knows how many others," she said.

"Where is Waylan Gage now?" Palmer asked.

Sawyer glanced at her notes. "It's been a week since he left Sacramento. He's already hit Oakland, Fresno, and San Jose. His next stop is Los Angeles, and then San Diego."

"And what are you proposing exactly?" Palmer asked.

"That we find a way to get Waylan Gage's DNA to check it against the unidentified DNA found in Kylie's apartment. I could fly to LAX myself. It's a short flight. I go to Gage's signing. I buy a book and grab his water bottle when I leave."

"Assuming he has a water bottle."

"Yes," Sawyer said.

"The answer is no," Palmer said. "You don't have my approval to go anywhere near Waylan Gage."

Sawyer crooked her neck in frustration.

Palmer picked up his phone and dialed a number. "But I do know someone who might be able to help us."

CHAPTER FORTY-FIVE

One week later . . .

"This apartment is perfect," Sawyer said as Derek Coleman followed her into the tiniest kitchen she'd ever seen in her life.

"This is not good," he said. "Too many overgrown trees and shrubs outside, leaving you wide open to be mugged. No bark covering the dirt and no sprinklers. The property is falling apart. Let's go."

"I can't afford perfect," she said.

"You said you wanted a downstairs apartment with one bedroom. This is upstairs with no bedroom."

True. It was a studio, nothing like the apartment she'd imagined in her mind's eye, but still . . . the price was right, and this was the fifth apartment building she'd been to today. She opened the cabinet, and the door toppled to the floor. "A broken hinge," she said. "Nothing I can't handle."

"It's not safe," Coleman said.

"Now you're being ridiculous," she told him. "This place has controlled-access entry with an intercom system. And on-site laundry."

She opened the oven door beneath the stovetop and tried not to cringe when she saw thick grime covering the racks.

"That's disgusting," Coleman said.

"I don't cook." She closed the oven door. "Problem solved."

"You'll have to park on the street, and that's if you can find parking. It's way too dangerous."

"Remind me again why I brought you with me?"

"Because this was as close as I was ever going to get to going on a date with you."

"Ahh. That's right." Sawyer moved on to the bathroom. "This place is within walking distance to all the best restaurants. The entrance to the American River Parkway is close enough that I can bike there in a few minutes."

"This place is too small. You can't fit a bike in here."

She pointed to the wall. "I'll hang it right there."

He shook his head in defeat.

"This is the only place that comes close to what I can afford. I'm going to take it. Because my only other option is to live with my sister and sleep on her couch." She lifted an eyebrow. "Plus, this place takes animals."

"That is a plus, since the cat can catch the mice and rats for you."

She laughed.

"Six-month lease?" he asked.

She nodded. "Six months." After another quick look around, she noticed Coleman looking at her. "What are you thinking?" she asked.

"Just that I'm happy to be here with you."

"Oh."

He smiled and said, "You were right about Waylan Gage. You do realize if it weren't for you, he might never have been caught?"

"I'll give Palmer some of the credit," she said, "for finding a PI friend to get hold of Gage's DNA. But yeah, I guess I'm sort of a badass."

"You're humble too. I'll have to add that to the list of things you told me about yourself."

She felt her cheeks flush. "I was hoping you'd forgotten what I told you when we talked on the phone."

"Sorry. It's all been burned right here into my temporal lobe." He pointed at the left side of his brain.

"Erase it," she said. "I made it all up."

"So there is no ex-boyfriend named Connor?"

She made a face. "That part was true."

"And what about him cheating on you?"

"Also true."

He took her hand in his. "What about the being-touched part?"

"True," she said, but she left her hand in his.

"More importantly," he went on, "I hope you don't remember any of the disturbing things I told you about me."

"Only everything," she said.

He leaned forward and kissed her. Not too hard. Not too soft. Just a brush of his lips against hers, and yet she had to resist the urge to push him away. Maybe over time she would find a way to let him into her life.

Sawyer got the feeling he knew she was uncomfortable. He let go of her hand. "Did you know that everyone's talking about your River Rock article?"

"Seriously? What are they saying?"

"That you brought transparency to a town riddled with secrets. Because of your story, the River Rock Rotary Club collected enough money to commission a bronzed statue of four girls."

"No way."

He pulled out his phone and showed her the drawing he'd seen. "It will be placed in the town square, where everyone can enjoy it."

Two life-size girls held the ends of a jump rope while one was getting ready to hop over it. The fourth girl was on a swing, high in the air, grinning from ear to ear.

"It's beautiful," Sawyer said, stunned.

"Your story made people see how important it is that victims of homicide not be remembered through hushed whispers of tragedy, but instead stand as a reminder to be grateful for the light that each of them brought to the world while they were alive. Those girls will not be forgotten."

Sawyer's gaze met his. "Thank you."

He looked around the apartment. "So this is where you're going to live, huh?"

She nodded. "It's perfect."

"Let's go find management," he said, "and tell them you found a winner."

She smiled as she followed him out the door and into the sunlight.

Harper waited for Nate and the kids to leave before she logged on to her computer and checked in with The Crew.

LILY: Have you seen the latest?

CLEO: Latest what?

LILY: Brad Vicente. The dickless moron. With the waiter's help, Brad has been doing his best to get the public on his side.

BUG: He's been telling the press and anyone who would listen that five female vigilantes wearing wigs attacked him and voted on whether or not to cut off his penis. When asked about the final vote, he said it was three to two not in his favor. He also said the "female mob" used nicknames like Bug and Psycho. Those were the only two names he remembered. He went on to say that he would seek revenge without resorting to such barbaric acts as those who dismembered him.

PSYCHO: And?

LILY: Sorry. I had to take care of a problem. Kid just got home from school. Back to Brad. At first his plan to gather sympathy was working. But two days ago, a young woman by the name of Mary McCoy appeared on the local news with her lawyer and stated that Brad Vicente had drugged her and held her captive inside his Midtown house for five days. He'd raped her and tortured her and threatened to kill her and her family if she ever came forward. But when Mary saw Brad on the news, she broke down, couldn't handle the lies, and she finally opened up to family and friends, who convinced her to tell the truth and go public.

BUG: I saw that some people were attacking Mary McCoy, calling her a whore because the dress she'd worn to dinner was short and too revealing. One bitch said, "What did she think would happen?" Others are saying she wants to be a part of the Me Too Movement and it's all for attention.

LILY: Yes. For an hour or two, it was bad and seemed to be drawing out bullies. But then another woman came forward with her own Brad story, and then another and another. In total, nine women have joined in. A few of them were able to show video and pictures of their date—Brad Vicente. Most of them saved email conversations that proved he knew them. And that, my friends, turned the tables. The bullies have been shamed and quieted.

PSYCHO: Amen.

BUG: I read that the police were able to restore Brad's videos, revealing images that the mayor of Sacramento is calling some of the most disturbing footage he's ever witnessed.

LILY: Correct. And the best part, drumroll, please: one hour ago, Brad was leaving the hospital when authorities cuffed him and put him in the back seat of a police vehicle. The reporter said he would be taken straight to jail, no passing "Go."

BUG: Yes! And hundreds of men and women had gathered at the hospital and were there to greet him with picket signs, letting him know they were standing with Bug and Psycho and against him and his waiter friend, sending a clear message to every predator out there who thought they could use and abuse and get away with it.

PSYCHO: Nice.

LILY: If it weren't for his ridiculous pleas to social media for justice, I don't know if things would have turned out so well.

CLEO: Hallelujah.

BUG: Not to piss on this party or anything, but I'd like to remind everyone that my reunion is coming up fast. Who's in?

PSYCHO: I'll be there.

CLEO: Let's start planning.

LILY: I'm ready to go.

Harper placed her hands on her belly. *Boy or girl?* she wondered. She thought of Nate and Lennon and Ella. It made her stomach queasy to think about what might happen if she were ever caught. Would Nate forgive her? The children had grown up in a bubble of love. How could they possibly understand? Sawyer was moving out, so she wouldn't be a problem, but what about Aria? She had eyes in the back of her head. Since returning from River Rock, Aria hadn't said a word about her comings and goings while Nate was gone. Neither had she commented on the book Harper had told her she was writing. Maybe Aria was so relieved and happy to have all three of them back in Sacramento she'd decided to let it go?

Or maybe she was watching her every move.

Dennis Brooks might be dead, Harper thought, but what he'd done to her would live inside her forever. Someday soon she hoped to practice what she preached and let it all go. But today wasn't that day. Harper reached for the keyboard and typed her answer.

MALICE: Count me in.

ACKNOWLEDGMENTS

My writing journey has been a long one. So many late nights, tears, and rejections, leaving me to wonder at times if my dream was too big. But determination, perseverance, and endless hours alone, clacking away at the keyboard, paid off in the end. As often happens in life, the struggles only served to make me stronger and more determined than ever to get my books out there in the world.

Don't Make a Sound is my fourteenth thriller with Thomas & Mercer. I am grateful for all the editors, past and present, whom I've had the good fortune to work with. After working with Liz Pearsons for three years, we finally met in person. Thank you, Liz, for all you do! I'm grateful to have you on my side. I'm also super lucky to again have had the chance to work with Charlotte Herscher. I don't know if I've ever met anyone who works harder. She knows more than most about characterization and plot and what makes a decent thriller. I think she's brilliant. Thank you to my agent, Amy Tannenbaum, for your knowledge and for being my sounding board for quite a while now. You might have the toughest job of them all. Cheers to Sarah Shaw for her never-ending enthusiasm. I'm also grateful for amazing copyeditor Karen B. Many thanks to super-helpful Sacramento detective Brian McDougle. He's always ready and willing to answer all my questions. My newest heroine is a journalist, and I must mention Bryan Gruley, an awesome thriller author, who has offered his forty years of journalism experience to help me out. All journalistic errors are his! Just kidding. I asked him one question, and he said, "No. Don't do that." If I'd had more time, I would have spent hours picking his brain. Next time!

No acknowledgment is complete without mentioning my sister, Cathy Katz. She's been reading my work and offering endless support and inspiration from day one. She is the female version of George Bailey on *It's a Wonderful Life*. Without her, the whole world would be less sunny and bright. My youngest daughter, Brittany Ragan, graphic designer and first reader, is the gift that just keeps giving. She's a natural at telling me which parts of my book suck and need to be fixed immediately. Thank you, Brittany! Thank you also to Morgan Ragan for being my social media expert and so much more! And to Joe Ragan, my husband of nearly thirty-three years, I give my appreciation, thanks, and much love for always being available to brainstorm and figure out how to get my characters and me out of a pickle.

To my readers, thank you for the thoughtful emails and kind reviews. Many of you have been reading my books since Lizzy Gardner and friends first made an appearance. I hope to continue to entertain you for years to come!

About the Author

Photo © 2014 Morgan Ragan

New York Times, *Wall Street Journal*, and *USA TODAY* bestselling author T.R. Ragan has sold more than three million books since her debut novel appeared in 2011. She is the author of the Faith McMann trilogy (*Furious*, *Outrage*, and *Wrath*); the Lizzy Gardner series (*Abducted*, *Dead Weight*, *A Dark Mind*, *Obsessed*, *Almost Dead*, and *Evil Never Dies*); and the Jessie Cole novels (*Her Last Day*, *Deadly Recall*, *Deranged*, and *Buried Deep*). In addition to thrillers, she writes medieval time-travel tales, contemporary romance, and romantic suspense as Theresa Ragan. An avid traveler, her wanderings have led her to China, Thailand, and Nepal. Theresa and her husband, Joe, have four children and live in Sacramento, California. To learn more, visit her website at www.theresaragan.com.